P9-CNG-403

"Are you trying to get out of the marriage?"

Shrugging his wide shoulders, he lifted his hands high in the air. "*I* didn't propose to you."

Now that he'd met her, he no longer wanted her. Deep humiliation stung her cheeks as she marched toward the center of town.

Even with his long stride, John had a hard time keeping up with her. "Sarah, it wasn't my doing. I only found out about you the instant you arrived. It seems my men...the officers...got together. As a prank, they wrote to you—"

"A prank?" She took a moment to digest it. *"A prank?"*

He looked at her with such pity in his eyes that before she realized what she was doing, her arm came up to slap him.

"Oww..." He cupped his nose. "What'd you do that for? I didn't orchestrate this! My men did."

"Well, pass it along!"

* * *

The Surgeon
Harlequin Historical #685—December 2003

Praise for Kate Bridges's latest books

The Doctor's Homecoming
"Dual romances, disarming characters
and a lush landscape make first-time author Bridges's
late 19th-century romance a delightful read."
—*Publishers Weekly*

"The great Montana setting and high Western action
combine for a top-notch romantic ending."
—*Romantic Times*

Luke's Runaway Bride
"Bridges is comfortable in her western setting, and her
characters' humorous sparring makes this boisterous mix
of romance and skullduggery an engrossing read."
—*Publishers Weekly*

The Midwife's Secret
"This is truly a story which will touch your heart
and stir your soul. Don't miss this delectable read."
—*Rendezvous*

"This is a lovely story and delightfully romantic.
Ms. Bridges is in a class all her own."
—*Old Book Barn Gazette*

DON'T MISS THESE OTHER
TITLES AVAILABLE NOW:

#683 THE IMPOSTOR'S KISS
Tanya Anne Crosby
#684 THE EARL'S PRIZE
Nicola Cornick
#686 OKLAHOMA BRIDE
Carol Finch

THE SURGEON

KATE BRIDGES

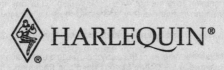

HARLEQUIN®

TORONTO • NEW YORK • LONDON
AMSTERDAM • PARIS • SYDNEY • HAMBURG
STOCKHOLM • ATHENS • TOKYO • MILAN • MADRID
PRAGUE • WARSAW • BUDAPEST • AUCKLAND

If you purchased this book without a cover you should be aware
that this book is stolen property. It was reported as "unsold and
destroyed" to the publisher, and neither the author nor the
publisher has received any payment for this "stripped book."

ISBN 0-373-29285-6

THE SURGEON

Copyright © 2003 by Katherine Haupt

All rights reserved. Except for use in any review, the reproduction or
utilization of this work in whole or in part in any form by any electronic,
mechanical or other means, now known or hereafter invented, including
xerography, photocopying and recording, or in any information storage
or retrieval system, is forbidden without the written permission of the
publisher, Harlequin Enterprises Limited, 225 Duncan Mill Road,
Don Mills, Ontario, Canada M3B 3K9.

All characters in this book have no existence outside the imagination of
the author and have no relation whatsoever to anyone bearing the same
name or names. They are not even distantly inspired by any individual
known or unknown to the author, and all incidents are pure invention.

This edition published by arrangement with Harlequin Books S.A.

® and TM are trademarks of the publisher. Trademarks indicated with
® are registered in the United States Patent and Trademark Office, the
Canadian Trade Marks Office and in other countries.

Visit us at www.eHarlequin.com

Printed in U.S.A.

Please address questions and book requests to:
Harlequin Reader Service
U.S.: 3010 Walden Ave., P.O. Box 1325, Buffalo, NY 14269
Canadian: P.O. Box 609, Fort Erie, Ont. L2A 5X3

Dedicated with affection and many thanks
to my editors—Ann Leslie Tuttle, who has
an uncanny skill with words and plot details and always
manages to pull out my best, and Tracy Farrell,
who gave me my first big break.

Chapter One

Calgary, early August 1889

It was a hell of a way to meet a woman.

Dr. John Calloway, a commissioned police officer and Chief Surgeon of the North-West Mounted Police, had just finished in the operating room and was striding down the hall of the officers' quarters toward his bedroom, fighting exhaustion. Drenched in perspiration, John struggled with his white shirt collar, undoing another button. Damn, it was hot inside the fort. Even the air smelled hot. Dry pine planks and leather.

"Evenin', Sir," said two passing officers.

"Evening." Was it John's imagination or did they elbow each other and grin as he passed? John glared at them. "Something on your mind?"

"No, Sir." The sergeant glanced down at the papers spilling from his youthful hands.

"Then I suggest you hightail it to the paymaster's. He's looking for the schedules you're holding. As for you, Corporal Reid, we could use your help dousing those vacated beds."

"Yes, Sir," came the response.

John shoved a hand through the thick brown hair at his temple, swallowed the dryness in his throat and continued walking. His own fatigue never usually hit him until the worst was over. Under normal circumstances he'd be heading to his private house in town for dinner, then to sleep for the night. But in the past week he'd had six men in surgery at Fort Calgary and he'd been too busy for sleep.

It was still undecided whether the constable John had just operated on would lose his leg. There had also been the constable who'd lost his eye on a runaway bronco; two others with second-degree burns from fighting forest fires to the west; and finally the two discharged this morning with bullet grazes from an ambush ten days ago by that damn cattle-rustling gang. For John, their discharge brought back a wave of remorse and grief for Wesley Quinn.

John's assistant surgeon, *his friend,* who was only doing his duty by racing to the ranch to help the injured, had been ambushed and murdered by the Grayveson gang. Blast them all to hell. Wesley Quinn had been a good man.

John rubbed his bristly jaw. He was starting to feel his age. He rolled his shoulders to loosen the stiff muscles.

Turning forty was a landmark, but why the hell did he feel so...*unsettled?*

The restlessness had started eight months ago, around Christmastime when Wesley had decided to get himself a mail-order bride.

No respectable man orders a woman from the newspaper, John had argued. *What kind of woman would answer your ad? A desperate one, with little backbone and no self-confidence.*

But Wes had just laughed and placed the ad anyway, claiming it was hard to meet a woman—an English one— with so few in the West.

And then he'd gone and got himself killed.

With a sigh, John neared his bedroom door. He stopped at the linen laundry basket. Although he'd worn a surgical gown, a few blood drops had still soaked through to his shirt. He peeled it off and tossed it in, knowing the clerk would need to boil it, too. Down to his sleeveless undershirt, he burst into his private room, glancing to his desk for drinking water.

He was shocked to discover a strange woman inside, who'd reeled toward him at the sharp sound of the door.

"Ah!" he yelped. She let out a choked laugh.

Standing at his open closet, she'd been rummaging through his uniforms. She dropped his scarlet tunic from her fingers like a child caught with something forbidden. A pink stain infused her cheeks.

A wall of curly reddish-blond hair, braided at the sides and clasped at the back, spilled down her shoulders. Finely arched brown eyebrows framed her clear gray eyes. Her lips parted in a pretty smile, revealing a front tooth that slightly overlapped its partner.

Her clothes were fancy for the West. Her heavily boned and corseted red jacket clung to her waist; a long red skirt with protruding bustle accentuated full hips. When one polished black leather boot peeked out beneath her hemline, he noticed a ridiculously spiked high heel. Why was she so dolled up?

He lurched back. His dangling suspenders slapped against the thighs of his tight black breeches. "How'd you get in here?"

She smiled but he didn't smile back. "Corporal Reid

let me in. I'm sorry for laughing. It's just…I was so nervous to meet you…and here I've made *you* jump.''

If Travis Reid had let her in, she must be here for a good reason. Was that why Reid had been chuckling in the hallway?

She took a step forward, holding out her hand. Happiness shone in her eyes. "I know this is a bit of a surprise, but I managed to pack up sooner than I'd thought. I'm Sarah."

Was he supposed to know her? He racked his brain, but no recognition came. "John Calloway."

Her grip was warm and soft and slippery, very different from the bulky, callused hands he was used to shaking. With the contact, his pulse took a leap. As their fingers parted, she glanced heatedly at his chest and he realized he was still in his undershirt. Good grief. What an indecent way to introduce himself to a woman.

She smiled timidly. *"Sarah O'Neill,"* she prompted louder, a deeper crimson flowing through her face. "I know I didn't send a photograph, but I didn't have one."

What was she talking about? If he'd ever met her, he was damn sure he'd never forget.

"Hey, Doc?" Corporal Reid's dark head appeared around the door. "Constable Pawson's wakin' up in a lot of pain."

John addressed the corporal, but his gaze still held the pretty woman's. "Give Pawson another drink of the laudanum by his bedside. I'll be right there."

The corporal glanced into the room at the woman, then cleared his throat. "I see you've met Miss O'Neill."

John's gaze pivoted to the corporal. Judging by the broad smirk on the tanned face, Reid knew something more.

"Can I speak with you outside, Corporal?" John nodded to the woman. "Excuse me, Miss O'Neill, you've caught me at a bad time. I've been in surgery around the clock."

There was laughter in her voice. "John, you can call me Sarah." Why was she smiling so much at him? Not that he minded, in fact, he was enjoying it...but who was she?

The minute they were out the door, John growled at Reid. "What do you know about her?"

Reid squirmed. "I have to get the laudanum."

John cursed. "You better tell me *right now*. Who is she?"

Reid's face paled. He lurched and hurried down the aisle.

"Maybe it wasn't such a good idea," he called over his shoulder. "Come to think of it..." Reid gulped and John felt a shiver of dread race through him. "Maybe it got out of hand.... We all chipped in for the newspaper advertisement and her train ticket...and ordered her for you."

John stalked after Reid. "Ordered her?" Was she a painted lady?

Reid began to run toward the doors of the hospital ward.

John said after him. "What the hell does that mean? *You ordered her?*"

Reid dove through the doors, escaping John's fury, shouting the explanation just before the thick door slammed in John's face. "She's...*your mail-order bride!*"

What? Stumbling back, John slumped against the hard wall.

What...in hell...had his men done?

They'd sent for a mail-order bride? For him?

After his criticisms to Wesley, was this some kind of joke? John had thought he'd seen it all in the fifteen years he'd been here. The pranks, the initiations, the tricks on the new recruits...

So help him God, he'd string them up one by one!

What decent man could do this? This was someone's life they were playing with! Maybe they thought it'd be a funny prank to play on him, but what about the poor woman in his bedroom?

He groaned. She was too innocent-looking to be a painted lady, to be part of a hoax. And Reid had been too scared to be lying.

Where had she come from? What was he supposed to tell her? How could a simple apology be anywhere near enough?

And why should *he* have to do it? The men responsible should. But...they were busy, and she was waiting.

She deserved an explanation—right bloody now.

Bracing himself, John walked back down the hall, rapped on his bedroom door, then entered.

She was standing at the window, letting the breeze roll over her face. Turning around, she met his awkward gaze with an awkward one of her own.

That's why she was so dressed up, he realized, glancing at her cinched waist. She thought she was coming to meet her groom. Just watching her, he felt his muscles tighten.

The air grew still between them. When her gaze hesitated over his bare shoulders, he wondered what she was thinking. That they would soon be married? That the two of them would soon be very intimate?

The thought brought a surge of heat to his own flesh. Then shame found him again, for how his men had tricked her. Looking down into her expectant eyes, he felt the hairs at the back of his neck bristle.

He tried to ease the news. "I'm not who you think I am."

"You're not?" Her generous mouth opened and she colored fiercely. "But you're John Calloway."

"Yes, but—"

They were interrupted again, this time by a sergeant running through the open door. "Dr. Calloway! You better come quickly! Pawson's tryin' to get up! The stitches in his legs are comin' apart!"

John leaped into action. "Get two more men to help us. We'll need to hold him down."

He grabbed a clean shirt from his closet and tugged it up his arms. "I've got to go," he yelled to Miss O'Neill, leaving her standing in his turbulence. "Wait right here till I get back! Don't go *anywhere!*"

What did he mean, *I'm not who you think I am?*

He was John Calloway. He'd sent for her! She had his four letters in her satchel to prove it. But an hour had passed and Sarah was getting the eerie impression something wasn't right.

Feeling ill again, she pressed a hand to her corseted stomach and tried to ease her nervousness. It was the same way she'd felt the whole eight days on the train. Motion sickness, the conductor had told her. There hadn't been much she could do except lay her head between her knees whenever she'd felt the urge to vomit. She did so now until the feeling passed. If she were already married, she might have confused her symptoms for those of childbearing, but she knew *that* was impossible.

Hopefully it would happen soon. A husband and children, a family of her own.

Maybe John was trying to tell her something minor. Maybe he wanted to clarify something he'd written in one of his letters. Looking at him in his undershirt had had her imagining what it'd be like to be his wife in the ultimate sense of the word. Oh, my. Sarah fanned her hot face. Rising from the chair, she walked to the window. As she leaned forward, it blessed her with a cool gust of air.

Why would a man like that need to find a woman by mail? She'd asked the troublesome question in one of her letters. He'd responded that he was looking for someone Irish, like himself, and there were no suitable choices in Calgary. When she'd read that, she'd felt as if her dearly departed father himself was guiding her.

The fact that John lived in Calgary was why she was initially attracted to his advertisement. It was rumored that her brother Keenan had moved West. Calgary, one of his friends had finally admitted to her. If she couldn't locate Keenan here, then she'd find a way to search other prairie towns.

The ache to find her missing brother wove around her heart. At first she'd search discreetly because she wasn't sure if Keenan was still in trouble with the law. She knew marrying a Mountie might help her search, since they kept records of settlers in the area, but she wasn't using John Calloway to find her brother. She wanted this marriage. John seemed like a kind man, writing about the busy frontier town and how much he appreciated finding a woman like her. After dealing with her father's sudden passing, then her mother's brutal decline, Sarah was ready for a new start. She ached to see the wide-open prairies for herself, to smell the flowers of the Rocky Mountains, to see an eagle or a wolf, to live in a place she'd only daydreamed of, in a house that didn't smell of sickness.

She had value and emotions and skills to offer the world.

Please let there be more to my life than what's been already.

In the West, she'd heard women had more freedom. When John had written that many women couldn't handle the danger and isolation of being a policeman's wife, she'd written back that she'd marry him on the condition he'd let her work. It would keep her busy when he traveled, and more independent.

She'd do everything in her power to be a good partner to John. She envisioned the intimacy of a lasting, bonding friendship that might someday grow into love. A love that had sadly escaped her parents.

Glancing around the room, she tried not to be intimidated. From her training, she always noticed two things when she entered a room, besides the people in it.

The guns and the clocks.

John had a pretty good gun. A great gun. The Enfield six-shot revolver sat in full view, slung in its holster over the dresser mirror. The beautiful contour of the mahogany stock glistened like new, but the tiny medallion screw needed tightening, and the holster hadn't been oiled in weeks.

Didn't they have a gunsmith who made regular checks? Then again, what doctor would make his guns a priority?

Compared to his gun, his wall clock was in precise order. It was Austrian with a gold-leaf frame, likely thread suspension with four quarter striking on coiled gongs.

Glancing at the time made her nervous again.

She'd been caught going through his closet, but only because she'd wanted to touch something personal. The most intimate thing she could find had been his clothing; not the botany textbooks lining his desk, not the private medical journal she dared not open, not the wall clock, nor the desk lamp. Even his bed with its plain brown blanket and squared corners looked bleak and detached.

Well, no more. They couldn't live here in the barracks, but she was definitely here *to mess up his bed.*

A shiver of anticipation coursed through her.

When the door flew open, she bolted straighter.

John strode through it. Again he wore only an undershirt. She gulped and glanced away. Blazes, maybe she wasn't as ready for this as she'd thought. Lord, the man liked to undress.

He left the door open. "Sorry it took me so long." He grabbed another white shirt from his closet, weaving his muscled arms through it. His skin was golden, his chest lightly matted.

His thighs flexed beneath his breeches and she abandoned herself to the dreamy thought of seduction. "You're busy. I understand."

"I've got two hours to myself. Let's go for a walk." He nodded toward the hallway. "Away from this ruckus."

Half a dozen men walked by, talking in crude language she didn't often hear—only sometimes when her father or brother or cousins had been too preoccupied in the shop to bother with politeness. When the policemen caught sight of her, one elbowed another and they grinned in her direction.

John stepped into their line of vision and, although she couldn't see his expression, it stopped the men cold.

"We apologize, ma'am," said one as they passed. Another man called out to John by some sort of nickname. "Sorry, Black-'n-White."

Black-'n-White?

John turned back to her. For an instant his face looked

racked with fury. Was he that angry about the coarse language? My, he was exceptionally decent.

The sun's waning rays caught the side of his short chestnut-colored hair and one plane of his handsome face, accentuating his black brows and brown eyes.

He smiled. Just a hint of a smile from one corner of his mouth, nothing overwhelming, but her body responded with a sensual tug.

She was a bit disappointed that he wasn't going to introduce her to his friends, but then…it was nice of him to want to spend time alone with her first. "All right then, John, you lead the way."

"Where are the rest of your bags?"

"I left them with the porter at the train depot. They were too heavy to drag along."

"You walked?"

"It's not far. Besides, I needed to stretch my legs from the train ride." *And wanted time to take it all in.*

"Then would you like to walk back again?"

"Sure," she said, hoping her voice sounded more credible than she felt. Her new heels were killing her feet, but she felt idiotic voicing a complaint. And they had to get back into town, as she imagined he'd be setting her up in a nice hotel room this evening. *After* they decided on a wedding date. As soon as possible, he'd said in his letters.

Grabbing the satchel's handle from her grasp, John's knuckles grazed hers. His touch made her instantly blush. He responded with an equally embarrassed look.

They had to get to know each other, that's all.

Her skirt and petticoat rustled as she walked. Her stomach growled from hunger and her tight corset didn't help. She'd changed into the clothes at the last station before they'd pulled into Calgary. She'd saved her best suit and brand-new shoes to meet her husband. Although joy bubbled through her, she prayed the nausea would fade.

The sun was setting on the prairies.. Dusk surrounded them. Stepping out of the newly built barracks, they walked shoulder-to-shoulder, weaving through the dusty log buildings. They passed the blacksmith's forge, the canteen, the chapel and, finally, the stables. When John stole a glance in her direction, a warm glow tingled through her. Her senses became saturated with the night scents of prairie wheat, rich loam and the hiss of insects. She felt fully alive for the first time in a long while.

The sound of clomping hooves on trampled earth filled the air. Men on horseback galloped past them. The animals were sleek and beautiful, fifteen hands high; the men, excellent riders. Judging from their uniforms of red wool jackets and dark breeches, they were training for an official event. Winchester rifles dangled in slings attached to the pommels of their compact saddles. Repeating rifles, eight rounds.

John's hand brushed the small of her back as he led her out the gate through a small crowd of men and women. He took charge with quiet confidence, and she liked that. Her pulse fluttered as she dipped beyond his grasp, her long hair swaying around her. It felt good to finally meet him after four months. She wished he'd be more daring and wrap his arm around her shoulders.

"It must have been a hard journey. How long did it take you?" he asked.

"Eight days."

He exhaled. "Eight…" His brown eyes sparkled. "Straight from…the east coast…?"

"Well, of course. Direct from Halifax."

"No one to talk to for eight days?"

"I met a few nice folks." Two very kind elderly

women in particular, Sarah thought, who were staying at one of the local boardinghouses. Sarah usually kept her private matters to herself, but over the course of several days, the two women had pried it out of her—that she was a mail-order bride coming to meet her husband. Once discovered, she'd been eager to share her news, and they eager to listen. Although surprised when she'd told them it was John Calloway who'd sent for her, they congratulated her with the warmest wishes.

Walking in anxious silence beside her tall surgeon, Sarah followed him onto the grassy path. It wound along the gently flowing Elbow River, leading to the steel bridge. The moving water whispered by. Blackbirds sang in the aspens. The fragrance of old summer leaves drifted between them.

John dropped her satchel beneath an overgrown willow tree. He moved with a restless energy and she was struck by a strange discomfort.

"Sarah, I don't know how to tell you this, other than to just say it."

Her smile faded. "What is it?"

"It's not good news."

She peered at his face, at the firm strength she saw in his eyes. There was a deeper significance to what he said. Her hands began to tremble. "You're not well?"

"No, no…it's not about my health."

"Then what? I surprised you. I came at a bad time."

"That's not it exactly, either."

She tried to force her confusion into order. Her pulse hammered at her throat. Something was terribly wrong. "We're soon to be married. Soon to be husband and wife. Please tell me what's troubling you."

Her words cut deep into his composure. His expression faltered and he looked suddenly off balance. Pulling in a deep breath, he struggled with the emotion in his husky voice. ''It wasn't me who wrote to you.''

Chapter Two

"*Then who was it?*" Nausea welled up the back of her throat. Sarah gulped to stay the taste of bile. Her fingers raced nervously over the pleats of her red jacket. She yanked back her shoulders and stepped away from John Calloway.

Struggling for words, he tilted his rough beardless face toward her.

She stared back, desperate for a plausible explanation. "I'm not sure who wrote to you."

She staggered back in disgrace. "Are you trying to get out of the marriage?"

He shook his head in dismay, then nodded, then shook it again.

"Yes or no?"

Shrugging his wide shoulders, he lifted his hands high in the air. "*I* didn't propose to you."

Now that he'd met her, he no longer wanted her. Deep humiliation stung her cheeks. With a sharp click of her tongue, she hoisted her satchel to her hip and marched toward the steel-and-iron bridge, heading for the center of town. Lights twinkled in that town's direction. He didn't want her. Her eyesight blurred with the sting of tears. What would be so terribly wrong to have her as a wife?

Even with his long stride, John had a hard time keeping up to her. "Sarah, it wasn't my doing. I only found out about you the instant you arrived. It seems my men...the officers...got together. As a prank, they wrote to you—"

"A prank?" She took a moment to digest it. *"A prank?"*

He looked at her with such pity in his eyes that before she realized what she was doing, her hand came up to slap him. He ducked and she cuffed his nose with a loud thwump.

"Ow-ww..." He cupped his nose. "What'd you do that for? I didn't orchestrate this, my men did."

"Well, pass it along!"

Spinning back to the path, she cursed under her breath in the same coarse language his men had used earlier. As her father would say, she felt like a whistlin' jackass. Not a penny to her whistlin' name.

Where to now?

Through watery eyes, she looked up past the bridge toward the plank buildings. Lamplights lined the dirt street, illuminating the crowd and the horses and buggies. The clatter of hooves and saloon music competed with the thudding of her heart. Her stomach fluttered with turmoil. Where to?

"Sarah, please, can we talk about this?" John dabbed at his nose. He swore when he saw blood. Served him right. Fixing a bloody nose was easy. Traveling eight days across the country for nothing wasn't!

Well... She'd return to the railway station to collect her luggage and make plans. That's what she'd do. Maybe at the boardinghouse, she'd locate the two women she'd met on the train. They might help her. Through a haze of distress, she realized she'd then have to explain that her marriage to the dashing John Calloway was a joke. Oh, and could they please pass the marmalade?

And how long could she get by, with only five dollars in her pocket? She'd done everything she could to speed her journey here, to pay the back rent she owed, to pay the creditors for her mother's funeral.

Much to her irate displeasure, John Calloway wouldn't let her escape. His long, limber body swung into step with hers. Blocking her path, he propped his hands on his lean hips. "Are you planning to *ignore me?*"

"Darn right! Maybe you're not used to being ignored at the fort, but I'm not one of your subordinates!"

She clamped her lips and stalked by him. In the adjacent pasture, plump brown-and-white cows peered at them over a dilapidated cedar fence, munching loudly, gazing as if they could understand the argument.

John raced along, stepping into her blasted path again. His massive shoulders blocked out the sun's dying rays, so she couldn't see his face. It was an etched block of darkness. "Let's talk about this, about what you're going to do."

She shifted her heavy bag from hand to hand and hip to hip. The future tumbled around her. Nowhere to go. Her dreams dashed. The utter shame of being fool enough to fall for this prank. Thank God her folks weren't alive to witness this. "Leave me alone."

She kept walking, her high-heeled boots echoing off the creosote railway ties of the bridge, but he shouted after her.

"I can't!"

She pivoted around to glare at the stubborn man at the other end of the bridge. "Why not?"

"Because…goddammit! I feel responsible!"

Her nausea took over. If she didn't get something into her stomach soon, she'd collapse. Slumping to the cement wall of the bridge to steady herself, she lost the satchel. It slipped out of her grasp, thudding onto the boards. She cradled her temples in the palms of her hands. When she opened her eyes again, John's boots were standing on the ground before her.

"Go away," she commanded the boots.

"I'm sorry. It's awful what the men did. There'll be hell to pay when I get my hands on them."

"It doesn't make me feel any better."

"But I'm still sorry."

She didn't move. Two strangers walked by, an older man and woman headed toward the fort. John nodded hello, squeezing his bloody nose. He had no handkerchief so the blood dripped on his boot. Sinking down beside her, he stretched his legs out in front of him. His white sleeve brushed hers.

Since it seemed she couldn't escape him, she opened her satchel, removed her lace handkerchief, then threw it at him. "Here!"

"Thanks."

She squinted up at him to assess the damage she'd done. There was no swelling, but the bleeding wouldn't stop.

"Don't worry," he said, with those glistening brown eyes that had *almost* been hers. "Luckily, I know what to do." He leaned forward, pinching his nostrils with her hanky, resting his elbows on his thighs.

"You're not supposed to lean forward and pinch your nose, you're supposed to lean back."

"I think I know what I'm doing."

She snorted in anger.

They sat like that for minutes, absorbing the awful reality of her situation.

"You honestly didn't write the letters?"

He shook his head. "Honestly."

She sagged back. In her gut she knew he was telling the truth. He'd been tricked, too, and his indignation was palpable. But his stakes were nowhere near hers.

"How many did I write?" he asked.

"Four. Oh, my God," she said, thinking of her letters.

"What is it?"

"Oh, my God." She clamped a hand over her mouth in embarrassment.

"What?" John's broad shoulders twisted to her direction.

A long groan escaped her. "When I wrote to you in my last letter, I disclosed something quite private."

"What?"

"Something I wrote in a hasty moment of honesty. I thought…you'd discover it on your own soon enough and thought I might as well confess." In truth, she'd thought if he discovered it on his own when she arrived, he might send her packing. There was no way she'd be able to hide it on her wedding night. It had been much easier to disclose at a distance, when she had so little to lose. *What a practical woman,* she chastised herself. "You'll no doubt hear it from your men…." She lowered her head and toyed with her hands. "I told you that I wasn't—" she lowered her voice to a whisper, reminding herself that he was a surgeon comfortable dealing with all sorts of subjects "—a virgin."

"You aren't?"

"You wrote back that you didn't mind."

"I didn't?" He paused with sudden comprehension. "Oh, my God."

She shook her head weakly. Thank God, she hadn't gone the full distance to disclose the how and why, or she wouldn't be able to look at him.

"Maybe it won't get out," he said. "Maybe you can trust them—"

"*Who?* Your band of merry men?"

When John rose slowly, he rubbed the growth of dark stubble along his firm jaw, and she knew he was affected. This was more devastating than any prank the Mounties could have imagined. This was her reputation.

Darkness surrounded them. When had it crept in?

Although she couldn't see his eyes, she felt John's heated stare as she rose and began walking. Shivering, she looked to the lights and sounds of the approaching buildings. There was a huge brewery to their left, a saloon across the road and stores lined up to their right. They passed a large sandstone building.

"How old are you, Sarah?"

She was twenty-eight but it was none of his business. "What difference does that make?"

"You're a little...*different* than I expected."

"How?"

"You remind me of a lot of friends I left back home in Toronto." He studied her intently. "And you're a bit older. Is that why you answered the advertisement? Because you weren't having any luck on your own?"

"For heaven's sake! I can't believe you're a doctor! You're not helping matters by saying aggravating things like that!"

A streetlamp flickered above John's dark head, weaving warm shadows around the two of them. When she started off down the boardwalk, John grabbed her gently by the arm. "Maybe not. Have there been any previous marriages?"

She tugged free, surprised at the impact of his grip, and his question. *"No."*

"Any children?"

She gasped. "How can you ask that?"

"Well, it happens."

"No!" She took a step toward him and turned the questioning around. "Have *you* had any previous marriages?"

He swallowed. "No."

"Any children?"

"For God's sake. *No.*"

"Well, it happens." Ignoring the curious looks of passersby, Sarah scanned the signs above the buildings, looking for a boardinghouse. "Your questions come too late."

"Do you have a place to stay? Where will you stay tonight?"

"I haven't really had a chance to make any plans," she said with cold humor. "Seeing that it's only been *ten minutes.*"

"Right. Of course."

She put down her bag. "Do you know... I mean, of course you'd know... Is there a pawn shop around here? A jeweler's?"

"What for?"

"I've got two fine watches...I might sell." The ones passed down from her grandfather in Ireland, the ones she'd vowed she'd never sell. Her stomach knotted as he appraised her.

After a moment of silent deliberation, he seemed to come to some sort of decision. "I've got a place you can stay."

"Where?"

"In my town house until we figure this out. I'll pay for your return ticket and anything else you need till you get home."

Home? Where was home?

"I'll see that the men responsible reimburse you extra for your troubles."

She scoffed. How much extra should she charge for a life turned upside down? She didn't recognize anyone or anything in this town. The noises were strange—tinny saloon music, eerie howls coming from the prairie grasses, the tap-tap-tap of cowboy spurs behind her. Glancing at the cold faces of strangers milling by on the boardwalk, Calgary suddenly seemed like a very lonely place.

John was the only person she sort of knew, and he *was* a doctor. Could she trust him to stay in his home? What choice did she have? Insecurity trembled down her spine.

As John picked up her bag, amusement lit his brown eyes. Was a smile hovering on his lips? "Did you tell me how you lost it?"

"Lost what?"

He leaned in next to ear and whispered. "Your virginity."

He didn't seem bothered by the news as many men would be, but then she no longer meant anything to him. She never had.

She wasn't ready to forgive him for the situation, and gave him a cutting glare. "No, but I felt sure you'd understand."

"Too bad you missed the party, John," his neighbor called over the fence from the wooden swing on her porch, greeting him and Sarah as they strode up his stairs to his weather-beaten door.

Heavy-set and in her early fifties, Mrs. Polly Fitzgibbon sat among a menagerie of pets. Her beautiful Irish setter panted at her wide-boned feet, the Siamese cat slinked behind her and her knotted black bun, the two newest kittens sitting on her lap pounced at her stubby fingers, and that irritating nuisance of a monkey was hopping along the handrail, eating an onion.

John groaned, wishing Polly would be inside her door for a change when he walked through his.

"Good evening, Polly," he hollered in the warm evening air. "What party are you talking about?"

"You remember, I told you two weeks ago my young nephew David was arriving from New York City. I know you've been awfully busy, but we had a birthday party for him last night. I baked an apple pie and George found streamers at the general store. We hung them all over. David's a nice kid, you'll like him."

"How old is the boy?"

"Just turned thirty-six."

"Oh."

"Who's your *friend?*"

John slid Sarah's satchel to the ground and, with his hand tucked around Sarah's slim waist, led her forward. She jolted at his touch and lurched away. It irked him. He was only being hospitable.

"Mrs. Polly Fitzgibbon, meet Miss Sarah O'Neill."

He watched Sarah nod slowly. A smile finally lit her face as she followed the movements of the scheming monkey over the fence, up one wall of John's house to peel off a piece of cedar roofing, then back to the ground. If the monkey kept this up, he'd soon have enough stripped pieces of the house to build one of his own.

"Now cut that out," John said, hiding his temper for Sarah's sake, diving for the shingle and grabbing it out of the pesky, hairy paws.

"Is that a monkey?" Sarah called over the fence.

"A chimpanzee, actually. There's a difference, you know."

He was still a scheming monkey in John's mind.

"I've never seen one before," said Sarah. "Where did you get him?"

"He followed us home from the carnival. 'Course, he hid in the trees for a couple of days, so by the time we noticed he'd flown the coop, it was too late to return him. His people were halfway to Minnesota."

"What's his name?" Sarah asked.

"Willie," said Polly. "He's our wee little Willie."

Sarah laughed softly but John rolled his eyes.

"Polly is my housekeeper," John explained to Sarah. "I'm glad I caught you, Polly. Looks like I'll be needed at the barracks for a bit longer still. Sarah'll be staying here for a day, maybe two. I'd appreciate if you kept your eye on her." *And be the proper chaperone,* he added silently.

"Be mighty glad to. Maybe I'll send David over to say hello. He's an accomplished photographer, you know. I'll ask him to bring one of his cameras and take your picture."

Polly's tendency for matchmaking never stopped. "Sarah prefers to rest."

Sarah shot John a quizzical look.

Now why had he said that?

"Well, I didn't mean tonight," said Polly. "Maybe me and George and David will all come callin' tomorrow, after I wash your floors. I'll make them nice and shiny for company—for us," she added with a laugh.

Sarah called, "That would be lovely."

John shook his head in exasperation. Why should Sarah bother to get to know the neighbors when she was leaving on the next train?

Polly stared at John. "What happened to your nose?"

John pushed the hanky into the pocket of his breeches.

Looked like it'd stopped bleeding. ''Someone punched me.''

Sarah shifted uncomfortably in her boots—*guilty*—while he shot her a smile of satisfaction.

Polly clicked her tongue with a noisy clatter. ''What you men go through in your line of duty.'' She focused on Sarah. ''You feelin' all right, miss?''

Sarah pressed her hand against her stomach. ''A bit of motion sickness is all. I spent eight days on the train.''

John noticed the pallor beneath her eyes. Why hadn't she told him she wasn't feeling well?

Why hadn't he noticed?

''Where are you from?'' asked Polly.

''Halifax.''

''Land sake's, I had the same thing happen on that steamer we took from Nova Scotia to New York two summers before last. You'll never get me to sea again. I was heavin' so much, by the end of it I was beggin' them to tie the bucket permanently around my neck.''

Sarah nodded then stumbled. John quickly unlocked the front door and led her into the front foyer.

''If I'd known you weren't feeling well, I would've…''

''Would've what?''

''…been a bit easier on you.''

She looked at him through cool gray eyes.

He lit the kerosene wall lamp. The glow spread. He watched Sarah glance up the curved staircase, then through the doors into the parlor. Wide oak planks shimmered beneath Turkish carpets, linen curtains adorned the sidelights of the door, and several fine pieces of Victorian furniture that John had ordered from a catalog salesman adorned the hallway, parlor, and upstairs landing.

He felt fortunate that his, and the other officers', high pay scale allowed them to transport a great deal of personal goods and luxuries not only to their private homes, for those who had them, but to their quarters at the fort. Unlike himself, most commissioned officers were descended from wealthy Eastern families, and had obtained their positions through influential connections. Many were second sons of wealthy Europeans who, having no rights of inheritance, had come to North America to seek their fortune.

Even Charles Dickens's third son, Francis, up until recently, had been a Mountie; John had worked with him once in passing. John, however, being from a modest family with no connections, had earned his position through hard work and a university education.

His home wasn't completely furnished yet, but it was comfortable, clean and spacious.

Looking at her ashen face, he realized she must be exhausted. "When's the last time you ate?"

"On the train sometime around noon."

John muttered under his breath. "Would you like a bite to eat now?"

"I'm not very hungry, but I should eat something, I suppose. Thank you."

She wavered on her feet. He lunged forward to catch her, but he'd overreacted. Her brows shot up and a flash of humor lit her face as she steadied herself.

Why did women wear those damn things, anyway? Corsets. As soon as they started breathing hard, the straps tightened around their ribs until they couldn't catch a breath. No wonder so many of them fainted. It was obviously part of her problem. He had a mind to tell her so, but didn't feel like getting punched again.

She followed him into the kitchen and sat at the table while he prepared the food. Ham from the icebox, two plums, a loaf of heavy rye from the bread bin and all the butter and preserves she could want.

He got so caught up in the meal preparation that ten minutes later, when he turned proudly to the table to lavish the food on her, she was in a deep sleep. She'd placed her head on the table and was out cold.

He watched her for a moment. Was she unconscious?

Setting down the plates of food, he checked her breathing and her radial pulse. Only sleeping, thank goodness.

What was he supposed to do? Leave her here? Wake her up to eat? Carry her to bed? He pulled out a chair and sat down, staring at her. The hair at her temples gently framed her fringed lashes and the rosy curve of her cheek. The neckline of her red suit dipped low to her curves, and her long red skirt swirled about her heels. She was far from being a spineless mail-order bride that he'd once described to Wesley.

When John had first signed with the force fifteen years ago, he was sent to the forts in Alberta before any settlers had arrived. He'd counted thirty-seven-and-a-half months before he'd set eyes on a woman. Then another eighteen months after that one. Even now, with Calgary's population hovering around four thousand, women were scarce and mail-order brides were not uncommon. Over the past ten years John reckoned about six or eight had arrived and passed through the area.

What were Sarah's reasons for responding to the ad? What dreams had she had in meeting him today?

God, the truth must have hurt.

She'd had a very difficult day and his men were to blame. As soon as she was settled, he'd return to the fort and speak to the guilty parties.

With the sting of exhaustion behind his eyes, he knew

it'd be another long night. When would John's pleas for additional medical personnel be answered? Dr. Waters, the town doctor, was useless; his whiskey had gotten in the way of his profession. The man was a hindrance because he couldn't even help the townsfolk—they were bypassing him and seeking John directly. In the past six months John had been caring for civilians as well as wounded police in the only hospital for hundreds of miles—the fort's.

But before John went anywhere tonight, he had to take care of Sarah. Slipping one arm beneath her soft thighs and the other beneath her shoulder blades, he lifted her yielding body and carried her up the stairs. When she moaned and settled against his chest, he sighed. Although he'd had his share of women, it'd been a long time since he'd held one in his arms.

When they reached his wide bed, he lowered her down.

The corset wouldn't do her any good. It impeded her respiration and surely hadn't helped her motion sickness on the train. How could she feel better if she couldn't breathe well?

And so, tugging in a breath of air to give himself confidence, wondering if he'd pay for it tomorrow, he did what any good doctor would.

He lowered his hands beneath the covers and, his fingertips brushing against her warm skin, he used his pocket knife to remove her corset.

Chapter Three

"How the hell could you do that to her?" Standing in the stables—the most private place to talk—while his good friend the veterinary surgeon, Logan Sutcliffe, groomed his stallion, John blasted the group of five men. He outranked them all.

The six o'clock sunrise peeked over their shoulders, flooding in from the open doors. They were dressed in their everyday working uniforms—white shirts, suspenders and dark breeches.

"We thought she might go over well, that you wouldn't mind," said one of the men.

"You heard my objections to Wesley when he placed his ad. What on earth would make you think I'd feel different now?"

The group was silent. Some kicked at the straw, some fidgeted with the sleek California saddle and the wool blanket slung over the stall.

"Well?" John bellowed. "I want an answer from each of you!"

They glanced uncomfortably at each other. Corporal Reid spoke first, playing with the brim of his wide brown hat. "We thought you'd see the humor."

"You thought I'd be *amused?*"

The veterinarian shrugged as he brushed the stallion's mane. In his mid-twenties, the youngest man here, Logan was being trained by John to help in surgery because John was so short staffed. Logan had been shot in the face by the Grayveson gang more than two-and-a-half years ago and left for dead. His cheek was bandaged from his own recent surgery to fix his droopy eyelid and to minimize the scarring left behind by the bullet wound.

Sid Grayveson, the man who'd shot Logan, was serving twenty-five years for attempted murder of an officer, but two of his vicious brothers were still at large.

Logan's young wife, Melodie, was carrying their first child. John liked them both. But it didn't change the fact that Logan was a goddamn horse doctor. John's wounded men deserved better. They deserved to be cared for by a trained surgeon.

"I tried to stop the prank but I should have said something more...the prank got out of hand," said Logan. "Wesley was so happy with the thought of *his* mail-order bride."

John scowled. "Don't keep using Wesley as an excuse. I know all about Wesley and his bride. *I* was the one who sent his fiancée the telegram telling her the news that she no longer needed to come." He turned to the two other men, the sergeant and corporal. "What are your excuses?"

"Beggin' your pardon, Sir," said Sergeant O'Malley, nervously patting his dark mustache, "but we can't forget about Wesley because the whole thing was Wesley's idea."

"*What?*"

"Wes said you always see things in such black-and-white terms, Sir. That maybe if you'd just meet a woman

we picked out for you, you might…see things from another angle.''

John leaned against the boards. The bulge of his shoulder flattened against wood. Wesley's doing?

How many hours had they spent working side by side
in surgery, on the fields and in the hospital? Wesley, with
the white-blond hair and friendly blue eyes, who was always ready for a good laugh. Such a damn good sport
about everything. Even when he'd lose in cards, or when
the men had secretly oiled his saddle with molasses that
had later stained his breeches beyond repair, or when he'd
gotten his paycheck and spent half of it on rounds of
Scotch for the men.

They'd been so close that Wesley had given him the
friendly nickname of Black-'n-White.

Because you never tear your hair out makin' a decision,
Wesley had said. *When the cook was caught stealin'
money, you said get rid of him. When the rest of us were
only suspecting old man Dubrowski was beatin' up on his
wife, you had him thrown in jail for seven days. When I
crushed my baby finger last year, you said cut it off right
away, but I said no, and with the infection wound up
losin' two instead.*

John didn't mind the name. Being able to see things
clearly had gotten him far in the police force. But with
women…cripes…with women….

Wesley had been behind it. What was John supposed
to make of that?

''What's she gonna do, Doc?''

John rubbed the kink at the back of his neck. Two
hours' sleep hadn't been enough. ''She's going home. But
before she does, I want each of you to make restitution.''

''How?''

''An apology for starters. And then you'll take up a

collection, so she won't go home empty-handed. I don't know what her circumstances are, but it's the least you can do.''

''Where is she stayin', Sir?''

John was about to tell them, then decided against it. ''I'll let you know later today. I'm headed there now.''

He'd see her as soon as he'd shaved and bathed. He should warn her to expect the men, to ask if she wanted to see them. He'd also stop by the train depot to ask for the schedule. There were two daily trains headed East, but he wasn't sure if both of them went all the way to Halifax.

The men edged toward the door, eager to escape his glare.

''Hold on,'' he demanded. ''Before you go, which one of you was the letter writer?''

''Wesley wrote them, but all of us—except Logan— dictated.''

John groaned. ''I want those letters returned to Miss O'Neill and I swear you all to secrecy. If one word gets out about their content, and you know what I'm referring to, I'll come looking for you.''

The men exchanged meaningful glances, nodding yes to John with a pronounced lack of enthusiasm. A sinking feeling wove through the pit of John's stomach.

Had they already started spreading the news about her chastity?

Half asleep beneath the comfortable down tick, Sarah stirred. The sun's morning rays slanted beneath the drawn shade, warming her face. She turned away from the sun's heat and buried her face in the unusual scent of the feather pillow. Whose scent was that? A hint of shaving cream mingled with a laundry soap she didn't recognize, mingled with the scent of a very faint male cologne...

Her eyes opened in wide alarm. This wasn't her bed!

She sprang off the pillow, causing the cover to dip around her shoulders. Her jumbled mass of red hair cascaded down her back. A cool breeze wafted beneath the nest of warm covers, stirring the hairs on her bare flesh, causing her smooth, flat nipples to tighten. She was naked!

John Calloway!

Her lacy white corset was lying on the dresser beside her, propped beside the candlestick. She'd bought it specially for him, but under far different circumstances. Not these!

When she picked it up, one side of the stiff whaleboned fabric fell open, revealing frayed ends. Her mouth dropped open in disbelief. He'd cut it off her! It was torn to shreds!

She shifted at the faint slam of a door in another part of the house. It echoed beneath the oak strip flooring of her bedroom. Struggling out of bed, armed with the shredded corset, she knew this room was his. They were *his* boots by the door, *his* denim pants over the upholstered wing-backed chair, and his checkered shirts folded on the dresser. This bedroom was totally different than his barracks. This one was warm and casual and reeking of masculinity.

The memory of yesterday's events came hammering down on her. It hadn't been a dream. It had truly happened.

How could he have stripped her of all her clothing?

Clutching the slippery cover around her, she raced down the stairs, her bare feet padding the floor.

Where was he?

She caught him in the hallway. He was bending to toss a duffle sack into the corner, dressed in off-duty clothes.

Form-fitting denim pants hugged his long legs, tanned cowboy boots encased his feet and another one of those billowing white shirts he liked so much spanned the breadth of his shoulders.

She stopped at the first landing and hollered down the stairs as if she were calling in a barnyard. *"Why did you strip me naked?!"*

He jumped at the sound of her voice. For a police officer, the man sure had skittish nerves. The sunlight caught his face and the twinkle in his eye.

He grinned up at her. God help him, he grinned. "Good morning to you, too."

The cover slid down her shoulders. She was too angry to care. She yanked it up, none too gracefully. The cloth was silky and she couldn't get a good grip. What did it matter? He'd already seen everything she had! ...Or had he?

"Who took off my clothes?"

His grin got wider. "You're looking at him."

"Ah-hh!" She threw the corset at him and it snapped him in the shoulder.

He dove and caught it. "Are you always this angry? Or is it just me you respond to?"

"How could you!"

He toyed with her corset in a manner that made her blush. "Is this mine to keep?"

"You owe me three dollars and ninety-two cents!"

"It's new then?" He snapped the lace and a mischievous look came over him. "That means you bought it for me?"

Her mouth opened in pure shock. "I bought it for my husband!"

"That would have been me, wouldn't it?"

"Give that back!"

"No...I think it's mine. You just gave it to me." He took the stairs one by one, appraising her up and down, from her squirming toes to her ruffled head.

"What are you doing?"

"I'm glad to see you're feeling better."

Her heart raced. She tightened her grip on the down tick and backed away. "You didn't answer my first question. Why did you take off my clothes?"

He held up the lace fabric as he moved closer. "Because you couldn't breathe in this thing."

"What? That's ridiculous."

His eyes roved her body. Good Lord, what was she doing standing in front of a man, in front of *him,* naked beneath this cover?

"Is it so ridiculous?" he asked. "Don't take this the wrong way, but when I removed your corset, your waist grew by a full three inches."

She gaped at him. Her face burned with heat. Why did she constantly feel like an idiot around this man?

"You know, most men would agree with me. These contraptions you women get into are highly unnecessary. Personally, I'd much rather see natural skin bouncing beneath a woman's clothing than this piece of armor."

He'd finally reached her and held up the corset, a foot away from her.

Gulping, she decided she'd better simmer her temper. He was getting far too close for comfort. "You tore my clothes to shreds. Why?"

"I didn't shred them all."

"Where are the rest?"

"Your satchel's in your room, on the right side of the bed. Didn't you see it?"

She shook her head a little too vigorously.

He nodded toward the front hall. "I had Polly wash

and press your red suit. It's hanging in the front armoire in case you'd like to check. After an eight-day journey, I figured you'd appreciate laundered clothes.''

"For heaven's sake, I didn't wear the suit for the whole eight days. I changed into it two hours before we pulled into the station. I'd prefer if you didn't touch my things, thank you very much!''

"I guess that explains why Polly said they weren't soiled.'' He grew bolder and stepped closer. Much too close for her comfort. "You changed into your lovely suit before the train rolled into the Calgary station? For me again?''

"No! For the man I thought I'd be marrying.''

"You're a very accommodating woman.''

It sounded like a compliment, but she caught the sarcasm.

The black flecks in his brown eyes sparkled. "How did you sleep last night?''

"Very well,'' she squeaked. She pulled in a nervous breath at the steamy way he was studying her, at the thought that she'd spent the entire night in this surgeon's bed. She cleared her throat. He must have gotten some rest, too. Even though there were a few sleepy wrinkles around his eyes, he looked fresher. "How did you sleep?''

"I got about two hours. It wasn't much, but I've got the next few to myself. I arranged for someone to take over at the fort so I could come to check up on you.''

"There's no need to check up on me.'' Another question gnawed at her. She had to ask. She needed to know for her own peace of mind. "How exactly...did you remove my clothing?''

"Are you sure you want to know?''

Swallowing she tried to say yes, but the word was inaudible. "Yes,'' she repeated, much too loudly.

"I removed them one by one." Leaning in, two inches from her face, he laid one palm flat against the wall behind her, grazing her hair.

A wave of heat shimmered through her. In a self-conscious gesture, she tried to smooth her tangle of hair, but it was no use trying. It was no use ever trying to smooth her hair.

"Your jacket slid off first. Quite easily, I might add."

"Humph."

"Then your skirt."

"Humph."

"Your petticoat was easy, too, because of the secret drawstring."

She heard a moan and realized it was coming from her throat. Heaven help her!

"Then the bloomers. They looked new, too. Did you buy them for me, as well?"

She didn't move. Didn't breathe.

He raised his other palm and placed it firmly on the wall by the other side of her head. She was trapped between his arms. His body was splayed before her. She recognized the faint scent of laundry soap that'd been on his pillow.

Her voice was a frazzled whisper. "Why...did you ruin my corset?"

"Because if I'd taken the time to unlace all those little zigzagging straps at the front, gently and carefully, and took the time to slip them up over your arms, I would have seen it all."

She gasped.

When his gaze dropped to the bare expanse of her throat, a suggestive smile curved his well-defined lips. He ran a long, tanned finger along the base of her jawline and her muscles quivered beneath his touch. She should drop dead here and now.

"Sarah?" he murmured.

"Yes?" she whispered.

"I'm going out that door, to the bakery. When I come back, I want you fully dressed."

A loud clang startled them. In the hallway below, a mop and bucket hit the hardwood floor.

To Sarah's mortification, staring up at them was a skinny, youthful man she didn't know. In front of him, Polly Fitzgibbon who'd just dropped her bucket, dressed in her washing clothes and kerchief, stood aghast. "Well, I do declare!"

The man turned his portable camera up the stairs. Sarah was blinded by the magnesium flashlamp as it went off in a cloud of smoke and ash. "Look straight at the birdie!"

Chapter Four

"Are they gone yet?" Sarah shrieked the question from behind John's bedroom door.

John hollered back from the hallway, still agitated himself but wondering when she was going to come out of hiding. "The house is empty. It's safe. They're both gone."

In the commotion ten minutes earlier, Sarah had dashed up the stairs and locked herself in his bedroom and Mrs. Fitzgibbon had huffed her way out the front door with her bucket, which had left her obnoxious nephew David alone with John to do the fancy footwork of explaining.

John heard a scraping on the floor, then Sarah asked another question. "Did you smash the camera?"

"I didn't need to smash it. Besides, it's private property and I can't do that. But I confiscated the photographic material."

"Did you smash that?"

"Yes." In his mind, the embarrassing photograph *was* John's property, no matter what David's flimsy excuses were for taking it—journalistic instinct for a great shot, his aunt Polly's request…. John rapped on the hard door.

His knuckles stung. "Come out and let's discuss this like two rational people."

"There's nothing rational about what Polly Fitzgibbon and her nephew witnessed."

"I'll admit they caught me off guard, too. But I'll go to Polly and explain."

"What will you say?"

He talked into the painted white wood. "That…that you were waking up and I was coming home from duty."

"And what? You were helping me to get dressed?"

Leaning back, he pressed his shoulders into the cool plaster wall. "I could tell them the truth. That we were arguing—"

"Because you slashed off my corset?"

He combed his fingers through his hair in frustration. Sarah was right. The truth would sound worse.

Sarah's voice got louder. "Polly's probably telling the neighbors right now what she saw—or what she *thinks* she saw—and David is probably writing home to New York City about the great Canadian wild."

"Polly won't spread gossip," John said weakly. God, he wished he believed it himself. "I asked her to keep it quiet."

"Polly Fitzgibbon is not one of your men. She won't be tried for treason or court-martialed if she tells people what she saw. And believe me, she won't be able to keep this quiet."

Sarah was right again. He knew that Polly Fitzgibbon had the biggest mouth in town; how he'd been so lucky to have her as a neighbor, he'd never fathom. "The police don't court-martial each other."

"Whatever."

John heard more thudding and furniture moving beyond the door. "What are you doing in there?"

She ignored his question. "What's your comeback about David?"

"I told him I'd have him arrested if he tried anything underhanded." But what John didn't tell her was that David took photographs for postcards and novelty buttons for distribution not only in New York City but across the country. A snapshot of John and a half-naked Sarah might have been amusing to any other person, but fortunately for him and Sarah, the picture had been destroyed.

The door opened suddenly, making him jump.

"You threatened David with arrest?" Smiling in deep approval, Sarah stepped into the hallway, fully clothed in a worn-out gingham dress. The collar couldn't be higher, going right up her throat, finished with a floppy lace flounce and a dozen tiny buttons, and the skirt couldn't be longer, sweeping her scuffed boots.

"Do you teach Sunday school in that thing?"

She patted the bun at the back of her head. How had she managed to capture all that beautiful curly hair into one tight bun? "It was given to me by my mother. As a matter of fact, it was my mother's."

He looked beyond her dress to the suitcases in her hands. Relief to see her finally packed and ready to leave settled on him. "There, you see. You'll be on the train in no time, David's photograph will be a bad memory and no one will even remember you were here."

His comment made her turn her head abruptly toward him. Her mouth twisted open in a stab of disappointment. The shoulders beneath the dress fell with his insult.

"I'm sorry, I didn't mean that no one will remember

you. That was a rude thing to say. I meant that no one will remember this incident.''

Well, that wasn't entirely true, either. *He'd* remember. He'd remember coming home to a beautiful temptress, *his* down cover spilling about her naked shoulders, the light of battle in her heated gray eyes. He'd never had a better welcoming. An unexpected smile caught his lips, but he thought better of telling her about the image he was savoring.

She stalked down the stairs. The bags, which he'd retrieved for her last night dragged behind her, thudding along each tread.

He followed, with a queasy feeling. ''You are heading to the train station, right?''

''I'm going to where I should have gone in the first place. To the boardinghouse.''

''Shouldn't we be going to the train station? I stopped by and got a schedule on my way here this morning. There's a train leaving this afternoon for Halifax, so there's no sense paying for a room at the boardinghouse.''

She threw her bags onto the Windsor chair by the door, then shoved past him to look into his armoire. To him, her nose seemed to get straighter the higher up in the air she held it. ''You came home this morning fully intending to get rid of me as quickly as possible.''

''That's not true,'' he said, stammering for an explanation, getting lost in the creamy skin of her cheeks and the finely arched brows. ''I was…I was going to the bakery to get us cinnamon buns.''

''And then after you fed me your hot-cross buns, you were going to get rid of me.'' She rummaged through his coats, his duster, one gentleman's overcoat and an oilskin slicker.

He reached past her to show her that none of her clothes were left inside the armoire. As his tight shoulder brushed against her soft one, she reeled back as if he'd bitten her.

Hmm… He watched the tide of crimson flood her cheeks. There could be worse things than biting Sarah O'Neill.

"It's not like I'm conspiring against you," he continued. "I had nothing to do with your arrival, remember? I'm doing everything I can to get you back home and to fully rectify the situation."

"Is that what I am now? *'A situation'?"*

He moaned. "You're exhausting." He'd never met a more argumentative woman. And he'd never been at more of a loss about how to remedy a difficult situation. Black-'n-White they called him? Well, things couldn't be grayer to him when it came to dealing with Sarah O'Neill.

"I'm staying here," she said.

"I beg your pardon?"

"I'm staying put. This is my home now."

"Sarah, maybe you're still not feeling well from yesterday." His hands waved the air. "There's no reason…there's no person…this wasn't my idea…you can't stay here."

She jammed her wide bonnet onto her head, then picked up her bags. As she stormed out the front door, she blasted him. "Don't worry. I mean, Calgary is my home now, not your house!"

Grabbing his Stetson, he dashed behind her as she strode down the sunlit front porch. "Let's both calm down. We're adult enough to speak frankly about this."

"Stop treating me like the doctor knows best."

Hell. John's temper rose another three notches. It'd been a long time since someone had argued with him like this, not since he'd been with his brothers and sisters back home, and they'd been gone for close to thirty years. John stumbled for a moment, hit by a pang of sorrow. He hadn't thought about them in that light for a long while, but the memories were nice. The last time they were together at the Toronto fairgrounds, the four of them had argued about whose turn it was on the carousel and whose turn to sit out. That was the last day he'd seen them conscious.

He heard Sarah huffing beneath the weight of her luggage as she reached the bottom step.

Racing to catch up, he tore the bags out of her hands. "Let me help you with those."

She yanked them back, nearly toppling over. "I'm afraid to let you help me. Every time you do, things get worse."

"Why do your words always manage to knock the stuffing out of me?"

A dog barked in the Fitzgibbon yard. Sarah and John turned to look and saw Polly drawing the shades.

John shrank in his boots. He felt awful about what Polly had witnessed on the stair landing. As a single woman alone in Calgary, Sarah's reputation was nothing to laugh about.

When he looked up the path two of his men, dressed in civilian clothes, were walking toward them. A wagonload of hay, pulled by oxen, creaked down the rutted street behind them. The cattle calls of the stockyards ten miles away echoed in the early morning mist.

Corporal Reid removed his broad brown felt hat and shifted his weight from one dirty black boot to the other. "Nice to see you again, ma'am."

Sergeant O'Malley dipped his hand into the inside

breast pocket of his wool jacket. When he removed a thick envelope, he passed it to Sarah.

"What's this?" She squeezed the envelope between her fingers. The lace trim at her wrist bounced.

"We were comin' to see the doc here, to have him pass this on to you. We had no idea that in our good fortune, we'd catch you here ourselves."

"Yes, it is a very fortunate morning, isn't it?" Her voice lacked the humor of her words. "It appears to be an envelope of money." She frowned.

Mrs. Fitzgibbon, who'd managed to sneak outside without being heard, peered cautiously over the fence. John refused to be intimidated by her scowls.

"It's the least we can do for you," said the corporal. "It was Dr. Calloway's idea. He thought the men should take up a collection, considering what we did to you."

Mrs. Fitzgibbon sniffed, then went back into her house.

What must the old lady think now? Sarah clicked her tongue at Mrs. Fitzgibbon, then at him. "I don't want your money."

"Please take it, ma'am. And our apologies for treatin' you...like you were a heifer for sale."

Sarah shook her head. "I wish I could say thank-you for the apology and all's well that ends well, but it isn't, is it?"

The two men lowered their heads. "No, ma'am."

Sarah colored beneath her bonnet. "I'd be most obliged if you'd return the letters I wrote."

"Oh!" The sergeant dug into his pocket again and handed her several envelopes.

She counted them. "One, two, three, four." She glanced at the sergeant.

He dug in and handed her one more.

"Five. Thank you."

"Please take the money, ma'am. It'll help you buy your return ticket, maybe a night or two in a fancy hotel, and it would sure make us feel better."

"Well, if it's to make you feel better—" She glared at the men with disapproval and it was the first time John had seen either of them blush with shame.

She tossed the envelopes into her satchel. "Thank you all for the most enjoyable eight days of nauseating travel. Good day."

While she stalked away, deserting them in the street, the three men gaped after her. Recovering quickly, John shooed away the other two while he ran to catch up. How on earth could she manage alone in town, knowing no one?

"Sarah, will you please allow me to help you?"

She fumbled with her bags, half dragging one of them on the back of her leg, balancing her satchel beneath her elbow and yanking on her bonnet to keep it straight in the gentle blowing wind. Silently they marched down the block to Macleod Trail and its wide boardwalk. Passersby nodded hello to him, gazing quizzically at the odd combination of the woman carrying everything while the man accompanying her strode empty-handed.

"Sarah."

"Ah, here's one."

She glanced up at the wood-burnished sign. Alice's Boardinghouse. John knew the woman inside to be older than the hills, but there was no telling what the two of them together might accomplish.

Much to Sarah's annoyance, he insisted on staying at the front desk while she registered for a room. The room wouldn't be available for two hours, though, so Sarah agreed to leave her baggage while she went outdoors again to run an errand.

Until Sarah was settled and he knew she'd calmed down enough so that she wouldn't do anything drastic, he couldn't leave her. It was getting awfully close to his two hours being up. He figured he had another half hour before returning to the hospital ward.

"You know, David told me he's a novelty writer." John tried to break through the danged wall of silence she'd erected.

"What's that?"

"He takes photos for postcards and novelty buttons, then writes captions beneath the photo, for amusement. That's how he earns his living."

"You mean, at this morning's photo, he might have written something like, 'Sarah gets her mounted man'?"

John laughed at her unexpected sense of humor. "How about, 'Another Eastern tourist arrives on the plains'?"

"'Another Mountie is brought to his knees.'"

"'A mail-order bride responds to an ad.'"

She laughed at that one. You never knew what would strike the woman funny, and what wouldn't. When she laughed, her entire face sparkled with warm spontaneity, her gray eyes glistened with flecks of blue and there wasn't an inch of skin that didn't glow with pleasure. The sound of her good humor rippled through him, gently arousing his senses.

They stopped at the corner to let a horse and rider pass. She followed the laughter of a group of children as they chased a mangy mutt around the water troughs.

Looking up at the buildings, they stood between Melodie's Bath and Barber House and Rossman's Mercantile.

"What are you looking for?" he asked.

"Work." She lifted her long skirts to descend the boardwalk and cross the road. "We passed a jeweler's on our way to the boardinghouse. Didn't you notice?"

"What do you call this one?" Standing inside the jewelry store, John leaned his bulky arms against the glass case.

Sarah laid her bonnet on the counter. "It's a singing bird box. You wind it up and a toy bird sings to you." She carefully lifted the gilded oval cover. A small bird with iridescent hummingbird feathers popped up, making her and John smile. "It's Swiss, I believe."

"That's correct, madam," said a female clerk, sidling up to the two of them. "It's vintage, and over sixty years old."

Sarah gently removed her hand from the box. "It's beautiful." She thought it strange that the clerk, who was about the same age, had called her madam and not miss.

"Good morning, John," said the clerk then, in a much more casual tone, causing Sarah's lashes to rise with suspicion. Not many people called him by his first name, Sarah had noticed. *She* had that privilege, but she'd almost married him.

"Mornin', Clarissa." John straightened, tall and lean, removing his Stetson but looking ill at ease.

"What brings you here?" Clarissa rubbed the waistline of her satin dress, fumbling with the pleats. She was pretty, with long brunette hair that she'd clasped at her temples with butterfly clips, and skin so white and smooth it looked like ice cream. When she swept her disapproving gaze over Sarah's best housedress, Sarah felt dowdy in comparison.

He introduced the women. They nodded politely, but

as he and Clarissa caught up with small talk, Sarah took her bonnet and stepped away to continue studying the merchandise. He'd already told her that Clarissa was the owner's daughter and didn't do the hiring. Sarah was waiting for Mr. or Mrs. Ashford to step out from behind the velvet drapes of the back room.

"It's a pounding right above my heart," Sarah heard Clarissa say. "Above my *breast*bone. Sometimes it's uncontrollable. What do you think it is? Heart palpitations?"

"Perhaps you need an examination," John replied, his dark features glued to the annoying woman.

Clarissa lowered her eyes coyly. "It would be in my best interest, I can't deny it."

"I'll set up the appointment this morning. I'll drop by Doc Waters's office and tell him to expect you."

Clarissa's look of surprise was equaled by Sarah's. "*Old* Dr. Waters?"

Trying to hide her amusement at Clarissa's disappointment, Sarah ran her hand along a carriage clock. Fancy pillars showcased an exquisitely painted porcelain dial and side panels. She turned to see John and an embarrassed Clarissa standing two feet away.

"I like the shape of that clock," said John. "It's massive."

"And see—" said Sarah, getting caught up with enthusiasm for the lovely items. "A lever in the base allows you to select silence, half strike and full strike."

"Yes," said Clarissa, rushing to take over the conversation. Was there some sort of bidding competition between the two women of which Sarah wasn't aware? The woman needn't feel threatened by Sarah, she had no hold over Dr. John Calloway. "The clock face has the name of the retailer,'' Clarissa added. ''Tiffany & Co., from New York. They're very prestigious.''

''Never heard of them,'' said John.

Clarissa smiled at him—a touch too readily, in Sarah's opinion.

Sarah raised her eyebrows as she occupied herself with something else. John and his taste for women were none of her concern.

But how could her life turn so drastically from one day to the next? Yesterday at this time she was on a train headed to Calgary, imagining her life with a tender doctor on the prairies, imagining the possibly of bearing their children... She glanced away in humiliation.

She still had Keenan to hope for, the only person left of her family. Did he even go by the same name, or had he changed it to protect himself?

One thing at a time, she told herself. If she took one step at a time, it wouldn't seem so overwhelming.

Staring into the glass counter, Sarah gasped. ''What an unusual watch.''

''Which one?'' asked John.

''The slender gold one. The ladies' pendant watch.''

Clarissa squeezed behind the counter, brushing against John in the process. ''Ah, yes. This came in this morning. I appraised and bought it myself, from a man I'm afraid wasn't fully aware of its value. It's truly a classic. Eighteen karat gold, from Geneva.''

Sarah frowned. ''What a shame about the crown.''

''What?'' said Clarissa, peering closer.

''What's a crown?'' asked John.

''The winder knob. It's off-kilter. Let's hope the movement inside isn't beyond repair.''

Clarissa colored and scooped the watch from the case. "It wasn't like this when I appraised it."

"Hmm," Sarah said softly. "Perhaps a switch was made when the seller got his money. It's a common scam."

"How do you know all this?" John whispered.

"My father was a clockmaker and owned a store for years in Halifax. He taught me."

He'd also taught Keenan. Not only had their father taught them clockwork, but gunsmithing. Most folks couldn't afford to own a Colt or a Smith and Wesson; town clockmakers often doubled as gunsmiths to make everyday guns for local folks. But gunsmithing was something Sarah had buried in her past, and fervently wished Keenan had, as well.

"That's very impressive," said a baritone voice behind them.

A friendly and handsome balding man smiled at them as they turned around. John introduced the dashing man as Mr. Ashford. Twenty minutes later, Sarah happily left the store as their newly hired clerk. Working here, she'd have to contend with Clarissa, but seeing that she had no romantic interest in the surgeon, Sarah didn't foresee a problem.

She tucked the escaping strands of her hair beneath her bonnet. "Are you finished drooling over Clarissa?"

"I was *not* drooling."

"Yes, you were. You were drooling all over each other. And I, for one, think you'd make a lovely couple."

It was a strange sensation, watching him flirt with another woman when only yesterday he was *her* intended. Try as she might, the prickly feeling wouldn't leave.

He shook his head. The sunlight caught his firm, black

temples. "I'd never go within ten feet of Clarissa Ashford. Her former lover is doing serious jail time for larceny and theft. He used to own a sawmill in the Rockies, and she ran off with him when she couldn't squeeze enough money out of his younger partner."

"Oh my goodness." Were these the kinds of people she had to contend with in Calgary? "What are her folks like?"

"They're honest and hardworking, near as we can tell. You shouldn't have trouble working there. There is one other jewelry shop you could try, but he just hired a new man."

"This one's fine. They told me I can start tomorrow."

John came to a stop on the sunny boardwalk. The mist had lifted, leaving behind a blazing blue sky.

For the first time in twenty-four hours, her future didn't look so bleak. Maybe she'd do well in this town. She'd found work and a place to stay, and she'd find her brother, too.

"You haven't stopped for one minute since your arrival. Look how much you've accomplished today." His smile was warm and true, and had a dazzling effect on her.

Her guard went up. She stepped away from him as shoppers squeezed by on the boardwalk. Sarah could still see through him. She'd found a place to live and a place of employment, so he was free of her. He was off the coals.

"Thanks for accompanying me. I'm sure your presence had something to do with Mr. Ashford hiring me. And now, I suppose you can rest your conscience."

Now that she was here, she was going to make the best of her situation. Maybe she'd give herself a time limit to find Keenan. The money the Mounties had collected would go a little way toward paying her boardinghouse, but if she couldn't make ends meet with her new job, she'd have to pack up and go somewhere cheaper.

She hadn't worked at her father's store for five years since she and her mother had sold it, and she wasn't quite comfortable with everything at Ashford's, but a little time and experience would polish her skills.

John insisted on following her right to the front desk.

"I can handle being on my own."

"But I'd like to see you to safety."

"Well, who do you think is going to walk me everyday to and from work? You won't be around and it'll be up to me anyway."

"Stop arguing with everything I say."

She groaned and kept walking. And groaned again as they entered the small doorway and encountered the two elderly women Sarah had met on the train. While Sarah had kept her personal business to herself for a thousand miles, she'd opened up to them halfway here, around Saskatoon. Sadly, it had been enough time to blab everything.

"Hello, Mrs. Lott, Mrs. Thomas," said Sarah.

"Why, hello young lady," said the thinner one, Mrs. Lott, with the kind wrinkled green eyes. "I see you're here with your new groom-to-be."

Sarah introduced them to John, who'd never met them. The sisters had obviously heard of him, though. Being the town's only surgeon, it was understandable.

Sarah squirmed under the sisters's scrutiny and John cleared his throat.

Mrs. Thomas, the one with the head of completely white hair, turned to John. The older women both looked tiny and frail standing next to his bronzed body. "Sarah told us on the train that she'd been corresponding with a lovely young man. Imagine our surprise when she told us it was you, Dr. Calloway. Have you set the date?''

Sarah swallowed hard and avoided looking at John. "There's not going to be a wedding."

"Dear me," said Mrs. Lott, clutching at her throat. "Why?"

"There was a mix-up, it seems. Dr. Calloway wasn't the... It wasn't the doctor who..."

John stepped in, removing his hat. "It was a miscommunication is what it was. I'm helping Sarah to settle in. She just found employment at Ashford Jewelers. Won't you congratulate her?"

The women gaily offered their best wishes, but Sarah knew she couldn't avoid the questions forever.

"Perhaps you ladies might keep her in mind if you're in the market for a lovely strand of pearls or a ring to adorn those pretty fingers."

The older women giggled. They did look rather wealthy, judging by their fine clothes and necklaces. "Why, Dr. Calloway, we didn't think you noticed such things."

As the conversation mellowed, Mrs. Lott turned to Sarah. "Would you and the doctor care to join us for dinner? We could meet here, later, say around seven?"

Sarah craned her neck awkwardly up at John, wondering what he thought.

His response seemed smooth and well rehearsed. "I'm afraid I must decline."

"But we insist," said Mrs. Lott.

"Unfortunately, I'm needed in surgery."

Mrs. Lott put her warm hands on top of Sarah's. "But you'll join us, won't you, dear?"

"Certainly." Sarah's tension eased. Perhaps it wouldn't be too bad living here. John's standing beside her indicated his support and respect in this town, and unless the Mounties leaked the truth, no one needed to know that her arrival had been a hoax. Perhaps she *could* hold her head high. Perhaps the town *would* welcome her.

"And where might you ladies be off to, this fine morning?" John inquired as they passed in a cloud of perfume.

"Why, you might call it a family reunion. Our young nephew is here from New York City, and we're off to visit our cousin, Mrs. Polly Fitzgibbon."

Chapter Five

"How on earth did you get a bullet lodged in your thigh?" In a sour mood and troubled by the man's injury, John asked the question later that afternoon at the hospital.

Sprawled on the examination table with his trouser leg torn apart, Corporal Travis Reid groaned in pain. John had given him an opiate, but hadn't wanted to sedate the man too heavily until after his anesthesia and bullet extraction.

"We were hunting. O'Malley thought he saw a doe scrambling through the woods. His shot ricocheted off a maple and hit me in the thigh."

Irritation nipped at John. The hospital needed more medical officers. Standing beside him on the surgical ward, Logan, the veterinarian, was ready with his doused rag of chloroform. *An animal doctor.*

"And now you're out of commission due to an irresponsible hunting accident."

Travis grimaced, trying to make light of the situation. "No venison for supper tonight, either."

John was beyond amusement. He was tired and hungry and mad at their carelessness. "Never mind the venison," he snapped. "Out of eighty-eight men, we've got eleven out due to injuries. The others got hurt in the line of duty, but this injury was totally unnecessary. Couldn't you be more careful?''

''Sure, Doc,'' Travis snarled. ''But not everything's always right or wrong. A man's gotta have distractions, not work all the time. But I reckon you don't know much about that.''

John balked. No one had ever talked back to him. And then his temper dissipated as he realized he was berating an injured man. ''Dammit, Travis, sorry.''

With a softer nod, Travis succumbed to the chloroform. John removed the slug then sutured the wound.

What was wrong with him lately? Why did he bark at everyone? When Travis was settled, John sought the privacy of his quarters. He tried to convince himself that he wasn't the lone man Travis made him out to be.

But since Christmas there'd been no time to spend with women, no time to take a leave, no time to go hunting or fishing, no riding to the foothills. The police were busy.

Just last week the Grayveson gang had stolen forty-eight mustangs a hundred and fifty miles to the south. By the time the Mounties had given chase, the outlaws had faded across the American border. Cross-border gangs had been one of the main reasons the Mounties had been formed by the federal government sixteen years ago. That and the illegal whiskey trade with the Indians. But the Grayveson gang would probably be back, selling the Montana horses and cattle they would probably steal next to the folks in Alberta where the brands weren't recognized.

Maybe Wesley had had the right idea. If it'd been John who'd died instead, would he have been satisfied with what he'd accomplished in his life so far? Poor Wesley had been robbed of his life; the loss had triggered John to think more about his own direction. Was work *all* that fulfilled him?

When he was a younger man, he'd envisioned himself in the future with a wife and children, maybe grandchildren in his retirement years. But he hadn't had the time or the inclination to look for a wife. There wasn't much choice, unless he went for a fifteen- or sixteen-year-old daughter of one of the ranchers, or the occasional European immigrant, or a daughter of one of the Metis Indians. And the years kept passing by.

John was forty years old today. Like most of his private affairs, he kept his birthdate to himself. But what had happened to his vision of family?

He sifted through the medical journals that he'd picked up from the train depot. He leafed through them with disappointment. It looked like this month's British medical journals wouldn't supply any answers to his other problem, either. During the twelve months he'd been treating the blacksmith on Angus McIver's ranch, John hadn't been able to pinpoint the man's illness. The blacksmith was only thirty years old yet sometimes he walked with a shaking palsy, like an old man.

Rubbing the back of his neck, John looked up at the wall clock. Six-fifteen. Sarah would be having dinner soon.

She could be a major distraction. Hell, she was already.

If marriage was what she wanted and why she was here, he was certain she'd soon find a husband. With her pretty smile and ready attitude for hard work, she'd have suitors begging for her company. Some men might consider her to be a handful, but her amusing tongue lashings reminded John of his younger sister. He and Beth had been closest in age and they'd argued night and day. After she'd passed away so suddenly, he'd felt guilty for years about their constant bickering, but as he'd matured, he'd realized they had only been children and the arguments hadn't meant he'd loved his sister less.

He missed Beth. And his younger twin brothers, Hank and James... Much to his mother's annoyance, John had been the only child who hadn't eaten any of the food at the fairgrounds that Sunday. He'd had an upset stomach and couldn't eat, but wouldn't admit to the nausea or his ma wouldn't have allowed him to ride the carousel. The rest had stuffed themselves with sausage and bread and vegetable soup and corn on the cob, then licorice and walnuts and mints. And lots and lots of water. *Contaminated water.* That's how they'd contracted the typhoid that had killed them. He and his ma and pa had been the only ones left standing. Ten other children had died that week, as well.

The wall clock chimed six-thirty. Why hadn't Sarah married before this? Why had she been so desperate to answer a newspaper advertisement and why so far away from home? Or was she simply as alone in the world as he was?

His stomach growled with hunger. Rising out of his chair, he strode to his closet. Donning a newly ironed dress shirt and his Sunday pair of pants, he headed out the door. It was his fortieth birthday, and what did he have to lose?

"Mrs. Lott, here I am!" Sarah rushed down the carpeted stairs, hoping to catch Mrs. Lott and her sister before they escaped into the milling crowd. The boarding-house owner had established a reputation as an excellent cook and there was often a lineup for her dining room.

Lifting the fabric of her finest blue twill skirt so she wouldn't trip down the stairs, Sarah waved again but the two women ignored her as they headed to the front door. They were going in the wrong direction.

Sara shouted louder. "Mrs. Lott! Mrs. Thomas!"

Weaving past a gentleman in a bowler hat, Sarah squeezed along the stair wall. When her sleeve brushed an oil painting, it jarred and she lunged to straighten it.

A hallway full of people stared. Some women averted their eyes and whispered to their friends. Sarah was struck by self-consciousness. She'd created a stir because she'd been too zestful in her shouting and clumsy with the painting.

However, the elderly sisters turned and waited for her. Like Sarah in her white mutton-sleeve blouse and cameo brooch clipped to her throat, the ladies were dressed in their finest.

Sarah squeezed past a man with a walking stick. Puffing to catch her breath, she felt herself flush with enthusiasm as she peered into the wrinkled green eyes of dear Mrs. Lott. "I've come to join you for dinner."

Ten feet past their shoulders, the stained-glass door opened. Dr. John Calloway strode through it.

With a quickening of her pulse, Sarah slunk into the corner, hoping he wouldn't catch sight of her. What brought him here? He'd said he was on duty this evening, so he must be on a doctor's call. In a glance, she didn't see a medicine bag, only an annoyingly handsome man with slicked-back hair and a white silk shirt. He loomed a good ten inches above the crowd.

Mrs. Lott had her back turned, so didn't see him. She wasn't smiling at Sarah as she had been that morning. "But we've already eaten."

"Oh—" Had Sarah made an error? She pivoted on her high-heeled black boot to glance at Mrs. Thomas. "But..."

Mrs. Thomas brought her leather gloves to her nose and sniffled. Her shock of white hair, pinned in billowing curls atop her head, shook with disapproval.

"But I thought you said seven o'clock. I'm five minutes early."

"Dr. Calloway declined, remember?"

"Yes, but I thought I'd mentioned I would join you alone."

"Sorry, there must have been a *miscommunication.*"

A burning heat slapped Sarah in the face. Polly Fitzgibbon had obviously done her work. She likely spread the gossip of Sarah's nakedness in John's arms and God knew what else.

John spoke beside her, causing her pulse to leap again. "Good evening, ladies. I see I've arrived in time. I'd like to join you for dinner if I'm still invited."

Trying to hide her disgrace, Sarah spun around to weave back up the stairs to the solace of her room. "It seems we're both late, Dr. Calloway."

He grabbed her wrist firmly and held it to his side, but smiled at the other women. "Late? It's not seven yet."

Sarah tried to wriggle out of his grasp, but he held her strong. A silent turbulence roared between them. Had he overheard that the sisters had declined Sarah? What was he doing? People were staring, and he was making the situation worse. It didn't help that his touch flustered her thoughts.

The two women puckered their lips. "We've already eaten, Doctor. Good evening." They strolled away.

Another couple brushed by John and Sarah. They mumbled, inaudible to most, but not to Sarah, which was the effect she knew they were seeking. "…caught red-handed with her clothes off. Phony mail-order bride. Wonder how much she charges…"

"Now just a minute," said John, red beneath his collar.

The sisters hesitated near the door, glanced back and fanned their faces with their gloves. Dead silence filled the hallway. Not a person in the crowd moved.

"John, don't—" whispered Sarah.

"Come back here, ladies," John commanded. "I'd like to explain something to you."

The women clicked their tongues. Someone held the door open and they slinked into the blue evening sky.

With a heated look of fury, John glared at the staring faces. He must have realized they were gauging his possessive hand on Sarah's wrist, because he dropped it quickly.

His absence left a cold spot on her wrist. She hadn't been touched like that for a very long time. It'd been a raw act of control, of possession. She fought the unwanted feeling of satisfaction it brought her.

"Good night," she said softly, rubbing her wrist, turning up the stairs, afraid to draw more attention to herself.

"Wait." John pressed his warm hand into her sleeve and held her back by the arm. Heat arced between them.

Judging by the murmuring and shuffling of feet, the crowd had lost their interest in John and Sarah. She stiffened her posture with pride.

When she turned around, a step higher and almost eye level to his handsome dark face and searching gaze, he added, "You still have to eat. There's a great steakhouse around the block."

The corner of his mouth twisted with a little smile. What would it be like to kiss that generous mouth?

"I don't think I'd be good company." She raced up one step and he followed by one.

"Better company than those two women."

His gentle attempt to make her smile worked. Why

should she run for cover? Who were they to treat her like that?

A teasing gleam twinkled in his brown eyes. Maybe she should keep her distance from John. He'd already rejected her once.

"Steak sounds good."

"If I can calm down long enough," John said an hour later over dinner, "I'll go to Mrs. Lott and Mrs. Thomas, and explain what happened. That you were caught in the middle of an idiotic game between my men, and brought here under false pretenses."

Sarah watched the golden candlelight flicker over the bridge of his nose and cheekbones, over the short wave of brown hair. The shadow of a beard and mustache added to his brawny appearance. Yet a white silk shirt draped from his wide shoulders, in soft contrast to his rough masculinity.

"I think that *they* think that once I met you…I no longer wanted—" he swallowed "—to marry you."

Sarah cut into her rib eye steak. "I'd prefer to explain it to them myself, thank you, when the time is right." She arched her shoulders against her high-backed chair, loosening the tension in her muscles. "But I'm no longer sure it's worth it."

John glanced over her ruffled blouse all the way down to her cinched waistline. She was covered from wrist to throat by fabric, but somehow John's heated glance made her feel as though her clothing was totally improper. How did he have that ability to make her so aware of her own sensuality?

"The rumors are spreading. Unfortunately, it's worth your reputation."

Her heart pounded in an offbeat rhythm. She knew he was right, but she wouldn't allow panic to set in.

He slid his empty plate away. "And as far as being caught this morning—together like we were—let me try to explain that to them, at least."

"Could you try to explain it to me first?"

She captured his attention with the remark. He laughed softly. "I see your point. Maybe it's best if we don't try to explain it at all."

He swirled his glass of white wine with one large hand, gazing into its depth. His fingers, long and lean, were tinted from the sun and exceptionally clean and trim. His hands were beautiful; a captivating paradox to the rest of his rough-and-rugged presence.

Then he sipped his wine, calling her attention to his well-defined lips. She wished she would stop noticing everything about him.

"What brought you here, Sarah? I mean, besides my so-called letters. Why did you come?"

Her body felt heavy and warm. This was her opening to speak of Keenan, but how could she reveal her brother? She didn't know who to trust in this town, and the more she kept her mouth closed, the better off she'd be.

"I think I've been waiting for this opportunity for years, but wasn't aware of it."

John gave her a quizzical look. She noticed a few other women in the room dining with their spouses, glancing in his direction. John seemed unaware of the envious gazes afforded to Sarah.

She finished with her plate and gently sipped her wine, welcoming the fruity taste on her tongue. "My mother passed away after a long bout with tuberculosis."

"Mmm," he said sympathetically, nodding his head. "That can be an awful decline. Did you have help?"

"There was no else at home—my father had passed away several years ago himself and…"

…and Keenan no longer lived with us.

John asked more questions about her life in Halifax, and the more answers she gave, the more he wanted to know.

She felt awkward at exposing herself, but flattered by his interest.

While they ate sweet plum dumplings, she asked, "Why did you become a doctor?"

A melancholy flitted across his brow. "Because of my family."

"They urged you?"

"No." His voice quaked. "Because of what happened to my family. My two younger brothers and one sister were very young…. They contracted typhoid and unfortunately didn't pull through."

Sarah winced, letting him go on, lulled by the serenity of his voice and this quiet, shared moment.

"There was nothing any of us could do to help. A few years later, I enrolled in medical school…"

"…because you never wanted to feel that helpless again."

He nodded in surprise that she'd finished his sentence. The candlelight flickered, her throat ached with sympathy, and he quickly went on to another topic.

Later, after they finished eating and were strolling back to the boardinghouse, she still felt a connection, as if he'd opened up and told her things perhaps he'd never said before. What an awful thing to lose his sister and brothers the way he had. Sarah couldn't help but admire the man John had become because of it. A doctor. Who else did she know who could reach beyond their own grief to see so clearly to the other side?

A purple half moon followed them, casting misty shadows on the uneven road. The scent of prairie flowers mingled with the scent of falling dew, and the lowing of cattle miles away nestled them in an intimate hush.

They were content to walk speechless in the tranquility. When they passed a streetlamp beside a deserted alley, Sarah stopped beneath it to say good-night.

She tilted her face upward and shivered in surprise when John cupped his fingers beneath her chin.

Riveted by the feel of his skin on hers, she parted her lips.

He fingered the cameo brooch at her collar. ''This is pretty,'' he whispered, then bent his head and kissed her.

It was an arousal, like a floating cloud of wispy lips brushing hers. She closed her eyes and let him draw her close against his muscled chest. Inhaling the scent of his clean skin and faint cologne, not able to breathe enough of him, she responded with an awakening.

The kiss was extraordinary. Supple and rich. She felt him growing urgent as he wrapped his heavy arms around her waist and shoulder. She responded with a torturous, teasing pleasure. Their tongues met timidly, like an exploration, then grew heated in desire…in the certainty of what could happen between them.

If they let it.

Awed by the feeling of being in his arms, of knowing who he was and where he came from and how he'd rescued her this evening, she lost herself in the universe of his body.

Why had it all been a hoax?

Why had she been denied the good fortune of becoming John's wife?

It seemed like they had only started when John ripped away from her aching body. Although his gaze was hungry and his lips swollen from their kiss, he drew away farther. His mouth quivered with unreleased passion.

His words were a murmured plea. ''Good night, mail-order Sarah.''

Chapter Six

For three days, sandwiched between his busy calls, John tried not to think of Sarah, the intimate evening they'd shared, or the tempting kiss. Why was it when it came to his work, he could make a judgment call in seconds, but when it came to Sarah, he wasn't sure where he stood or what he wanted?

He was much safer dealing with his men.

On Monday he was busy changing burn dressings on the two constables who'd suffered in the forest fires. Fortunately the fire was under control and their burns healing.

On Tuesday and Wednesday John was critically busy with Constable Pawson, the man who'd sliced his thigh clear down to the bone in a train door while foiling a robbery attempt. The inflammation might have turned into gangrene if John hadn't applied the poultices frequently and stayed up all night tending to the fever.

Finally, Thursday morning after a good night's sleep, he was paying his routine weekly call to Angus McIver's ranch. John was walking beneath the clump of pines with Angus as he headed to the buggy. He'd tended to Angus's flaring gallbladder, treated the ranch cook for severe sunburn to the back of his neck, checked up on the blacksmith's trembling hand—still puzzled over the symptoms—then treated the foreman's youngest daughter for a patch of poison ivy.

"Anyway," said Angus, pressing closer to John as he helped him to the buggy, "next time you come, maybe you could convince Sheila to let you examine her again."

John tried to saying the words kindly, knowing how much it affected Angus. "We've been through this before. It's not easy for you to hear, but you're the one who's likely sterile."

Angus clenched his jaw. In his fifties, he was tall and brawny and as heavy as an ox. Widowed early from his first wife, he'd married Sheila in her twenties, but in their ten-year marriage, they hadn't produced any children.

It was sad to see how desperately Angus wanted them. Sheila had resigned herself, content to mother her dozen nieces and nephews who lived down the road, but Angus owned one of the busiest cattle ranches in southern Alberta and had often told John he only wanted to pass it down to a son—or a daughter.

Someone tugged John's knee. One of the blacksmith's children peered out from John's pant leg. "Are you gonna help my pa get better?"

John smiled at the slender eight-year-old boy. His name was Russell but most called him Rusty because of his orange hair. "I'm trying."

"Why was his hand shakin' so much this mornin'? It hasn't done that for a long time."

"I'm looking for the reason, son."

"When are you gonna find it? What kind of doctor are ya?"

"Shoo," said Angus with a laugh. "Us adults are talkin'."

Angus tried to make light of what the boy had just said,

but John sobered and watched Rusty run back to the stables in his dirty overalls and blackened bare feet. What was John missing in his readings? What couldn't he see?

Sergeant O'Malley strode through the pine trees, ready to hop into the buggy beside John and return to town together, as they'd come.

"Any new information?" John asked him.

O'Malley shook his head and peered at Angus. "They got away with only one steer this time, but they attempted the entire herd."

"Goddamn bastards," said Angus. "If I hadn't hired more men and bought more guns to protect myself, I'd be penniless by now."

"The Grayveson gang has returned in full bloody force," said John softly. "We've all got to protect ourselves. After what happened to Wesley..." His rage flared. The four sentry posts nestled among the ranches were useless unless they could be manned twenty-four hours a day. The Grayveson gang knew exactly when to strike, during unmanned hours.

"Stay away from those rich foods, Angus," said John as they rolled away. "They're bad for your gallbladder."

Their drive back to town was quiet. At the fort, John had a few hours to himself. He combed through the journals again, but hungered for fresh air. He wondered where Sarah was, how her day went at the jeweler's and who she was eating with tonight. It was eight o'clock and he'd already eaten, but he decided to ride to the boardinghouse to see for himself.

Galloping into town atop his mare, John was surprised at the anticipation he felt. After the last four days of strain at work, he almost ached to see her. He imagined Sarah with a shawl draped across one high shoulder, her body moving gracefully beneath her skirts. The last time he'd been with her, her face was staring up at him, her ruby lips stained with his kiss. He couldn't deny the spark of excitement at the prospect of maybe kissing her again.

What was it about this woman that created such an urgency inside him? Over the years he'd held the company of several women. Some he'd slept with, some he'd only dined with. With Sarah, he wanted to do both. If there was a deeper significance to why he felt this way, more than just physical attraction, he wanted to know what it was.

The boardinghouse owner was commanding the front desk when John strode in. "Sarah hasn't returned yet for the day."

The jolt of disappointment he felt had nothing to do with reason. "She's still at work? This late?"

The elderly woman eyed him carefully. Unease clouded her gaze. Looking at her frail figure and hunched back, most folks wouldn't recognize she was as nimble as Willie, the chimpanzee. "When's the last time you spoke to Sarah?"

"Sunday evening," he said in a panic to the woman's glumness. "Why?"

"Can't say for sure how much longer she'll be stayin'. Yesterday, she got fired."

Half an hour later John bolted down the other side of the road, looking through the lit store windows, questioning people if they'd seen Sarah. When they answered no, the alarm that tore through him didn't make sense, but he didn't stop to analyze it. When he finally saw her exiting Rossman's Mercantile, his body screeched to a halt.

His feet pounded up the boardwalk stairs to her side. "Sarah. Here you are."

She was wearing her high-collared Sunday school dress

again, but this time it almost looked provocative. The starched collar and overly stern pattern were a sharp contrast to the blossoming curves beneath and the sharp warm wit it concealed.

Sarah came to an abrupt stop and blinked up at him. "John. Hello." She fumbled with a hand on the railing. Her gaze darted to the well-dressed couple passing by. Was she self-conscious of being seen with him? A stone skidded off the boardwalk beside her foot and plopped into the water trough below.

Embarrassed to be seen *with him?* Humiliation crept up his neck.

"What happened?" He squeezed in tight beside her and cupped her elbow, leading her to the alley where they might talk privately. Her warmth seeped into his body and it felt good. He lowered his head to her ear, beside her bonnet, and whispered, "Alice told me you lost your job."

Sarah wheeled around. Even in the dimly lit street, he saw her eyes flash with anger and that stubborn chin tilt upward.

"Who asked you to leave?" he said.

"Clarissa."

His temper burst. "She has no authority—"

"Her father told her to." Sarah pulled in a deep breath, stepped out of the path of two cowboys, then lowered her voice. "When I confronted him, he said he didn't want to listen to the rumors at first because of the headaches he'd gone through with rumors about his own daughter. I guess he was referring to her former beau being in prison. But when his customers asked *not* to be served by me, he said he had no choice but to let me go. He said folks know Clarissa because she grew up in this town and are forgiving of her, but they don't know me."

John figured Mr. Ashford to be a straightforward man, and it must have been difficult for him to confide about his daughter's downfall. But dammit, it was unfair to fire Sarah. "What rumors about you is he talking about?"

"A few things about me have surfaced." She tilted her head and her red curly hair came tumbling around her shoulders. Her nostrils flared with indignation. "The contents of my original letters to you—*to your men*—got out."

John groaned and closed his eyes. "You mean—"

"There's been a question about my virtue."

It sunk like a stone between them.

"Hell, I'm sorry."

What she'd written to John in confidence, hoping to be honest with her groom-to-be, had backfired. She was a phony mail-order bride, caught naked in his arms, and every time she turned around to try to improve her situation, she sank lower into the mud.

As a physician, he could name half a dozen women in this town who'd delivered their babies only six to seven months after their wedding day, which meant their holy attitude was a sham.

As a man, he was curious how Sarah had lost her virginity, but he was damn sure it was none of his business. It struck him how both he and Sarah were intertwined in the same story and resulting ugly gossip, but while he'd managed to escape the hostile remarks, she was paying the consequences.

"Who leaked it?"

"I don't know. Apparently some of the married Mounties had told their wives about the letters, some of those wives had told their neighbors."

John kicked the ground and swore. He tried to focus on what she might do to regain her footing. "You could find other employment. You could try the other watch-maker in town.'' John stepped forward, urging her to fol-low. ''We'll go now. I'll help you.''

Sarah shook her head in disgust. She stayed put.

''You were right about the watchmaker. He told me he just hired a new man and doesn't need another clerk.''

All right, then, they'd try another approach. With his hands on his hips, John glared at the sign swaying above her head. ''How about Rossman's Mercantile?''

''*Mrs.* Rossman wouldn't look me in the eye, but she just told me—'' Sarah cast her shiny eyes to the street, ''—she said they don't need to hire any women like me.''

John winced. He focused farther down the road. ''The bank?''

''When I inquired there, I heard the manager behind a wall, whispering to the clerk to tell me he wasn't in.''

John cursed again. ''How about the restaurant—''

''She told me she's a church-abiding woman. That was her answer. I could tell you about the other places I vis-ited, but they all said the same thing.''

John's stomach twisted with the injustice. ''All of them?''

Sarah's posture softened as she marched to the board-walk stairs. She lowered herself to the stoop. John braced himself then walked over and sat next to her. For a brief second their thighs touched and his pulse raced. She pulled away and he wished he could do something to right this awfully desperate situation.

''The schoolteacher said she could hire me as an assis-tant,'' Sarah continued, ''but if folks don't want me look-ing after their children, there isn't much she can do. It's too humiliating to try.''

She flushed, but remained silent. If he reached over and touched her hand, he was sure he'd feel her trembling. He couldn't remember the last time he'd felt as terrified as she must feel at this moment. He'd never been surrounded by complete strangers, ones who didn't trust him.

Shame at what his men had gotten away with, at what they'd done to Sarah, and shame at his accidental role in her life numbed him.

"At least in Halifax, people wouldn't know the rumors."

He turned to stare at her silhouette, blanketed by the darkness. "Is that what you want to do? Return to Halifax?"

"It's not what I want at all." Her voice dropped to a bare whisper. "The other night when you walked me home from dinner, someone saw us kissing."

His muscles squeezed. "Since when is kissing a crime?"

"It's adding to what people think of me."

They listened to the soft evening sounds of trampling feet behind them on the boardwalk, to doors opening and closing, to the call of children down an alleyway.

She toyed with her fingers and said absently, "I've misplaced my gloves and I don't recall where."

"You know, Wesley Quinn had ordered himself a mail-order bride. He was two weeks shy of marrying her when he got killed."

"Who was Wesley Quinn?"

Sarah listened quietly as John explained about his friend. "He was trying to tell me something…by ordering you for me."

"I had no idea that Wesley had been behind the letters. It's too late to blame him." Sighing, she added, "I'm sorry that your friend was killed."

Tenderly, Sarah leaned forward and rubbed his arm. He reacted with a downpour of sensations. The gesture was comforting and soothing, at the same time electrifying his desire. His defenses weakened and a raw sensuality coursed between them. Heat followed her touch.

The light rippled over her downy cheeks and parted lips.

He reached forward to cup her chin. "If this involvement with you were happening to any other man but me, the Mounties would be putting pressure on him to do the right thing and stand by you. To make restitution. I know we would. We've forced a marriage in far less scandalous circumstance."

The fact that she didn't draw away made his heart beat faster.

"What's done is done." Her lashes lowered. She gazed at his mouth. "We can't ask Wesley why he did it."

John traced his thumb across her lip. "But I'm getting away with this because of who I am. You're paying the cost."

He felt her respond beneath his touch.

"I prefer to focus ahead, on where to go from here."

The thought came to him slowly. At first he ignored it, but it kept popping back into his mind. Why couldn't he do it? Why shouldn't he ask her? They seemed like they could be compatible, and both had much to gain from the proposition.

If she said yes, it would easily correct her tarnished reputation.

And to *his* benefit, he'd gain the companionship he craved, and perhaps a family down the road. Children he'd often considered having. He was forty years old. Sarah O'Neill was a good woman.

He wiped a sweaty palm on his pant leg. *Stop,* he warned himself. *Think this through.* His pulse galloped ahead. His breathing doubled.

"Sarah, would you consider marriage? To me?"

Chapter Seven

Sarah simply stared, thunderstruck, at John's proposal. Heat pounded in her temples. She smothered a groan, leaped off the stoop, brushed off her skirt and stalked away. Why had she agreed to come to this town? Why couldn't she have been...*smarter* and seen through the letters? Only an idiot would fall for it twice.

"Where are you going?" John hollered.

"To get my gloves. I remember where I left them."

"Won't you answer my question?"

"It's another hoax."

John struggled to keep up, but she didn't care. He followed along the main street, squeezing between the men exiting the saloon. "I'd never joke about marriage."

Piano music drifted through the breezy night air. Her pace increased. The wind snatched her hair and tossed it over her shoulders. "Then you'd like to marry me out of a sense of duty."

Breathless, he pulled her back by the arms and held her in front of him, frowning as if to say, *What's wrong with that?*

There was plenty wrong with it. She squirmed out of his grasp. "At least when we were writing to each other,

I thought you wanted marriage because of *me*. It may have started as a mail-order ad, but you'd written that you'd received several offers and you thought *we'd* be most suitable.''

''Ah-hh,'' he said in frustration. ''We keep arguing about imaginary letters that I didn't write.''

''I still believe suitability is the prime consideration. Not scandalous circumstance.''

She heard his heavy footsteps come to a grind behind her. ''Sarah,'' he called.

Despite her better judgment, she slowed to a wavering stop.

John drew up behind her. His voice probed deeper. When he stroked her arm, the touch sent a tingle to her fingertips. ''Would you let me read your letters?''

Oh, the embarrassment. ''No.''

From the nickname she'd heard his men call him, and the way he'd come to her aid the other night when Mrs. Lott and Thomas had been so condescending, Sarah knew he followed protocol and had a deep sense of obligation. He was offering to marry her because he thought he should.

But that's not the kind of marriage she wanted.

She wanted friendship and companionship that could grow into love.

Finally she turned to meet the overpowering strength in his firm, clear features. Could their relationship flourish and develop into something more?

After all, marriage to him was the reason she'd come West.

''Tell me why you want to marry me,'' she said. ''Not just any woman, but me.''

He tugged in a long breath, likely knowing how important his answer was, how perilous his position. "Because you stayed."

She blinked.

"Because after you found out my men had tricked you, and even though you didn't know anyone in town and didn't have a place for the night...you stayed." He stepped closer, close enough that she felt his warm breath on her throat. "That took more courage than I've seen any woman display. My work's not easy. Sometimes I travel with the troop for hundreds of miles to field injuries, or when we're chasing outlaws or fighting fires. I say this as a matter of fact, not from arrogance—courage is a necessity for any woman who chooses to be my wife. So you see, we are suitable. And I'd be honored to have you as my wife."

It was more than she'd hoped to hear.

He brushed the wisps of hair from her cheek, riveting her into place at the mouth of the alley. "And now that I've met you, there's an attraction here I can't deny. Can you deny it?"

She gasped with delight, ever so conscious of where his flesh touched hers. So he felt the physical desire, too, the heavy aching in her limbs whenever they came close. "Do you suppose that attraction might grow into something more?"

She silently pleaded for his yes. The muscles rippling beneath his shirt, so close against her breast, quickened her heart.

His lips curled into a dangerous grin. "It might."

The compelling depth of his humor, the confident way he thrust his shoulders and then leaned forward to cradle her in his arms, caused her to succumb.

Here was the opening where she should speak up and say that she was here to look for Keenan as well as to marry John. But may God forgive her, she felt every time she opened up to disclose something of herself, it only came back to hurt her.

John held her in a steel grip, exploring the hollows of her back, running his fingers along the curve of her spine and setting her face aflame. Then in a sudden grip, he pressed her up against the wall. Cold, hard sandstone pressed against her back while hot temptation pumped through her veins.

His profile grew serious. A tendril of his dark hair ruffled in the breeze. He placed his large palm against the wall beside her head.

"Ask me for a kiss," he murmured.

"Kiss me," she begged.

His lips became hers, soldering them together in the shadows, awakening her intrigue for this man to a height she never thought possible. She could only imagine what it might be like to lie naked beside him. And all she had to do was say yes.

His gentle tongue swirled against hers in an exquisite union. She felt and heard him shudder against her breast, and the thought that she could do this to him, to Dr. John Calloway, drained her of all resistance. Nibbling on her throat, he loosened his hold so that she wasn't completely crushed against him. His kisses grew feverish as she arched her neck. She trailed her fingers up and down his back until he groaned, then he slipped his mouth over the fabric covering her taut nipples. She gasped in sweet ecstasy while he came back and brushed his lips against hers.

"Marry me, Sarah."

"When?"

"Tomorrow."

"Yes."

* * *

It was her wedding day, but no one spoke of love.

Sarah awoke with the rising sun peeking beneath the drawn shade of her boardinghouse room. Stretching in her creaking bed for the last time, she scooted to the edge and gazed at her luggage. She was packed and ready to go. John was needed in surgery today, but after their ceremony this evening, she'd be moving into his town house. He'd dropped her off last night, saying he had to race back to the fort to get permission from the commanding officer to marry.

It was only a formality, John had said; a requirement for all policemen. He'd also said that if by chance there were any delay, he would let her know. Since she hadn't heard, Sarah assumed all was well.

She rose and drew the shade, basking in the sun's warmth. Today she would become Mrs. John Calloway.

After she changed into a housedress, she walked to her dresser and fingered the intricate lace of her wedding gown. It was the dress her mother had worn, yellowed with age so it looked more cream than white, but the beads were pretty, spanning the fabric from its high collar all the way to the floor. The white silk sash, yellowed, too, was broad and would hug her waistline and the voluminous sleeves added to its weight.

Her parents would have approved of John. It was Sarah they never would have approved of, had they known.

She wasn't the virtuous person they'd thought she was. Her parents hadn't known just how far, at the awkward age of fifteen, Sarah had gone with Tavish McNamara. If they had, they might have thrown her out of the house as they had Keenan.

It's your duty, her mother had whispered when she'd first been diagnosed with consumption, ten years earlier.

You're my only daughter, and it's your duty to care for me.

Sarah had done it not because she was the only daughter, but because she cared about her mother. Ma had grown frailer, more surly and resentful from her illness as the years passed. Her ugly tone had driven away two serious beaus Sarah had brought home. When she'd privately told the men that she intended to live with and care for her mother till the end, both fled in panic. But Sarah chose to remember earlier years, when Pa's business had been lucrative, when their family had lived in the bigger house and times together had been calm and pleasant.

Yet, in their household they'd never spoken words of love. Some people just didn't. Sarah had always thought there was love there, buried somewhere, but they never spoke tenderly to one another. The arguments about money and striving to put dinner on the table and shoes on their feet had consumed her parents. After Keenan had fallen in with a delinquent group and the law had come pounding on their door, then a new terror had consumed them. *Look what he's done to us,* her father had screamed. Within the year, Keenan had disappeared, their father had died accidentally in a summer thunderstorm, and it was up to Sarah and her mother to feed themselves.

Toward the end of her mother's decline, Sarah had once leaned over the bed and whispered, *I love you, Ma.* Her mother had nodded, but like Sarah's father, had never offered the words to Sarah.

Keenan had rebelled against their father's controlling hand by spending more time away from the house and eventually being charged with gunrunning. When Sarah's sole companion of friendship and tranquility had been kicked out of the home, she'd silently rebelled and taken up with a delinquent friend of Keenan's.

To the young and dashing pickpocket—Tavish McNamara—Sarah had spilled her heart. It was Tavish who'd told her where her brother's visions of becoming a rancher might have led him. Keenan's law-abiding dreams were new to her for he'd been a pickpocket like Tavish. Then Sarah had declared her love to Tavish, but he'd laughed and called her sentimental. In the end, she'd walked away more alone than ever, and he'd moved out of the neighborhood.

A loud knock sounded at the door. "Sarah, it's Melodie Sutcliffe. A message has arrived."

Sarah bolted to the door. "Thank you." She flagged Melodie to enter, took the envelope and ripped it open.

Sarah,
I don't want you to worry. Permission has been granted and we'll meet tonight at seven, as planned. See you then my lovely bride.

John.

Although she wished he'd signed it with more affection, Sarah clutched the note to her chest and smiled.

"Good news?" asked the pretty black-haired woman.

"Everything's going as planned." Sarah held out her hand to the smiling woman, who was obviously a fair bit along in her pregnancy, judging from the size of her belly. "I'm Sarah. Thank you for agreeing to this."

Melodie scoffed at the outstretched hand and stepped closer to hug Sarah. "Not at all. Logan explained the circumstances to me last night, and we'd both be honored to stand up for the doctor and you. Have you had breakfast yet?"

Sarah shook her head, eager to make a friend, but shy.

"Then come with me to my home and I'll fix you some.

My sister's looking after our bath and barber shop today, so I'm blessed with time. Let me do your hair real pretty for the ceremony, and we'll soak your nails in rosewater.''

"That sounds heavenly."

They left the boardinghouse with Sarah's bags.

"Please don't tell anyone about the wedding yet," said Sarah as she entered Melodie's breezy kitchen.

"Mercy, why not?"

"When I first got here, I was blabbing about being a mail-order bride…maybe you heard about me?"

Melodie looked away in slight embarrassment. "Logan told me about the prank. They're not a bad bunch, you know, but I gave them a sharp piece of my mind when I found out what they did to you."

Sarah's heart swelled at the woman's kindness. "I blabbed on about how I'd be marrying the surgeon. This time, for good luck, I'd like to wait until afterward before telling anyone."

"I understand. Now where's that mirror?"

The women spent the day together. Melodie did most of the talking, but Sarah enjoyed the spark of a budding friendship. The other woman was married to the veterinary surgeon, but as policemen's wives, they had much in common. John had explained to Sarah about Logan's disfigurement, about the bullet wound he'd received to his face when he was ambushed by the Grayveson gang almost three years ago. Melodie must have gone through hell when it'd happened, thought Sarah.

"…and then Mrs. Lott suggested I might stay indoors until my confinement was over, so as not to offend anyone with my condition. Well! You can imagine what I told her."

After a very pleasant afternoon, Sarah had her hair washed, pinned and set, agreed to borrow Melodie's long white gloves for the ceremony, then carefully dressed in her gown. She wondered what John would think of it.

"Something old." Sarah pointed to her mother's gown. "Something new." She indicated her new stockings.

"Something borrowed," said the other woman, pointing to her gloves. "And something blue." Melodie gave her a blue hanky.

Seven o'clock finally arrived. And went.

At seven-thirty, Sarah's fears fluttered inside her stomach while Melodie tried to reassure her. "Policemen don't abide the clock when they're sometimes caught in duty."

At seven-forty-five, Sarah declined the tea Melodie offered and wondered if John had changed his mind.

"Don't you worry, there's good reason for their delay. Why, my own Logan was late two years for his own wedding night."

"Beg your pardon?"

"Ah, it's a long story. One you needn't worry about now."

At eight o'clock, Sarah sat quietly in the kitchen rocking chair, wondering what had happened. *Not another raid*, she fretted. *If John wants to walk away from the wedding, I can live with it, but please don't let him be hurt.*

When Logan finally stumbled through the door at eight-thirty, apologizing profusely, Sarah heard Melodie whisper behind the door as he changed. "For heaven's sake, it's the man's wedding day. Couldn't he postpone the cleaning of his instruments for twenty-four hours?"

Sarah was so relieved to know John was safe and the wedding hadn't been canceled, she waited quietly with no complaints.

Cloaked by darkness in their biggest buggy, Logan and Melodie delivered Sarah and her bags to the fort chapel.

Earlier she'd gone to the garden with Melodie and picked a bouquet of wild Alberta roses, a burst of brilliant pinks, which Sarah clasped in her sweating palms as she slid from the buggy seat. Inside the small room alongside the priest, John was waiting.

Dressed in high uniform, which the Mounties wore only on formal dress occasions, John stood tall at the altar in his scarlet tunic and black breeches, swallowing hard when Sarah walked in. Her body electrified with the energy of his presence.

Newly shaven and hair still a tad wet from his bath, he was exceptionally handsome. Black brows framed his intense gaze; pride rippled in his square jaw and one sleek dark cheek dimpled with a threatening grin.

His gaze moved upward along the swept curls of her hair to the top of her head. She wore no veil, just two beautiful golden combs Melodie had provided to sweep the tresses from her cheeks. Then John's gaze drifted downward, to the sash at her waist and the movement of her hips as she strode down the aisle toward him.

Tonight would be their night. She felt humbled and exhilarated for what their future might hold, and trembled as she imagined what the night ahead might be like, bonded in intimacy with John.

When she reached the altar, Logan and Melodie whispered something to the priest, but John and Sarah remained silent, watchful of each other. He held out his hand and she took it. The feel of his hand in hers eased her tension. She would do everything in her power to be a good wife and partner.

The ceremony was brief. Their words echoed in the hollow spaces of the wooden pews and walls. John removed a brand-new gold wedding band from his pocket and slipped it on her finger.

"And do you John Calloway take this woman, Sarah O'Neill, as your lawfully wedded wife in sickness and in health, till death do you part?"

Her body filled with waiting.

He smiled at her profile. "I do."

Chapter Eight

It was their wedding night, but no one spoke of love.

The warm night air tingled against John's skin, blowing over the hairs at the back of his neck, arousing the sweet scent of wildflowers that bloomed along the road's edge.

In the hazy moonlight, he helped Sarah off the buggy, took her luggage and said his thanks to Logan and Melodie as they raced off. It was ten-thirty. The street houses were quiet and settled for the night. Most folks arose with the rooster's crow at dawn to prepare for the hectic workday ahead, as would John in the morning.

With Sarah's traveling bag and suitcase in his arms, he glanced hesitantly in her direction. "Did I tell you how beautiful you look tonight?"

Beneath her clinging bodice, he saw the quick rise and fall of her breathing. She didn't wait for him at the threshold, she took a bag and helped him carry her things up the porch and through the door.

When they got inside, he lit the lamps on the wall and lost himself in the wholesome sight of her. In the room's glow, her small figure radiated strength and goodness.

"I'm not sure I'm the right man for you. I've had a lot of women and—"

"Shh," she whispered, rising on tiptoe to kiss his lips. "We're married now and we'll make it right."

His muscles tightened beneath his suit. He felt the warm grip of her fingers on his and his instinctive response was how much he wanted her. What was it about Sarah that had that affect on him? Was it purely physical?

As she pulled away, he noticed her hand trembling. She was more affected by his presence than she let on. He didn't want to frighten her by starting things too quickly. He wanted them to come together slowly, relishing, tasting, feeling every moment. "Would you like me to draw you a bath?"

Her gown swept the floor as she stepped back beside her bags. "Yes, that would be relaxing."

"Which bags go upstairs to the bedroom?"

Her cheeks flushed at the implication that they would soon be sleeping together, but she steadied her hands and pointed to two.

Lifting the small remaining carpetbag, he led her down the hall toward the bathing room. She carried a lantern that swung in her hands, casting rhythmic shadows along the walls. Recently he hadn't given the room much thought, but he was relieved now that when the home was built, he'd ensured the room was large, airy and warm. He supposed his attention to hygienic detail came from his medical background. The room doubled as the spring room, which meant a water pump had been set up against one exterior wall so that fresh water could be pumped without going outdoors. When he'd ordered his furniture from the Eastern catalog, he'd ordered a luxurious porcelain tub, unlike the practical tin tub available for use at the fort. A long dresser and washing stand had been positioned across from the tub while beside it stood an oval mirror that swiveled on a pine base. A fieldstone fireplace spanned the entire north wall, with cauldrons used for heating water.

Damask wallpaper infused the space with a pleasing pattern. In the center of the room, in front of the fireplace, a plush Turkish rug draped the floor. It was thick and soft, riddled with a thousand different strands of colored wool to mark its beauty, and felt like velvet beneath bare feet. The pattern was called *The Tree of Life*, and John had chosen it because the woven tree overflowed with images of birds and animals and people.

He placed Sarah's bag on a dresser, allowing her a moment to adjust while he stacked logs and lit a fire. He heard the clicking of leather straps and buckles, then the thud of toiletries as she unpacked her things on the dresser towel. The noises made him smile. He and Sarah were a couple.

Still in his red uniform, he pumped water into two cauldrons, then hung them over the fire. He hauled two more and dumped them into the tub.

When he finally turned around, Sarah was seated in the satin upholstered chair, perched on the edge, staring at the fire. Lights meandered across her smooth forehead and down the bridge of her nose.

"Well," he said, fumbling for words. He wanted to say something profound or intelligent. Yesterday he'd had no problem with conversation, but tonight during the ceremony and afterward, he'd found himself straining to divulge anything private about himself. "The water's almost ready. I'll stay to lift the heavy pots into the tub."

She nodded. Her lips lifted into a dreamy smile, giving him a glimpse of her pretty teeth.

Then his eyes traveled over her ivory-lace bodice and the supple curves straining beneath the buttons. His pulse stirred and his arousal deepened. To kiss those lips and nibble on that skin…

"The water's boiling," she said, nodding gently to the fire.

"So it is." It took him no time to pour the scalding water into the bath. When he dipped his hand into the tub, it stung. "It's still too hot. You'll have to wait a few minutes."

The air was getting moist and steamy. Tiny rivulets of perspiration glistened at Sarah's temples, and his own tunic felt suddenly warm.

She fingered her high collar, rubbing her throat. She stepped back against the wall for him to leave. He felt the charge between them. He took two steps toward the door while she reached out and grasped the key in the lock, preparing to close the door behind him. Was she actually going to lock it? As he brushed by her shoulder to leave, he heard her quick intake of breath. He quivered at the sound, inhaling the sweet air around her, and allowed his desire to respond.

Slipping behind her instead of in front of her, he pressed himself against her back, reached for her hand that held the key, slowly closing the door with his other hand, then intertwined their fingers, turning the key to lock it, trapping them in together.

She gasped.

"Sarah…" From behind, he buried his face into her soft neck. "What are you doing to me?"

He kissed the silky tendrils that escaped her golden combs and his heart soared when he felt her skin turn to gooseflesh in response.

She moaned and fell forward against the door, flattening her palms against the wood to brace herself.

When he spun her around, he cupped her feminine chin

between his strong fingers and couldn't believe he'd soon have her naked and writhing beneath him.

Gently, he lay her down on the Turkish rug, basking in the sweet torture of anticipation. It took her a moment, then she began unbuttoning his tunic with such eagerness it made his blood pound and his raw instincts surge. Her buttons were delicate and he strained to withhold himself from ripping them apart. Lord, she had a million of them, but he took his time unwrapping her, gasping when her wedding gown parted to reveal an intricately boned corset that thrust her creamy breasts almost up and over the edge. A hint of rosy areolas dimpled at the corset's edge, which he hungered to touch.

"Another corset?"

"I didn't lace it up so tight this time…" she said in explanation.

"Mmm…" he said with open desire.

"Take off your jacket," she murmured.

Eagerly, he slid it over his biceps and let it fall around his waist, revealing a white cotton undershirt wrapped around his chest, tucked into tight black breeches. His desire for her was so intense, his erection strained against his pants.

Her eyes shone. She ran her hands up along his thighs.

He groaned. "I won't last if you touch me like that."

On his knees, he straddled her body and peeled off her gown, first dipping one sleeve over a bare creamy shoulder, then the other, then yanking the billowing fabric over her full, tantalizing hips and silky bloomers.

Tugging at her silk stockings, he pulled one off until her hot foot rested in his huge palm. "You're so small."

Everywhere he touched her, her skin heated—a combination of him and the crackling fire. He kissed her foot, up along the ankle bone, then the dimple in her calf. She responded with a shudder and a sigh, sinking back into the plush wool, one leg dangling on top of his thigh.

With a startle of surprise from her, he thrust his hands behind her backside and tugged off her bloomers. He took a moment to savor the vision, her bare thighs rippling in the golden light, leading to a triangle of hair he ached to explore. With one fingertip, he slowly traced her flesh from her knee to the muscle of her soft thigh to the crux where it joined her hip. She trembled and grasped his hand to stop him, but he smiled and traced the other leg. Then he did it again up to the swell of one gorgeous cheek.

Unbuttoning her corset, he opened the fabric as he would split open an apple. Acres of milky flesh greeted him in reward. Her breasts jiggled and he covered one sphere with his mouth, gliding his tongue over the smooth tip until it turned into a button. He sucked the other one while she ran her fingers up his spine. It tingled where she touched him and they arched together in a long embrace.

"Shall we get into the water," he whispered. "While it's still hot?"

"John…I can't wait."

Laughter caught him. He was pleasantly surprised at Sarah's response to him. He'd thought she might be more reserved, more conservative, but was blissfully confounded by the desire that sprung to match his own. "Yes you can, my lovely wife."

He lifted her and dipped her slowly into the liquid heat. It felt astonishing to hold her naked, her moist skin sliding against his muscled waist. Her face mellowed into such a relaxed state, he said, "I hope you don't fall asleep."

She leaned back and pressed her head against the porcelain. Her eyes were half cloaked by lowered lids. An easy smile trembled along her mouth. "Rest assured, John Calloway doesn't put women to sleep."

"I'm happy to know that." He eased himself into the water. The heat soaked into his muscles, along every limb and cell. The tub was tight and he had to tuck his legs beneath hers. The intimacy between them grew. After a minute gazing at her with her eyes half closed, he took a sea sponge, dipped it into the water, then swirled it around her breast.

She opened her eyes and gazed back at him. He watched the droplet trickle down her breast to the rosy tip, then balance there before it dribbled off the fleshy cliff, landing on her rounded stomach, finally losing itself into a mirrored sea and a mound of curls below.

"I want you, Sarah."

Her eyes glittered with an emotion he couldn't read. She looked almost pained by what he'd said. Was she expecting him to say more?

He felt a pang of inadequacy.

He'd try his best to be everything she might want in a husband, but he could only give what he had. Then the expression flitted across her face and was gone as quickly as it'd come, making him wonder if he'd imagined her fleeting sorrow. It was replaced by such a fervent look of wanton desire it made his pulse careen.

"I want you, too. Make love to me, John."

In the tub, he lifted her gently to sit on top of his lap, easing her slowly onto his erection until they fit together like hand in glove. He shuddered as her heat cupped him in astonishing pleasure, driving him to the peak. While they tenderly kissed, Sarah rode him, faster and faster. Pulling back, he caught a glimpse of their entwined limbs in the standing mirror across the steamy room, her spine and muscled back and the side of her swaying breasts glistening in the fire glow like sculpted clay. He grasped her breast and led it to his awaiting mouth, swirling his tongue around the softness until he and Sarah finally succumbed together, united as man and wife.

More than an hour later, after John had added additional hot water to the tub and they'd bathed each other, Sarah reveled in the soft graze of his fingers as he unclasped her hair and it tumbled down her naked back. Wrapped in thick towels, they were seated in the corner on the upholstered chair, she on his lap, making love again.

She allowed herself the indulgence of appreciating his touch and his body, and its awakening effect on her. The smooth, lustrous skin on his rippling shoulders and chest brushed against her nipples and she reacted with a delightful quiver. Highlights in his dark hair glowed in the light as he smiled his warm, private grin. His lips sought to capture hers and in one swift movement he lifted her then planted her on the thick rug. The towels spilled around them.

Sarah recalled that with Tavish McNamara, the act had been quick and covered by blankets. He was the one who'd enjoyed the sex itself; she'd gotten much more pleasure from his kisses and his hugging.

With John, it was different. He ensured that her curiosity in his body—and her own—and her erotic appetites were being satiated, too. He was an older man than Tavish had been, much more experienced and confident. Even so the moment was speeding along much too quickly. She wanted him to take it slowly.

She tried not to think of the lovers either of them had had before this night. None of them mattered anymore.

John moaned aloud in pleasure. "I never imagined it would be like this between us."

"You take away my shyness."

"You surprise me," he whispered, entering her again while kissing her face and throat and shoulder.

He filled her body; she felt herself stretch around him. She arched to meet his hungry mouth, astonished by the intensity of her need. He'd brought out her provocative nature in ways she'd never experienced before.

When John looked into her eyes and brushed the mass of strawberry-colored hair from her cheeks, she wrapped her legs up and around his waist and tugged him closer. His self-confident smile and the proud way he carried himself made her yield to the tremor inside her heated thighs. In a burst of throbbing sensation, she gripped his back.

He whispered her name. "Sarah…"

When at last he carried her up to the bedroom, wrapped in a dry towel, naked but holding the carpetbag on her lap, she felt drained of all energy. And yet, there was something missing between them that amplified her loneliness.

With a playful toss, he threw her onto the bed, then covered her body with the warm feather tick. It was much cooler in the bedroom than the bathing room, but once she grew accustomed to the cooler air, and her body was totally dry, she sat up and watched him prepare his clothes for the morning.

She glanced at the clock on the dresser. One-fifteen.

He pulled out a white nightshirt, about to pull it over his head.

"Don't," she said. "Let's sleep like this."

His jaw clenched as his gaze traveled over her nakedness. She felt no shame. He was her husband.

He growled like a hungry bear and planted himself on the bed, towering over her and demanding another kiss.

"Sorry, sweetheart," he said in between soft kisses and bouts of laughter. "But I have to get up at five and go to work."

"You work so hard."

His expression grew serious. "If these were calmer times, or if I had an assistant, I'd take a leave and we could go to the mountains—"

"People need you," she said, hushing his apology. "They depend on you."

But still, a tiny thread of disappointment, and that flicker of sadness that wouldn't go away, that kept reminding her that he wasn't in love with her, wove its way through her, and wouldn't cease.

The noon sun cast a sharp blue shadow of Sarah's hand across the garden dirt as she picked a ripe tomato. She held it to her nostrils to savor the sharp aroma of the tomato vine where she'd snapped it, then added it to the basket that already contained two onions, a bulb of garlic and three yellow peppers. She didn't expect John for lunch, but she was anxious to share a hot meal with him when he came home for dinner.

He'd allowed her to sleep in this morning while he rose before the sun. She felt guilty at her laziness; it wouldn't happen again. She'd be as productive as he. She'd find work in town and begin her search for Keenan. After lunch she'd go for a stroll, retrieve her lost gloves that she'd forgotten two days ago when John had proposed and plan her next move.

Her legs felt soft and spent from the evening's activities. The vivid memories of intimacy brought a bounce to her walk and a flush to her face. There was so much possibility awaiting her in her life with John, if only he would open up. Their night of lovemaking had been quiet, with very little spoken. It had fulfilled her physically and yet…

A crackle over the neighbor's fence startled her. She looked up through a cluster of thick cedar trees to see the hairy monkey, little Willie, balancing himself along the top rail while the Irish setter barked below him. Sarah laughed. She bent and pulled out an onion from the garden, offering it to the monkey.

He chattered and raced toward the prize.

"Willie!" Mrs. Fitzgibbon called from the other side.

Sarah peered through the cedar branches, catching a glimpse of the older woman's flowered hat from fifty feet away. Polly must have caught sight of her, too, for she spun on her heel to leave, hollering over her shoulder, "Willie, come here this instant!"

The sting of another insult burned Sarah's flesh. No one knew yet that Sarah and John had wed last night. What must Polly think?

"Polly!" Sarah called, meaning to extend a cordial hello and explain.

But the old woman had already retreated. The monkey clacked, raced away with dangling limbs and disappeared with his owner.

Well, thought Sarah, Polly Fitzgibbon would know soon enough. John had told Sarah that Polly was still hired to do the floors and clean the house, so the two women would soon come face-to-face, whether Polly approved of her or not.

Weaving through the broad gardens of fruit trees and flowers, Sarah loitered around the herbs. She recognized basil, parsley and dill, but hadn't a clue about the others. John also had a carefully tended rose garden along one wall, which bloomed in beautiful colors of yellow and soft orange.

So he enjoyed gardening. She enjoyed discovering it about him. What else did he pursue in his leisure time?

Crossing through the back door, Sarah slid off her straw hat and placed it on the rack beside John's Stetson, his wide brown Mountie's hat and a white pillbox helmet that was likely part of his formal uniform. She'd never seen him or any of the Mounties wearing the pillbox. They preferred the broader brown hat to guard from the weather and the flies, she supposed.

Although she was his wife, a nervousness engulfed her as she made her way into the kitchen, feeling strangely like an intruder. What she wanted to do was to throw open every cupboard door to see what secrets it unearthed about her husband, but she stifled the urge. It would be snooping.

When she passed by John's cramped office, she glanced at the examining chair, a glass cabinet of bottles and tonics, and several crutches and splints on the cabinet counter. He obviously took calls here at home as well as at the fort.

Passing the library, she caught sight of his desk. A massive block of cherrywood, it was stacked with papers and journals. One journal was labeled *Records*.

What sort of records? Records of townsfolk? Names she might skim to search for her brother?

Unable to control herself, she wiped her hands on her apron and gently opened the cover. Leather creaked as the first page fell open. Lines of neatly inked names rose to meet her.

"Sarah!"

She dropped her basket in response to John's booming voice. Onions and peppers rolled along the floor. She dropped to her knees and hastily fought to catch them.

John peered around the corner, a dark tower of masculinity. "There you are." He picked up a squished tomato from the floor. "What happened?"

"You startled me."

She took the tomato from him, holding it in her apron. "To what do I owe this surprise?"

He lifted her to her feet. Tentatively his hands slid up her waistline then he yanked her against him, crushing her chest against his. The basket nearly toppled out of her hands again, but his possessiveness pleased her.

"We've got three hours to ourselves," he whispered in her ear. His hands lightly traced a path over her cheek; her skin warmed instantly beneath his touch.

"Three hours is a long time."

He agreed. "We could do just about anything."

She laughed and struggled to free herself from his grasp. "It will allow me to make you lunch. Are you hungry?" She made her way to the kitchen, conscious of his penetrating stare on her back.

"Starving," he said with amusement. The unspoken implication wound between them.

She felt that same breathless pulsing that she'd felt in his arms last night. "Well, you'll have to pace your appetite," she replied to his laughter.

"Who says I do?"

She ignored his innuendos and turned her back to begin chopping the fresh vegetables.

"Sarah, I'm not hungry for peppers."

She turned her shoulder playfully away from him to the counter. "You have to eat. You'll lose your strength. Then what will your commander, Superintendent Ridgeway, I think you said his name was, think of me?"

"Every man in the troop envies me this morning, and so will he."

So John had told them. It wasn't a dream in her mind; they were married.

In an instant she felt his hands move magically over her shoulders, caressing her soft muscles with the strength of nimble fingers. Aroused, she leaned back, drawing herself closer.

His hands explored the lines of her waist and hips. When they slipped toward the front of her blouse, he began unbuttoning. She lowered the knife to the cutting board then let it fall altogether.

He slid his tender hand between her flesh and corset, uncovering one breast then the other. He pinched her nipples and tugged on them till they grew long and round. The cool sensation of air mingled with the heat of their bodies.

She shifted with pleasure. When she turned around, he pressed her against the table and claimed a kiss. His tongue traced a path along her lips, while the shapely beauty of his body beneath his billowing white shirt taunted her.

She was in John's experienced hands, so proud to be with him. Honored and thrilled that he'd chosen *her*.

With a slow deliberation, he swiped the empty pots off the tabletop. They crashed to the plank floor as he lifted her by the buttocks to lay her gently on the table.

He hoisted the fabric of her heavy skirt to uncover her hips, then slid his hand over her bloomers and down along her bare thigh. They kissed each other's throats and lips, unable to get enough of each other. When he slid his hand lower, claiming her center, she twisted beneath him, arching against his firm touch.

He pleased her like that, teasing her body until she climaxed. She ached to please him, too. He slid off her bloomers until they dangled from one ankle, while she released his pants. She moaned as he lowered himself completely inside her. It felt good. It felt right.

They were too aroused to take more time, but she welcomed him to her bosom with ardor. In her heart, they were equals in every sense. She unbuttoned his shirt, revealing the quivering muscles of his chest, caressing his warm skin as they rocked together. Her body flushed as he came inside her. To her, this would always be the symbol of their loving vows, till death do them part.

After they'd both collapsed in a laughing jumble of arms and legs and naked parts, she kissed his temple. "Lunch is served."

John laughed and kissed her breast in such a gentle manner her heart ached. Would he ever turn to her and tell her that he loved her? What would that moment be like? And why, after they'd just made love, did her heart falter? She should be savoring what they shared rather than noticing what was missing.

Untangling his limbs from hers, he pulled her to her feet and rocked her in his arms.

"The rocking's nice," she whispered, wishing he'd never let go.

An hour later, when they'd finished with their meal and could barely stand from their exhaustion, John leaned across the table. "What have you got planned for the afternoon?"

Sarah slid her plate on top of his. "I'm going to retrieve my gloves—the ones I lost—then perhaps take a stroll down the boardwalk to see if I can find work."

"As my wife, you no longer need to work."

"I understand that and thank you, but I prefer to do something with my time. Until—" she dipped her head and added with a smile of hope "—until children come."

His warm expression deepened.

"You said yourself, John, that you'll be traveling when duty calls. This will give me something to occupy my time until you return."

He nodded and cupped her hand with his. "Where do you think you left your gloves?"

"At Ashford Jewelers." Sarah squirmed on her chair, anxious at the thought of bumping into Clarissa.

"Then let me come with you," he said to her surprise. "It's about time I introduce you as my bride."

Chapter Nine

"What are you doing?" Sarah asked John as they prepared to leave for their stroll.

John stacked the journals on his desk, feeling refreshed from the coffee they'd just shared and welcoming a walk with his wife. "When we come back, I'm taking these records to the fort. Since Logan's filling in for a while, I want him to review these."

Oddly, Sarah began to stammer. "M-maybe you could…leave them here. We could invite Logan and Melodie for dinner later this week, and you could talk business while Melodie and I have a nice chat."

He rubbed his cheek and wondered why she was interested in his records. "It's more convenient to have them at the fort."

"All right." Hesitating, she smiled then removed her apron. "I'm ready to go."

He forgot about the incident as soon as they left the house. With Sarah walking beside him, he placed his arm at the small of her back. The sky was blue and clear, one of those beautiful prairie days that made him grateful to be living in the West. Wagons creaked by, teams of horses neighed, folks hollered across the street to one another.

John recognized that he and Sarah had a long way to go as husband and wife. He enjoyed her company, liked the way she handled herself; she was a kind, fair person. Still, they were almost strangers. She seemed withdrawn at the oddest moments. But judging by their compatibility in the bedroom, they'd do fine. Physical attraction between a husband and wife was not the most important value in a marriage, honesty meant more, but sexuality was a healthy fact of life that John and Sarah both seemed to enjoy and hold in high regard.

Nothing wrong with that, he thought with a grin.

When they crossed the road and passed the newspaper press, Sarah stopped. "Could we buy a paper? I'd love to read about the town."

"Sure." They stepped inside and came out with last week's issue. For some reason, Sarah had insisted on buying all the back issues they had for sale, four in total, so John indulged her.

As they walked by the Land Registry, Sarah turned to look at the sign and to peer through the large front windows. "They keep records and things in here, don't they?"

"What kinds of records are you interested in?"

Sarah shrugged. "Well, I—I'm interested in everything about the town, and about the homesteaders you'd once mentioned."

"For a minute there, with all the questions about newspapers and land registries, I thought you were a secret bank robber plotting to steal a bag of gold."

Fumbling, Sarah rubbed her arm. When he laughed softly, she relaxed at his side.

"Don't worry," he added. "You'll get to know everyone in no time. You'll fit right in." He tugged her closer and saw the color infuse her cheeks. "By the way, I thought we could throw a party and formally announce our marriage.''

Her gait slowed. "That would be nice."

"Two weeks from Saturday would be good. I've already invited some of my friends and their wives. Logan and Melodie think it's a wonderful idea. I have to speak with Polly yet, to ensure she's available to cook, but even if she's not, there are several women in town who could help."

Sarah stiffened. "You mentioned it to Logan and Melodie before you mentioned it to me?"

"Only because you weren't with me at six o'clock this morning when I thought of it and told Logan. When Melodie dropped by to see Logan for lunch, you weren't there, either."

Sarah smiled and the tension left.

"Shall we have a large party? Say fifty to sixty people? If the weather's nice, it could spill into the garden."

Beneath the shade of her bonnet, Sarah's expression grew keen. "I'll set up the chairs and tables. I already know the tablecloths we can use, I saw them in your chest of drawers."

Cow bells clanged across the street. Dust filtered up to the boardwalk and tickled John's nostrils. "My grandmother sent me those linens when I first came West fifteen years ago. I could have used new boots, new gloves, another hunting knife, anything for basic survival. What does Grandma send from Toronto? Eight linen tablecloths she brought on the boat from Ireland. May God rest her soul, I now cherish those linens more than anything else I own. She'd be proud if you used them for our wedding party."

Sarah wrapped her arm through his elbow.

He pressed closer, his lips skimming the cotton fabric

of her wide-brimmed hat. "I want you to sit back and enjoy the preparations. Let the hired help do the heavy work."

"It's been a long time since my parents had hired help…I'll feel spoiled."

"They'll be paid well and happy to have the work, so don't be concerned." John glanced down the stretch of stores to Ashford Jewelers, a block away. "When did your parents have hired help?"

"When my father's business was doing well. We lived in a bigger house and had a housekeeper and butler. As the city grew, though, three more men opened watch shops within several blocks of my father's store. The competition knocked the coins out of my father's business and it was never the same. After he passed away, my mother and I struggled to keep it going for several years."

"That was tough luck." It must have been difficult for Sarah, being the only child. "You said there was no one else to help you when your mother got ill. Did you have any other relatives around?"

Their stroll ended at the jeweler's door. "There were some…distant cousins."

"One relative in particular…we were the best of friends, but—" she scanned his face, almost as if she were gauging his reaction "—he was in trouble with the law."

John's brows arced in surprise. "What did he do?"

"He was young and foolish, that's all. Fifteen and a bit of a…a pickpocket."

The policeman in John surfaced. "Did he get away with it for long?"

She colored. "No. The authorities suspected him."

"*Good.*"

"But fifteen is very young. He was a boy, not a man."

"Fifteen is old enough to know better. Pickpocketing

can develop into something dangerous if the boy isn't brought to face the consequences early.''

There was a tremble to her soft lips. ''I knew about it and tried to convince him to stop, but…''

''He didn't, did he?''

She shook her head.

''And it got worse, didn't it?''

Her eyes flashed and he knew he was right.

His voice strained. ''I'd have no patience for it myself.''

She shriveled at his tone. ''You'd turn him in?''

''It might seem harsh, but in the long run it would be better for the boy.''

She turned glum, as if she'd been reprimanded herself. John wondered if he was being too harsh, too judgmental. But what was right was right. There was no excuse for breaking the law.

''Sarah, I've often seen delinquency start, and some of those young men are now doing time in federal prisons. Good thing your cousin was caught when he was.''

She paled but didn't respond because the door opened in front of them. Two customers walked out. John led her through, appreciative of the fact that she'd told him about her family, even the things that were difficult to tell.

''Hello, John.'' Clarissa stooped behind the counter. Her smile was warm and ready, and he groaned at her predictability.

''Hello, Clarissa,'' said Sarah, stepping to the glass case. ''I've lost my gloves. I wonder if I've left them here.''

Clarissa slid the glass window of the pocket watches closed, locked it and shoved the keys into the bulging pocket of her brown puckered skirt. ''Would they be white?''

"Yes, white cotton with a leather button in the upper corner."

Clarissa sniffed with disdain. "I wondered who left those stained gloves behind. Why the fingers are almost worn through to the fibers."

"I—I dropped them in the road on the way to work that last morning. They're only dusty, not dirty."

God, thought John, glancing at Sarah's embarrassed face, humiliated himself at having to witness her defense.

With her glossy brown hair, Clarissa was pretty and turned many heads, but the woman could be a witch when she wanted to be. Did she think none of the men around her noticed? He stepped up alongside Sarah and draped a casual arm around her waist. The move wasn't lost on Clarissa.

"We'll have to take you into the clothing shop around the corner sometime soon," he said to Sarah. "So you can buy yourself what you need." Then he turned and smiled at Clarissa. "Did I mention Sarah and I were married yesterday?"

Clarissa stumbled. She grasped the counter with tight fingers. "Uh?"

John noticed that Sarah seemed to get no pleasure from Clarissa's comeuppance, but he was ashamed to say his smile deepened. "Yes, we were married last night. I knew when I first laid eyes on Sarah that she was someone special."

"John, please," whispered Sarah, and he knew he'd said enough.

"Married?" asked Clarissa. "I had no idea…I thought the mail-order ad was a hoax."

"That's what you get for listening to rumors."

Clarissa's face turned scarlet. "I…congratulations."

"Thank you," Sarah and John said together.

"The gloves?" asked Sarah.

Clarissa disappeared behind the velvet drapes of the back room. There was a lot of whispering, then Mr. and Mrs. Ashford stepped out.

"I hear congratulations are in order." Mr. Ashford shook John's hand first, then Sarah's, followed by his pretty plump wife, a brunette who looked much like her daughter. How did folks like these wind up with a vindictive daughter like Clarissa? They had two other sons, but they were quiet, decent ranchers north of town.

Three other customers spun around at the news, eager to offer their congratulations. When the door creaked open and two more folks stepped in, Mr. Ashford stepped back to gaze at the friendly group. To John, Mr. Ashford seemed particularly interested in the folks' warm reaction to Sarah. It irked him that only two days earlier, Sarah'd been shunned by everyone. Now it appeared she was respectable.

The old gent took her hand. "Mrs. Calloway, would you still be interested in working here?"

Two hours later Sarah gripped her gloves and tried to balance the packages in her arms. She clenched the four newspapers beneath her elbow, eager to get home to scan them for Keenan's name. With a carefree spring to her walk, she crossed the boardwalk. John had left her at the clothing store, insisting she buy what she needed. She insisted she didn't need much. One formal dress for the upcoming party celebration, a new blouse and skirt, a new pair of everyday gloves and a striking shirt she couldn't resist for John.

Saturday shoppers filled the town, but there was one in particular whom she noticed across the road. She shifted beneath his uncomfortable stare. He was an older man, tall and thick as an elephant, with white hair at his temples. He wore a suede vest and double holsters with Navy Colts.

She'd have to get used to remembering names and faces, for John was well known and liked in the community, and she wanted him to be proud of her standing at his side. She turned the corner and walked the two blocks home. As she struggled up the porch, a man called her name.

"Miss O'Neill!"

Sarah spun around. One of her packages slipped out and fell at the feet of David Fitzgibbon.

He bent over and picked it up, tall and thin, flicking his yellow hair past one eye. She tried not to let her embarrassment show. The last time she'd seen him, he was telling her to look at the birdie. He was obviously unaware she was no longer *Miss O'Neill,* but what did he want?

"May I help you with those?"

"I can manage, if you'll stack it on top of the pile."

He gingerly replaced it. "I'd like to apologize for our last meeting. I had no idea I'd find you in there like that."

Huh, she thought. Why had he needed to snap a photograph? Greed? She stared coolly at his freckled nose.

"I was wondering if you'd like to accompany me to dinner this evening."

He wanted to court her! "No, thank you."

"But I do like adventuresome women. Perhaps tomorrow evening?"

"I don't think my husband would approve."

"Your husband?"

"Yes, Dr. Calloway. You've met?"

His fleshy cheeks turned red. "Well, yes…well I…I suppose…I had no idea…" He turned and yelled across the fence. "Aunt Polly, did you know that Dr. Calloway and Miss O'Neill *are married?*"

"Excuse me?" Polly charged down her porch to stand at the foot of the fence, peering at Sarah. "When did this happen?"

"Yesterday."

The older woman ran her hands along her apron. "Well, I do declare. Does this mean you won't be needin' me to wash your floors anymore?" The agonized look on Polly's face indicated she still wanted the work.

Sarah descended the porch stairs to meet her at the fence. "We still need you, Polly, if you'd be so kind. I'll…I'll be working at Ashford Jewelers five mornings a week."

"Workin'? Whatever for?"

"For…the pleasure."

"Pleasure?" Polly laughed. "Must be nice to be rich."

"I'm not—" Sarah began, then held her tongue.

"Working girls. That's a great angle," said David.

"What's an angle?" asked Sarah.

"It's the way we journalists talk. An angle is the way you approach a story."

The only angle Sarah was interested in was the angle of his head as he left her property.

Sarah said to Polly, "I'll come by later this afternoon to discuss your hours. I'd also like the return of our house key. You won't need it anymore because I'll be here to let you in."

As Sarah made her way back up the porch to her front door, Polly snorted. "…wants her key returned."

David stepped closer to the door. "As I was saying, I'm writing an article. May I interview you? I'm not sure yet where I'll send it back East, but it'll be a newspaper or magazine. Heck, maybe both. It's going to be about the Mounties and their wives. It'd make a real nice folksy kind of story. I was thinking of calling it 'The Wild West Life of a Mountie's Wife.' Whaddya think?''

"I thought you took novelty photographs.''

"I do, but journalism would gain me more…*respect* among my colleagues. Mrs. Melodie Sutcliffe has already agreed to an interview. You're both working women. That might be my angle.''

She didn't need a reporter following her as she searched for her brother. "No, thank you, I'm not interested.'' She set her packages down on the stoop to remove her key from her dangling satchel.

"But if I get your husband's permission—''

"No,'' she repeated. "This is my decision and I say no.''

"Are you related to those other O'Neills?''

Sarah spun around. "Which O'Neills?''

"I ran into a fella at the newspaper office yesterday. O'Neill was his name. He was placing an ad to sell his horse.''

Sarah rubbed her throat, hoping the pounding in it didn't show. "What's his given name?''

David scratched his ear. "Not sure. Something similar to Nelson, or Keith or Kyle.''

The shock of possible discovery flamed her cheeks. "Where exactly does he live?''

Chapter Ten

"I've added more people to the guest list," said John three days later while finishing his after-dinner brandy. "The guest list has grown to sixty, but Polly insists she can handle the numbers, especially since we've hired another woman to do the cooking. David offered to come with his camera."

"David?" Sarah exclaimed, trying to contain the agitation rising up her throat.

"Sure," said John, putting aside his brandy to pick up the leftover canned peaches. He followed Sarah into the kitchen.

"But how can you trust him after the sneaky way he acted, barging into your home?"

"He's harmless. But if it bothers you, I'll tell him no. He's the only photographer in town and I thought since we didn't get any wedding photographs, you might like to get some of the party."

She slid the dirty bowls into a soapy bucket in the wooden sink. She would have preferred if John had asked her first. She had the feeling he was making all the decisions in the house as if he were still a bachelor. He'd lived alone for years before she'd arrived, a high-ranking officer used to making quick decisions by himself, but didn't he value her opinion?

Or was it all in her imagination, and was she being overly sensitive?

"It's fine," she relented. "Photographs would be nice."

John came up from behind and nuzzled her neck while she washed the dishes. His arms felt solid wrapped around her. It was the first dinner in three days that they'd spent together. On two previous nights, he'd tended to the man with the infected leg at the hospital past eleven o'clock when she'd already gone to bed. She'd tried to stay awake, but had finally succumbed to her heavy lids. And last night just as they'd sat down to dinner, a neighbor knocked on the door needing immediate help because his wife had slipped and broken her ankle. Fortunately the poor woman was fine, but it had meant another meal eating alone.

Sarah was humbled that John was needed by everyone in town, and grateful that he had the skills to help, but she couldn't help feeling deserted. It was difficult to make friends in town during the day because everyone had chores or work to do. She rambled around the house with long stretches of afternoon time, waiting for John. They hadn't had time to be intimate since the day after their wedding when he'd come home for lunch.

John planted a soft kiss along her neck and it fired through her body.

"Thank you for my new shirt. I haven't had a chance to try it on, but I saw it by my bedside. I'll wear it to the party."

She'd never bought a shirt for a man before, and felt especially proud that she'd been able to find John something he liked. "You're welcome."

"I've given David permission for the interview."

"You did what?" Sarah propped the last plate in the drying rack. "Permission for the article on Mounties' wives?"

"He said he spoke to you about it."

She spun around. "I told him no." How dare David go behind her back to her husband, as if her word was worthless. And how dare John speak for her.

"Now I can see you *are* angry with me." His boyish smile faded. He leaned back against the counter and crossed his arms.

"I'd prefer if we discussed things first, before you make decisions for the both of us."

John unhooked his hands and they fell at his hips. His broad cheeks flashed beneath his dark hair. She was breathless at how handsome he looked when he was tired and disheveled, at the same time frustrated that a man could look so good but be so contentious.

"An article like this would boost the morale in our troop, and it's good for people back East to know what a Mountie's life is like. If the article is sold to the Ottawa papers, like David suggested, it might attract more recruits. *We've* been trying to muster interest in our cause for years."

Sarah sputtered. John made it sound as though she and his men were on opposite sides of a team. "But I'm your wife. Couldn't you please talk to me first?"

John glared at her. "I'm not used to someone finding fault with my decisions. These are work issues, not personal ones."

Sarah winced. "This morning I had breakfast with Melodie Sutcliffe. She told me that Logan told her that you're thinking of moving from this house and building us another one, where you can be closer to the fort, and perhaps add more rooms for our children, when they come. That's a personal issue, and I had to hear it third-hand.''

He frowned. ''What's wrong with wanting that for us?''

''John, you open your heart to your men more than you open it to me.''

His expression grew solemn, as if he'd been mortally wounded.

She feared she was speaking too fast, but couldn't stop herself. ''It hurts when you treat me like a subordinate. You're not a commanding officer in our marriage, I'm hoping that we're equals.''

A muscle in John's jaw flickered.

''You've got good reason for wanting the article written,'' she added, ''but maybe I've got good reason for not wanting it.''

''Such as?''

''Perhaps I prefer my privacy.''

''Privacy?'' John ran his fingers through his hair. ''Where were you on Sunday afternoon, Sarah, while I was at the fort?''

She opened her mouth in surprise. How had he known that?

''I've been waiting for three days for you to tell me about what you've been doing with your time, but you've never offered a word. Why?''

''There's nothing to tell. It's been going well at the store and I've been getting to know our neighbors.''

''And on Sunday?''

There was nothing to hide from John. ''David had told me about a family south of town with the name O'Neill. He wondered if I was related. I didn't think so, but my curiosity was raised and what harm was there in going to visit?''

''You took one of my horses from the backyard stable

and rode out alone, ten miles south without telling a soul.''

His steady gaze bore into hers, making her pulse drum. The trip had been awkward. She was used to riding side-saddle, but John only had Western saddles. It had taken her four hours to go there and back—including several stops for her motion sickness—and in the end, she'd come home with an aching rear and a terrible disappointment in not finding her brother.

John crossed his arms in military style, making her feel as though she was being interrogated. ''And are you related?''

She pulled out a dish towel and dried the platters. He could still throw her out on her rump and tell her to go back to Halifax. The marriage could be broken as quickly as it had begun.

''No.''

David had been mistaken. Mr. O'Neill's first name had been no where near Keith or Kyle or Keenan. It was Entwhistle. How on earth could David forget a name like that? He should rethink his desire to become a journalist, for his memory skills were dolefully lacking.

John continued his interrogation. ''What were you doing yesterday at the Land Registry?''

''Are you having me followed?''

''Of course not. But I've got many friends in this town, not to mention the police on duty. They're just as curious as I am to know what my wife's doing racing about town. Do you think they wouldn't report back to me, Sarah? How clueless do you think I feel when they ask me these things?''

She felt her chest prickle with heat.

He continued. ''What were you doing at the registry?''

She'd been looking for Keenan's name, but she would

darn well keep that to herself. All she needed was for John to find Keenan first. God only knew how her rigid husband would react if her brother weren't on the right side of the law. Suddenly, she felt engulfed by her problems and almost as lonely as the first day she'd arrived.

"I—I was reading. Getting to know the layout of the town and the history of the folks behind it."

"Just reading, huh? How gullible do you think I am? What are you doing here, Sarah, and *why* did you come to Calgary?"

She clamped her mouth tight, unwilling to respond.

"Perhaps we don't know each other very well, after all," he said softly, leaving the room and her, standing there staring after him, dumbstruck at the severity of their first married argument.

Sarah was wrong.

John respected her a great deal, but what could be equal between a husband and wife? They were different in every way. It would be like comparing a flower to a boulder of granite. Most men in town would laugh if they heard she'd even mentioned the possibility!

He'd defended her and married her and had helped her to find work, hadn't he? What more evidence did she need about how deeply he felt about her?

Going out on his planned night calls with his medical bag tucked beneath his arm, he cursed the night air. It would be easier if he hadn't fallen for her like he had, if every time he looked at her, he didn't recall the taste of her lips and her skin. Maybe they should have gone slower, gotten to know each other more before they'd married.

If she expected him to come to her every time a decision needed to be made, she'd be mistaken. Hell, he was letting her deal with all the household decisions, but when it came to his work and confiding in her before he confided in his men…well, his friendships with the men in his troop went beyond question. Dammit, their lives depended on their trust for each other.

What did Sarah expect from him?

Too damn much.

And what was she doing, snooping at the Land Registry and reading all those newspapers?

John wasn't sure what to make of her. And that gnawing little scrape at the side of his gut wouldn't go away, reminding him that maybe he'd made a mistake in marrying her.

When John entered the warm fragrant kitchen the next morning at five, he was surprised to see Sarah. It was obvious to him that she'd been crying. Last night, he'd come home late after checking on three patients. He still had reading to do, so he'd taken the lantern from beside Sarah's sleeping face and took to the spare room, where he'd slept.

Sarah's eyes were puffy and red. He felt guilty for causing her misery, but pride held him from reaching out, for saying sorry, for apologizing for something he wasn't sure he should apologize for.

"Good morning," she said curtly, standing by the stove.

"Good morning. You've never been up this early before."

She gave him a weak smile. "I've made coffee. Would you like a cup?"

He was aware she was trying hard to please him, but unfortunately he couldn't spare the time. "No thanks, I'm expected at the fort by five-thirty. The cook makes me breakfast.'' Usually, John galloped in around dawn, as the bugle sounded for reveille and the flag was being raised.

Her look of disappointment shot an arrow through his heart, but it was something she didn't understand. The fort ran like a synchronized clock. The men had duties to perform and were expected there on time. He supposed he could suggest he and Sarah rise half an hour earlier at four-thirty if they wanted to share breakfast, but four-thirty was so damn early he said nothing.

They didn't see each other again until eight that evening. By that time, John had been on his feet for more than fourteen hours and was exhausted.

When he stepped through the front door, the smell of smoke alarmed him. Racing into the kitchen, he found Sarah opening the stove door and fanning smoke coming from her brand-new skirt.

He leaped at her legs with a towel, snapping at the final sparks, but she'd already put them out.

''What happened?''

She looked down at her ruined skirt. ''You'd obviously missed dinner, but I was making something for myself.'' Turning around to mop up the mess, she grew silent.

''Sarah, I'm sorry I'm late. I stopped by the saloon—''

''The saloon? You're avoiding me, sleeping in the spare room and not even sharing conversation. For pity's sake, John, our party is little more than a week away. Should we cancel it? Because I can't put up a front!''

He said what came to mind first. ''That's what I like about you...you don't hold back on your sentiment.'' Unlike him.

''At least there's something you like about me!''

There were a few things. Another thing he liked about her was the soot on her nose and the black fingerprints at the side of the new, long cream skirt that clung to her legs, which he could see she was furious at ruining.

He slid out the stove's ash pan drawer and scooped the fallen ashes off the floor. "I wasn't in the saloon for pleasure. There's been an outbreak of..." Should he tell her? Would she keep it confidential? "...of gonorrhea. I treated one of my men with it today—or treated the symptoms I should say, since there is no cure—and once I discovered where he got it, I headed there to treat the saloon girls. We've got a few saloons in town. It's the cheap one off the main trail. The disease spreads easily and I forbade the women to ply their wares, or I'd shut down the alcohol sales, too."

When he looked up again, Sarah's glare had mellowed to deep embarrassment.

"Dr. Waters was there when I arrived."

"He'd...he'd already begun treating the women?"

"No, the son of a bitch was drinking. After I finished my work, I grabbed him by the scruff of the neck and hauled him to dinner at the café. I thought I might hammer some sense into the man, to sober him up and urge him to continue with his practice, but he's too far gone to be useful."

"Why does he drink so much?"

"He's a compulsive drinker. An alcoholic. He can't stop himself."

"But maybe he's got a deeper problem. A difficulty of some sort—"

"We all have difficulties. He could put his experience to good use and help the folks in this town, but the son of a bitch chooses..."

His voice trailed off when he saw Sarah flinch. He knew he was being hard on the old doctor, but hell, patients were suffering because they had to wait longer to be seen, if at all.

"Black-'n-White," Sarah said softly.

At the opened back door, sliding the ashes into the bigger bin atop the stoop, John faltered, stunned at her assessment. Then he clenched the wire handle and scrubbed the ashes with fury. She was judging him again.

In his line of professional duty.

"What about the party, John? Let's postpone it till we've both had more time. Till you're better rested."

He fought his anger. Time would tell what Sarah was made of, whether she'd decide to pack it in and leave. Hell, it made him sick that the party was only days away, but canceling would mean admitting defeat.

A pounding on the front door broke their conversation. John swore at the interruption. He slammed the ash pan back into the bottom of the stove. "The party stays."

Chapter Eleven

"**W**hy is it so smoky in here?" Eddie Dickson, a short, muscular young man whom Sarah recognized as a worker at the livery stables, gripped his sore stomach as he stumbled into the front foyer. She fetched John, and he directed Eddie toward his office at the back of the house.

"It's smoky from my cooking," said Sarah, concerned about the injured man and trying to make light of the situation. Eddie had an injury, he'd declared, that needed attention and that's why he'd come.

"Ah," said Eddie, glancing at her burned skirt. "I remember the first two years with Hattie. She couldn't cook eggs and always overboiled the coffee. I had to do most of the cookin'."

Sarah smiled. She'd met his wife in the mercantile; they were both buying honey. There was a toddler wrapped around the woman's legs at the time and an older boy who carried her basket.

"She's caught up now. Best cook in town, if you ask me, so don't give up, Mrs. Calloway."

Sarah nodded at the kind remarks. She could cook just fine. It was starting or dousing the fires she had problems with. But kind remarks in this house were hard to come by.

When they reached the office door, John wasn't smiling. "I can manage," he said to Sarah, making her feel as if she'd been dismissed.

She held her tongue. Eddie had mentioned he had a deep gash on his stomach that he'd bandaged himself, which had led her to believe that John might need her help. Surely she could do something useful. "I'll boil water then for your instruments, and bring fresh towels."

John leaned against the door, indecision written across his brow. My, he looked tired, Sarah decided. His dark expression tightened, accentuating the circles beneath his eyes and the strain in his jawline.

Looking from husband to wife, Eddie leaped in. "Let her help, Doc. Women like to feel needed."

Sarah responded with a warm smile. Eddie was much younger than John, but seemed to read her mind better than her own husband.

When John relented, Sarah rushed down the hall and into the kitchen. She put a pot of water on to boil. John couldn't do everything alone. She'd tried to be helpful this morning by providing breakfast, but he'd walked out on her.

When it came to matters of his work, there was no criticizing him. Not that she did it purposefully, but it seemed to come out that way. Wouldn't it be better for him, too, to lighten up on his rigid standards, to ease the work strain from his body and mind? To share his problems by opening up to his wife?

All the things that'd initially attracted her to him, his deep sense of duty and obligation, his confident aura and the firm way he made decisions—*the things which made him strong*—also made him unapproachable. And drew her anger.

Would he share her bed tonight? Had it all been only physical on their wedding night?

Maybe if she proved herself indispensable, he'd lighten up with her, see that she was trying hard to make their marriage work.

Brightening at the thought, she hummed to herself as she prepared the towels. When she knocked gently at the door and entered, Eddie was sprawled out on the examination chair, half reclined. His shirt lay unbuttoned and a cloth had been spread across his lowered pants.

She got a glimpse of the wound, gasped in shock and staggered with the water, nearly spilling it.

''Whoa,'' said John, helping her to set down the bowl.

She turned away from the injury. There was no other way to describe it, other than that the three-inch gash looked…rotten.

''My missus can't look at it, either,'' said Eddie. ''You remind me a lot of her, ma'am.''

Sarah rubbed a trembling hand across her forehead, then stacked the towels, trying to ignore the putrid smell. ''How long have you had it?''

Towering beside her, John peered from her to his patient, watching Eddie rather intently. In the crammed space, she felt John's arm brush her own and wished he'd do something to comfort her.

''A couple of days.''

Remorseful at her first reaction, she tried to silently apologize by pretending it no longer bothered her. But she made sure to keep her eyes on Eddie's face, well above his wound. ''How did it happen?''

''…I was lifting the sickle to its peg on the wall, and

it slipped and hit me in the gut. It took a chunk of flesh out.''

Sarah shivered.

''I figured I could bandage it on my own, but...when I took the bandage off this evenin', it don't look good.''

''I'll need to drain it,'' said John as nausea welled up Sarah's throat. ''And cut away the infected skin. You'll need Hattie to apply these poultices three times a day. If you do that, and stay away from work for four or five days, I reckon you'll be fine.''

Sarah's moan of relief was louder than Eddie's.

John turned to her in surprise and she felt herself color. What sort of help was she? She couldn't even stomach looking at the patient.

She'd had the misfortune to be born squeamish. She got motion sickness at the slightest provocation, and the presence of blood turned her stomach inside out.

As a matter of fact... ''I'll be right back,'' she said, stumbling out of the office.

She ran to the kitchen, heading to the back door for the privy but only got as far as the slop bucket before she fell to her knees and vomited.

One good retch was all she usually needed, then she'd be fine. It took her fifteen minutes to clean her face, scour the bucket and dump the rinse water outside. When she returned to the office, John watched her enter. She silently pleaded that he wouldn't discover her weakness.

John must have already finished with the draining and incising, because he asked her to hand him the long roll of gauze bandaging.

There was a glass needle on the counter, so Sarah assumed Eddie had received an injection. He appeared quite at ease. His talkative nature made Sarah relax. She'd even laughed at one point when he told her how decent she was.

An hour after he'd arrived, Eddie was ready to leave.

"Let me walk you home," said John.

"No, Doc, you've done enough, and I thank you."

"Are you sure?" said Sarah, appalled that the man would walk himself home.

"I'll be fine. I'm just around the corner." True to word, the man was steady and strong on his feet. Must be from the hard work of roping cattle and exercising horses, thought Sarah.

The door had hardly closed behind him and John was putting on his wide-brimmed brown hat.

"Where are you going?" She couldn't believe he had to leave again. She'd been hoping that they could talk, perhaps read a book together, or do *something* that a normal husband and wife did in the evening. Maybe even share a quiet hour that might lead to making love.

"The superintendent's house."

"Why?"

John analyzed her for a long moment. "Sarah, as my wife, you'll be privy to a lot of confidential matters. I expect this to go no further. I'm going to report Eddie."

"Report him?"

"The wound's a lot older than two days. And I've seen enough wounds in my lifetime to know that this didn't happen from a sickle. A sickle wound, like a knife's, would be straight and clean. This gash has ragged ends."

"Then how did it happen?"

"It's a bullet graze."

"A gunshot?"

"That's right. Several days old. Which might place him on the McIver ranch during the rustling."

Sarah gasped in astonishment. "But he was so…so kind to me."

"That's the other thing that strikes me funny. He's normally a quiet man who says very little. He went out of his way to compliment you at every turn."

Her temper flared. "Maybe he appreciates me." Which was more than she could say for her husband.

John's deep dark eyes flickered. "Maybe he's trying to cozy up to you to deflect any questions I might have."

Her lips thinned. "You're a very suspicious man."

She watched John tense as if he'd been insulted. "Maybe it's part of my nature."

She pleaded, "But he's got a wife and two children."

"That's something he should have thought of before. Hattie has a large family with several sisters living in the area. If need be, his children will be well taken care of."

John had already thought that far ahead, in case Eddie went to jail? "But you're a doctor. Isn't there a measure of privacy between you and your patient that shouldn't be breached?"

"I'm a doctor, but I'm also a police officer. I can't cut myself in half. This is who I was before you married me, and this is who I am, Sarah. If Eddie's put one person in jeopardy because of anything he's done, then it's my duty to report him."

Sarah understood John's duty to protect the town, but in her heart, she believed Eddie was innocent. "But John…his wife…"

His voice dropped to a hush. "You're so soft, Sarah. Maybe this *isn't* the right life for you."

She staggered at his words. How could he say that to her? *"Have you no compassion?"*

John winced, and she felt the final wedge of distrust lodge between them. A glimmer of vulnerability flashed across his face, replaced by a coldness that sent a tremor through her.

"Lock the door behind me."

When he slammed it, the sound reverberated through her spine. God help her brother, if or when she found him, if he was still in trouble with the law. And God help her with her marriage.

"Would you quit taking my photograph?" Exiting her front door, Sarah darted past David on the porch, clutching her satchel and arranging her bonnet on her way to the market.

David wiggled out from beneath the black cloth of his standing camera. "Would you quit walking away? I need time to focus!"

"I don't like being chased and followed."

"Your husband said you'd enjoy it."

"Heaven forbid I go against my husband's wishes!"

The thin man and the monkey on his shoulder looked like they belonged in a circus. And with tonight being the evening of the big party, it would be a circus.

A circus with her standing in the center of it for everyone's entertainment, a hangman's noose being lowered over her head. How could she survive the seventy-five pairs of eyes upon her and John? The party she'd thrilled to when he'd first suggested it had degenerated into a party she had to endure.

John hadn't come back to her bedroom since the first night he'd left.

If she confided this to anyone, if the lovely image she and John were portraying were shattered by the truth, it would likely dampen the chance of working out their problems. John was a very private man who disliked the intrusion of others, and Sarah was certain if details got out, he'd be utterly disgraced. So would she.

David left his photographic equipment and leaped beside her as she strolled down the road. Willie cackled on his shoulder.

"Where are you headed?"

"I've got flowers to pick up at the market. Perhaps grapes and almonds, too. My new gown is too long. It's being hemmed by the seamstress and I need to pick that up, as well."

"I'll tag along and help you carry everything. In the meantime, I'll squeeze in a few more questions. Pretend I'm a journalist."

That would take a lot of pretending. He was not conscientious when he jumped out from bushes to ask her questions or to take her picture, never having his equipment ready nor questions planned out.

"What made you answer the mail-order ad?"

"I thought Calgary would be a nice place to live."

"What's the real reason?"

"You just asked that."

"The first answer people give is never the real one."

Maybe he'd be a better journalist than she thought. She blinked. "I thought it would change my world. I thought I would fall in love. I thought…I thought someone would finally appreciate all that I had to offer."

She reached the boardwalk and headed south to the open market. It was held every Saturday morning, she'd heard.

"Has it changed your world?"

Sarah's lips quivered with sorrow. "Yes."

But not in the way she'd intended, although she wouldn't tell David. It had turned her world upside down and made her realize that it was *she* who had to make her life better, *she* who had to learn to appreciate herself and not depend on a stranger. On a stranger who happened to be her husband, who didn't seem to appreciate anything about her.

She'd been so naive when she'd written those letters.

When they reached the flower market, she was still talking. She wasn't quite sure what she'd said aloud and what she'd kept to herself, other than being aware not to disclose anything private about her deteriorating relationship with John. She spoke about her own life and feelings. The words flowed and it was a welcome relief to speak to someone who was truly interested in listening.

The open-air market buzzed with a throng of farmers, sellers and buyers. Heavenly scents wafted through the air, of fresh-cut flowers, squash and onions.

The rest of the hour went quickly. David helped her choose the prettiest flowers, the Dutch gardener took her address and promised he'd deliver them before noon, and the seamstress had Sarah's gown pressed and waiting when they arrived.

"Willie," said David to the monkey as they approached home. "When did you steal that marigold? You little thief."

Willie sniffed it and Sarah laughed. "I'll mention it to the gardener when he arrives and it'll be put on our bill."

"Thank you," said David. "Now I'll leave you to get ready."

Laden with packages, Sarah stepped through the front door. White-haired women nodded as she entered. The home smelled like baked strudel and fresh air. Outside on the half acre lot, the side of beef donated by a rancher she hadn't met yet, Angus McIver, was turning on a spit. Several Mounties who were off-duty had already arrived to help, although John himself was at work. Sarah was struck by the lost opportunity of making true friends with these fine folks. How could one make a true friend if one never revealed their own true face?

John had told her yesterday—only when she'd asked, she thought with rising temper—that Eddie Dickson hadn't been charged with anything yet, and that John and the superintendent would quietly conduct an investigation without tipping their hand to Eddie or his wife.

"My, what a pretty gown," said Melodie, pushing past the older women carrying plates outside, to the stairs where Sarah stood unwrapping her dress from brown paper.

Sarah stifled a sob, wanting so desperately to confide in Melodie, knowing the consequences if she did. Melodie shared everything with her husband, and Sarah worried that every word she might say would go to Logan's ear and then perhaps the rest of the troop.

When the afternoon arrived, despite Melodie's awkwardness due to her pregnancy, she arranged Sarah's hair, helped her dress, then left for home to prepare herself.

At quarter to six, fifteen minutes before the guests were to arrive, Sarah made her way down the stairs to find John.

Two dozen people were there already, milling through the front room and spilling into the gardens, standing around the fire and the barbecued beef, the men with ales in their hands, the women with punch.

Through the crowd, Sarah felt the burn of someone's eyes upon her. When she turned past the others, she saw John standing at the outdoor fire thirty feet away, his dark brooding gaze riveted on hers. Not a smile broke his features, just that unreadable mask assessing her, sweeping her from top to bottom then up again, his lips twitching in response, silently mouthing her name. *"Sarah."*

Her pulse spun. Her chest tightened beneath her gown. He would not break her spirit.

His rugged black figure pulled her like the stars to the sun. He stood in lean black pants and black boots, with a sleek black leather vest and full-cut white shirt and blue cravat. She tried to quell her rising tide of desire, fighting the images of John making love to her in the bath, the golden light skimming over the sinewy muscles of his backside, reflected in the mirror, and then John pressing her to the kitchen table because he'd told her he couldn't wait long enough to carry her to the bedroom.

Now, while he stood at the fire with one large palm straddling a glass of ale and a long, taut leg propped on a log, Sarah noticed other women glancing in his direction. She felt her back stiffen. He was still hers, as long as she had breath to fight.

The new white shirt she'd bought him hung gracefully from his wide shoulders. Wearing her gift was a nice touch of deception on his part, wasn't it?

Smiling as she said her soft hellos, she wove past the couples to join her husband. She could also play this game. She'd play the role of loving wife to perfection.

Chapter Twelve

"Hello, darling."

Sarah's low voice made John's heart crackle against his chest. In the setting sun of the garden, she raised herself on tiptoe to brush her lips across his cheek, so steady, so confident in front of the others, but her slight tremble belied her self-assurance. Sarah was unsure of *him,* and he wanted her more because of it.

He allowed her lips to linger as he floundered in her aura, captured by her faint scent of roses and strudel and evening air. She had no idea how much he wanted her physically, or what she did to him standing here in her floor-length green gown, the peplum springing from her rounded hips and the bodice clinging tightly to those creamy breasts he dreamed of nightly.

The modest neckline revealed the naked, tender hollows of her throat, golden skin against a glistening gold chain, a throat he imagined kissing with the same explosive passion she'd kissed him with on their wedding night.

Thinking of her bare, throbbing body beneath his with her legs wrapped around his waist made the blood pound in his arteries. He had to pull away because they were in public.

She gave a soft gasp at his brisk withdrawal, mistaking his reaction for one of rejection, not arousal.

No matter. She was a mystery to him; she'd come into his life when he was feeling sorry for what his men had done to her. Yet her criticisms of his very nature, questioning his motives toward his patients and his compassion toward her, insisting he put her first, before his men...had insulted him beyond words.

Why, Sarah could make fog out of a clear blue sky. The woman had definitely flung everything he thought he knew about himself one hundred and eighty degrees into the clouds.

Dammit, though, he'd never let any woman affect his work. Until Sarah learned to devote herself to her own life and not to changing his, he saw no common ground by which they'd unite.

But then again, perhaps he'd take her physically if she offered. After all, she was his wife. She'd seemed to enjoy the erotic pleasures as much as he. Was she offering herself now, by the hidden meaning in her kiss?

Before he could read her expression, the crowd around them began introducing themselves. The two men on either side of John, one a wheat farmer and the other a cattle rancher, hadn't stood together for years, John observed, not without fighting. At least the party served the purpose of bringing the town's two feuding men together. They were head-to-head competitors for the best grazing land in Calgary.

Standing to John's left, Slade Phillips reached out to shake Sarah's hand. "Congratulations, Mrs. Calloway, and pleased to meet you."

John introduced Slade as the head of the Wheat Growers Association, then his wife.

Angus McIver stepped up, white hair at his temples, as

big as an elephant, and shook Sarah's hand. "Howdy, missus. You've got a fine man here as your husband."

Sarah smiled and John noticed whatever insecurity she may be feeling, she kept it to herself. Then Logan and Melodie arrived, and Sarah greeted them warmly.

"Mr. McIver, is it?" said Sarah, turning back to Angus. "Have we met before?"

"I don't think so," said Angus, stretching an arm around his young wife, Sheila.

"But I think we have…uh, I know where." Sarah planted a delicate finger in the air. "I noticed you across the street one day while I was shopping. You were wearing a set of Navy Colt .35s. We didn't speak, but I had the impression you knew who I was."

Angus squirmed. "I remember. Sorry if I was staring. Someone had just told me you'd married the doctor."

Other men cut in, Travis Reid, balancing on a crutch, and Sergeant O'Malley beside him, ribbing Angus for staring after a pretty woman, but Sarah and Angus's wife took it in cheerful stride.

Sarah's comments seemed to pass over everyone's head except John's. As a woman, how had Sarah known the make of Angus's guns? It was an odd thing to recall. John's curious gaze caught the veterinarian's, but neither man said anything about it.

As a matter of politeness, no man was visibly wearing his guns at the party.

Then other people poured in, and John and Sarah left as a couple to greet their guests, shake their hands and offer a kiss on the cheek. Under different circumstances, John might have found it pleasant to be standing with his wife, but the insincerity of pretending they were happy chafed against his pride.

More people arrived, including Clarissa. Her parents followed, then a subdued Mrs. Lott and Mrs. Thomas.

"I'd like to take some photos before the sun sets completely," David hollered at the newly married couple.

John watched Sarah's body tighten beneath her fine twill fabric.

"After you," he said softly, causing her to clamp her lips together.

He had an urge to laugh at her expression.

"Do you laugh at me?"

"Not at all," he murmured with amusement. "If you feel uncomfortable in the situation, you've brought it upon yourself."

This seemed to anger her more. "It's not all my doing."

As she breezed by him, the sting of her words pricked his cheeks. The way she sashayed into the garden, attracting every bachelor's eye, made John feel like taking her over his knee.

The thought of her on his knees made him wilt.

Frustrated by his pent-up energy, he followed behind her with more vigor than he'd intended.

"I've set up here," said David, indicating a garden bench beneath an arch of carefully tended wild roses. "Have a seat, both of you, while I adjust my lens."

Sarah plopped herself down into the corner, adjusting her skirts and clutching a matching parasol.

A congregation of heads and bodies formed a ring around the couple, making John feel like they were two polar bears on display at the zoo.

"Come here, *sweetheart*," said John, lowering himself close to Sarah. If she thought he was going to sit in the other corner, she was mistaken.

While the others watched, sighing in pleasure, Sarah's

cheeks turned crimson as he pressed against her and wrapped an arm around her shoulders. "Luckily, the photograph is not in color, like in real life," he said, referring to her blush.

The listening crowd laughed with great merriment, but Sarah glared at him with vexation.

"Your sentiment is so easy to read," he whispered as David scooted beneath his camera's long black cloth.

"That's because you bring out such a strong reaction...in my heaving *stomach*."

John stared straight ahead at the camera, holding his pose. "And perhaps even lower?"

She snorted through her frozen expression, but he felt a definite pinch on the side of his thigh.

"Ow!" He jumped so high he nearly slid off the bench.

The crowd snickered again and Sarah bent to his side. "*Darling*, are you all right?"

"I think I got stung by a bee."

"It may have been a queen bee," she said as she tugged him back up beside her. "One who felt threatened."

"A crazed hornet, I suspect."

"Bees?" said someone in the crowd, looking around the empty air. "Hornets?"

"Well," said Sarah, adjusting her hand on his for the photograph, "perhaps if you sit quietly this time, you won't provoke any more bites."

The camera clicked loudly.

"David," shouted John, "how about one with her on my knee?"

Sarah gasped as John grabbed her and slid her onto his lap. She tried to fight but he held her firmly. "Now, now," he whispered. "We've got an audience."

"Looks good!" hollered one man, whose wife cuffed him playfully with her gloves.

John fought the sensations of Sarah on his lap, her sweet breath and moist skin dangerously close to his own. The heat of her legs seeped into his thighs, melting his resistance, reminding him again of their wedding night.

"Watch out, Sarah," he whispered as David prepared for the next photo. "You always give me a strong reaction, too."

She shifted her soft bottom on his legs, then surprised him with a soft tumble of laughter.

Their situation struck him as comical, too, and his laughter joined with hers.

"Stop laughing," shouted David. "Be serious, or you'll look ridiculous in the photograph!"

They calmed down, David took his photo, Logan and Melodie, best man and matron of honor, joined them for another, then a final one with simply John and the other Mounties, standing around the well-done side of beef just before two men removed it from the spit.

At what seemed like the first opportunity, Sarah ran from him and into the fold of her female friends. The women disappeared into the house while the men carved the meat onto platters.

They'd be eating outdoors. The borrowed tables were set around the perimeter of the fence, four tables deep, five wide.

Before dinner was served, John nudged Logan. "Any more word on Eddie Dickson?"

"No. But if he stole that steer, or any of the others that have been disappearing for the last several months, he has easy access to the livery stables and good opportunity to get rid of the cattle without being caught."

"I've been thinking the same thing. The brands would be visible, but with the hundreds of animals coming and going at the livery, not to mention some of the seedy characters who pass through, stolen hides would be easy to sell.''

''When did Eddie move into town?''

''About three years ago, but I don't recall the month. I've got a police registry of births and deaths in my office. I started recording them around that time. It should have a record of his youngest child's name and birthdate. Let's take a look.''

John led them into his study and headed for the pile of journals he'd brought home this evening. He was done with them at the fort.

He rummaged through the pile. ''That's funny. I could have sworn I brought them all. I was thinking about leaving one or two behind, but I could have sworn…''

''Dinner is served,'' said Polly, peering into the library dressed in her starched black dress and crisp white apron.

Logan shooed John out the door. ''We can't be late for *this* dinner, even though I know how much you like to work.''

When they entered the gardens, darkness had fallen and candles glowed in their path. Kerosene lanterns hung from the fence, casting swaying shadows against the fruit trees, flowers and herbs, creating a magical atmosphere.

Sarah, standing in a circle of friends with a glass of wine in her hand, timidly met John's bold gaze then smiled softly. Why did the woman have such a hold over him? Could they diffuse their anger long enough to meet on neutral territory?

''Come sit with me.'' John excused his wife from Melodie's conversation and led her by one soft shoulder to the head table, beneath the same arch of wild roses they'd been photographed with. Someone had moved the bench away so that a table could be placed for the two of them, along with their best man and matron of honor.

"Where else would I sit tonight?" Sarah asked.

"I can never predict what you're going to do, so I'm playing it safe by telling you."

"Why must you always tell me what to do? Why can't you ask me?"

"Sarah...sometimes you've got to give in. That's what marriage is about. Compromise."

"As long as *I* compromise to *you*."

"Ahhh! Do you search for these things to criticize? Or do they come naturally?"

"As near as I can tell, they come naturally to you."

"Sit down."

"Say please."

"...please."

"Ask me nicely."

"Would you please have a seat, Mrs. Calloway? I would be ever so grateful for a little of your sweet company."

"That's more like it," Sarah whispered.

"Oh, how nice," said Melodie, coming up from behind. "Did you hear, Logan, how John speaks to her?"

John was certain heat was rising from his ears, but Sarah simply fluttered her lashes and with a great show, proceeded to sit down and unfold her napkin.

When the tables were seated, but before the hired ladies began to serve the dishes, the veterinarian rose to his feet. "I'd like to give a toast."

The crowd hushed. People filled their glasses with the champagne bottles opened at their tables.

John shared a nervous glance with Sarah, running his fingers over the creamy linen tablecloth that his grandma had provided and cherished all the years before she'd passed it down to him. Would she be proud of him now?

Masquerading in a marriage that perhaps neither he nor his wife were ready for?

Logan lifted his glass and the crowd did likewise. "I'd like to give a toast to my dear friends, John and Sarah. May your marriage always be strong and healthy, blessed with all the children you desire, and may your home never be short of love."

John heard the catch in Sarah's breath. When he turned to her, her eyes had misted. Her stoic silence caused a lump to form in his own throat.

He nodded in sad acknowledgment to his friends. They drank, and when they turned to John, he realized they expected him to give a toast, as well.

He rose on shaky legs. Lifting his glass high in the air, he was forced to look at Sarah. She met his gaze with unwavering strength, but her eyes glistened in watery pools.

"Look," whispered one of the women to her friends at the closest table. "Sarah's crying. Look how happy she is."

John knew it to be far from the truth, and the realization shamed him to the bottom of his boots.

"To my beautiful wife," was all he could say at first.

The crowd hushed and waited for more. Sarah bowed her head then glanced up again, her lashes clumped with moisture.

The moment seemed to stretch forever. He ached to say something nice about Sarah, something gentle and appropriate, but he couldn't lie, he told himself. He couldn't lie while he stood at his grandma's linens, he couldn't declare a love he didn't feel, and so he searched for the sentiment that was truly in his heart.

"Sarah, I know that it was difficult for you to come

here. I admire and respect the courage it took. And I greatly admire the woman behind it.''

''Hear, hear,'' folks called, then drank.

Sarah's eyes spilled over and John's chest felt like it was about to burst.

He sipped, then sat down, placing a gentle hand on her firm back, hoping to soothe her if he possibly could. How had they gotten themselves into this forlorn situation?

He reached below the tablecloth where no one could see and gently stroked her thigh. ''To my queen bee,'' he murmured, desperate to cheer her, make her smile—even to make her angry—anything but tears.

''To my crazed hornet,'' she replied, mustering a smile in his direction and wiping away a final tear. It didn't cheer him.

His heart felt pierced. He'd never been in love before, but if he were to fall in love with Sarah... *if he could*...this would be one of the reasons why. It was Sarah's gutsy determination to mount any hurdle and overcome any difficulty, even in the face of her own pain.

''Thank you for coming,'' said John at the door, to the superintendent and his wife who were one of the first to leave.

Sarah stood beside John in the brisk evening air, smiling graciously and looking fully recovered from their earlier encounters. Her long hair swirled and swung around her, framing her cheeks and large eyes, lulling John into a soft hypnosis. He wondered if she felt as composed as she appeared. Or, was she as stirred by him as he was by her?

Sarah waved once more, then pressed the door closed. ''Well, I guess the worst is over.''

''Was it really that awful?''

With a pronounced hesitation, she rubbed her slender hands over her green skirts. "Not all of it."

John felt a pang of disappointment. Was he expecting that she'd jump with elation at how the dinner had gone? That she'd fall into his arms and plead forgiveness for any strain she may have caused in the marriage?

No, not his Sarah.

He opened his mouth to begin a conversation, but she brushed past him. "We should join the others. It's still early."

It was only half past eight. The folks with children had left for home to get them settled for bed, which left the singles behind, or couples like themselves with no babies yet. Some of John's closer friends were still in the garden. They'd built a bonfire and were roasting husks of corn in the glowing coals.

For the first time since the evening began, John couldn't wait for the guests to leave. Then he could be alone with Sarah. To do what, he wasn't sure. But whatever it was, it would be damn entertaining.

At the fire, while Sarah whisked away to join Melodie and the other wives at one side, John squeezed to stand in between Logan, the other Mounties, Angus McIver and Slade Phillips.

It seemed John had stepped into the middle of an argument.

"The homesteaders are free to do as they please," Angus was saying, "and most choose cattle ranchin', just like I recommend." As head of the Cattlemens Association, his recommendations went far in Calgary.

But hell, thought John, why'd he always have to bring it up? John wondered what the women were talking about. Across the circle of fire, the flames were almost as high as Sarah's throat, but her face glowed in the orange flickers and the animation in her expression held him rooted.

"Hell, Angus, would you listen to yourself?" asked Slade. He was scrawny in comparison to Angus's thickness, but Slade always delivered his points with emphasis, one finger jabbing the air. "Grain is going to take over the prairies. Then you'll be sorry that you missed out on the money to be made. And—" Slade's face grew redder "—and you'll be responsible for takin' down good men with you!"

Angus leveled his gaze like a shotgun on a flying duck. "Like hell it will. You people still can't grow a wheat hardy enough for our climate. What'd you earn last year, Slade? Care to compare?"

Slade cursed and stepped forward with fists clenched.

John dove between the two. "What the hell's going on here, boys? Calm down. This is my party." He tried to laugh it off, and glanced to see if the women had noticed the raised voices. They hadn't. The sizzle and pop of burning logs and the new batch of charred corn they were pulling out from the fire seemed to occupy them.

Slade backed down, still fuming over the remark. John would be, too, because Angus had nailed the problem. Slade's wheat crop last year hadn't totally ripened in the short growing season, and he barely scraped through the last winter supporting his wife and three kids. On the other hand, Slade was often the aggressor in these arguments, and John felt sorry for Angus. Slade seemed gleeful every time word got out that Angus had another steer or horse stolen, or that the Grayveson gang had attacked his ranch.

"We might get some of those new homesteading laws changed that you helped set up," Slade hurled at Angus. "To favor us more by giving wheat farmers the most fertile soil around Calgary. Grain is the future!"

"It's prime grazin' land around Calgary, and you think we're gonna give up our rights for more of your failed attempts at wheat farmin'?"

This time Slade lurched forward before John could get between them. "You think I don't see what's goin' on around here?"

"What the hell are you implyin'?"

"Bribery."

Angus's face turned white. His lips drew into a tight line. "You better not be accusin' me of it."

"Everywhere the police go, there's Angus McIver, drinking among them. The Mounties need something? Ask good ol' Angus. If his cattle get stolen, why he gets more guns and better protection. One of the Mounties needs a side of beef for a wedding celebration? Never fear, Angus will donate it."

It began. Angus swung his fist at Slade but the veterinarian caught it in midair, and before Slade could lunge, John twisted his arm behind his back.

John swore. Slade was insulting not only Angus, but the rest of them standing here. "Get the hell of my house, both of you. I'm not going to put up with any of your goddamn fighting. The two of you use up more manpower for your squabbling than a cartload of thieves."

John flung Slade away from the fire. "Now you'll politely find your women and say good-night."

Angus paled and clutched his side.

John softened when he saw the man's misery. As Sarah had once aptly pointed out, John was a doctor as well as a policeman and yes, he did have compassion. He patted Angus on the shoulder and helped him locate his coat. "One of these days, Angus, that gallbladder will need to come out."

The older man straightened and grinned weakly. "No surgery for me. No one's cuttin' me open."

As much as Angus feared it, John knew there was a good chance it would happen. He hoped not, because odds of survival from gallbladder surgery were barely better than fifty percent.

When they left, John turned to Logan. "Do you think we should put a few men on the detail of watching Slade and the rest of the wheat growers? Maybe there's a connection between Slade and the Grayveson gang."

"I was thinking the same thing."

First Eddie Dickson and now Slade Phillips. Others might construe it as paranoia, but John saw it as being cautionary.

Ten minutes after Angus and Slade had left with their wives, more folks shuffled out the door. With Sarah standing beside John doling out jackets and cloaks, he noticed something strange out the front door, and a hollow barking in the distance.

He peered into the clear evening and saw the shadow of a group of…boys across the street. They were dressed in rough clothes, overalls and denims and short summer jackets. A couple of the older ones were surrounding one boy in the middle. John couldn't make out any faces in the darkness. They were fifty feet away.

Something was wrong. An eerie feeling crept up John's spine.

He jumped onto the porch, pushing past David. It looked like the gang was headed toward John's house. "What's going on?" he hollered.

"What is it, John?" Sarah had reached his side on the pathway. There was dread in her voice. Gripping the top of the gate, she peered in the same direction.

The center boy was limping, with the other ones helping him walk. The group was deathly silent. That's what was wrong—for a group of scruffy-looking kids, they were too quiet.

John flew to the injured one, recognizing him as Eddie Dickson's oldest boy, ten years old. He met them in the middle of the road and swooped down to the boy's level. "What is it, son?"

The white face strained with pride. "It's nothin'. I got bit, that's all."

"By what?" John scanned his body, but there was no obvious indication of what had happened. In the pitch darkness, John saw no torn clothing, no cuts visible on the denim trousers of his right injured leg.

"Just a dog."

"A mangy old dog," said one of the heavier boys.

Relief washed through John. "You've come to the right place. I think I can help you with that. Your name's Eddie Junior, right?"

Eddie Junior nodded.

"Step this way and I'll wash it for you with soap and water."

"Doc?" said the youngest boy dressed in overalls and boots too big to be anything other than hand-me-downs. John recognized him as living around the corner.

"Yeah?" John wondered how parents could allow these children to be on their own this late in the evening. What was it? Nine? Nine-thirty?

"The dog…the dog…he had a soapy mouth."

"Shut up," said the limping boy.

John quaked with horror. "What do you mean? Was his mouth white and foamy?"

"Yeah. And he kept growlin' and walkin' funny."

Sarah choked out a cry, but John tried to not let his

reaction show. "It's good you came to me. How long ago did you get bitten?"

"Ten minutes."

Thank God it was minutes and not days or weeks. There was no treatment for rabies after the acute symptoms appeared.

Sarah had recovered and scooted to Eddie Junior's side. She put her arms around the silent boy. His chin quivered; he looked like he wanted to wrap himself in Sarah's arms, but held himself in check.

"What's going on?" The veterinarian came up behind John, followed by the last dozen guests from the house.

John ignored the circle of adults. "Was the dog alone?" he asked the boys, praying for a yes.

None of them spoke.

In a panic, John turned to the littlest one. "Was the dog alone?"

"No. There was a pack of 'em."

"You're not supposed to tell!"

"I'm glad you told me. I'm a doctor and I'll help you. Did any of the rest of you get bitten?"

One by one, the boys shook their heads.

"Are you sure?"

They nodded.

"Did any of you get the foam from the dog's mouth on your hands, or on any cuts?"

They mumbled no.

John swooped the injured boy into his arms. "I've got special medicine in my house. You'll be fine. We'll bring your folks here and we'll get your friends home safely."

Sarah comforted the younger ones, while the other Mounties, headed by Logan, sprang into action, grouping the men into clusters of three to chase and capture the diseased animals. To the casual observer, the Mounties looked unarmed, but guns appeared from beneath jackets, having been tucked in shoulder holsters all evening.

Sarah's quiet poise brought a calm to the children, even to some of the adults, John noticed. But the severity of the incident finally dawned on the others.

"A pack of rabid dogs!" one fellow yelled in terror, madly running down the street, acting worse than the children.

John knew the townsfolk had to be informed for their own safety, but didn't want a panic on his hands. But sure as hell, the man shouted out the fatal illness that had rooted the world in terror for centuries, running door to door and knocking, his voice resonating into the sleepy street. *"Canine madness!"*

John understood where the man's terror came from. Rabies had been the scourge of Europe for centuries. Three to twelve weeks after being bitten, it caused an inflammation of the brain—encephalitis—that took root in a person's body, progressing to confusion, delirium, hallucinations, then death. Some people killed themselves when bitten by a rabid dog, knowing the horrible outcome. John had never witnessed it, but people with acute rabies were known to bite other people, thereby transmitting the disease. In fact over the centuries, human 'vampires' may have been confused with humans suffering from rabies.

Then four years ago, Louis Pasteur had developed the life-saving serum, one John could now miraculously offer to Eddie Junior.

John ignored the temptation of grabbing the screaming man by the scruff of the neck to calm him down, trusting in his men to do it.

With coaxing arms, John pressed the boy to his chest and raced into the house, flanked by Sarah at his side.

Chapter Thirteen

"**W**hat are you gonna do to me?"

A minute later, John set Eddie Junior down on the examination chair. "I'll explain everything as we go, okay?"

The boy didn't reply. His arms tightened in wary preparation, ready to flee at the slightest provocation, John imagined.

"Shh," said Sarah, sliding a stool to the boy's side and stroking the bare part of his arm that poked through the short-sleeved plaid shirt. John was grateful she was here, soothing the child.

He tugged at his blue cravat, removing it altogether and undoing his collar's top button so he could breathe.

He quickly surmised the situation. He'd never given the vaccination before, although he kept a small supply available. He estimated he'd need to give Eddie Junior only four days' worth of the vaccine. One needle a day.

"Dr. John knows what he's doing," Sarah said to the child. "I bet he's tended to lots of young boys like yourself."

"Name one," said Eddie Junior.

The boy was smart. John fidgeted beneath the boy's

perceptive stare. While pouring fresh water into the basin to wash his hands, John had to think about it. "Well, I helped deliver the Rossman boy last year."

"He's a baby. He's not a boy."

John cleared his throat. The truth was, Dr. Waters had tended to most of the townsfolk and their children for several years. "Oh, I remember one. At the fort last year, the superintendent's daughter got stung by a bee—"

"She's a girl."

"Then I guess the cook's daughter on the McIver ranch wouldn't impress you, either."

Eddie Junior pressed his lips together and narrowed his eyes. "What'd she have?"

"Poison ivy."

"Haven't you looked after any boys before?"

"Can't say I have, not recently."

"Humph."

"How about anyone with…cane…canine madness?"

"You don't have canine madness, son. If I didn't treat you, you'd get it, but you don't have it now."

The boy's tension eased somewhat. "What is canine madness?"

"It's another way of saying rabies. You'll hear that word a lot. If someone gets bitten by a rabid dog, then that person will get as sick as that dog."

"You mean I'm gonna be spittin' soap from my mouth?"

"No, no, no. You won't get sick at all. But I have to give you the medicine four days in a row."

"Will it hurt?"

John braced himself for the reaction. Honesty was always the best route. "Yes, it will, but only for a moment. The needle—"

"Needle? You ain't givin' me no needles!" The boy

jumped off the chair but John caught him before he reached the door. When John closed the door firmly, the boy screamed. "Let me out! You can't keep me here!"

Sarah held Eddie Junior by his shoulders. "No one's going to hurt you. The doctor and I are trying to help you. The needle will pass quickly, you'll see."

"No needles!" He punched Sarah in the arm, she fell backward and, horrified, John lunged to help her. Her green party gown swirled about her new leather shoes.

The office door opened and Sergeant O'Malley poked his head through. "I heard the screamin'. Need some help?"

John hated to do it, especially without the parents here, but if the boy didn't get the injection it meant life or death for him. "Could you hold him down while I clean the wound and give him the injection?"

"*No!*" Eddie kicked at the air.

"John, don't," said Sarah, springing forward. Taking a big chance at being kicked again, she stepped in front of Eddie to protect him from the men. "Let me talk to Eddie. Don't hold him down. I'll explain what he needs to do, and when he's ready…" She craned her neck slowly to peer at the top of the boy's head. "…I bet when he's ready, you won't need to hold him down. He'll cooperate."

The boy's tough front crumbled. He sobbed.

Sarah turned around and cradled him. "You won't fight me anymore, will you, sweetheart?"

His chest heaved into hers. "No."

"You're just as scared as I would be and that's natural. Why I bet even these big men wouldn't like it if we turned around and gave them needles."

"No, ma'am," said the sergeant, disappearing behind

the heavy wooden door after John had signaled him to leave. "Eddie's a lot stronger than me."

As John watched Sarah coaxing the boy, talking to him like an adult, John realized that what he would have done by force—if necessary—Sarah was managing to do by kindness and explanation.

She was interfering again in his work, but this time, unlike the other times, John could have kissed her.

Why couldn't he say it? Why couldn't he reach out, bury his pride in his pocket, and admit that she was sometimes right?

Sarah tucked her silky hair behind her ear. "All right, John. I think we're ready."

The boy hopped up on the chair. He let Sarah lift his pant leg so that John could have a close look at the bite. It was sharply gashed and bleeding.

After a quick cleansing, John opened the glass cabinet, retrieved the rabies vial, then prepared the syringe out of view.

Sarah kept the boy busy with banter, asking him where he lived and how his father was doing so the boy focused on her rather than the needle when the time came.

Eddie recoiled but didn't fight the inoculation in his upper abdomen. He clung to Sarah.

John recalled that days earlier when Sarah had tried to help John with Eddie Senior's wound, her face had turned purple with nausea. John had suspected she'd left so she could vomit, and this time, he saw her face turn just as squeamish when she saw the needle coming at Eddie Junior. But she stomached whatever displeasure she felt and tended to the boy.

Within minutes it was over. By the time his folks arrived, Eddie was sitting up in the library, enjoying a piece of party cake.

"Junior!" Eddie Senior came hobbling through the front door. "What happened?"

The boy's mother wasn't far behind. When she reached Junior, she buried him with her hug. "We thought you were in bed!"

The boy smirked. "Sorry. Everyone was sleepin' and I snuck out."

"You're never to do it again," said Mrs. Dickson as she led him outside. She and her husband thanked John and Sarah profusely for what they'd done.

"I'll come by to see you early in the morning," John said, along with his goodbyes.

When the family left, John turned to Sarah.

Say it, he urged himself. *Tell her how helpful she was.*

With a timid glance in his direction, which made his pulse quicken, Sarah pulled back her hair self-consciously then turned and went into the library. The bustle on her green gown amplified the swell of her hips and the tempting curve of one long lean thigh. "I need to tidy up."

John followed her into the room, determined to sort out their differences, to mend the problems in their marriage and make her understand how much his men and his work meant to him, but also how much she did. "Thank you for your help."

Sarah bent to pick up the magazines that people had been reading at the party and had left sprawled on the end tables. The *Illustrated London News* and *Paris Match* shuffled between her slender fingers. "My heart went out to the boy. The next few days aren't going to be easy for him, getting those needles."

It was a pleasure to watch her move. Her long hair shimmered around her temples, framing her eyes and full, glistening lips. The gold necklace around her throat captured the intricate planes and curves of her skin.

"Would you come with me in the morning?"

She smiled, disconcerted by his question. "If you want me there."

"I'm sure Eddie would like it."

Her smile disappeared as she picked up a messy stack of newspapers. "I'll do it for Eddie, then. Now that I've met the boy, I feel even worse for the suspicions you hold against his father."

"Sarah..." John stepped closer, a foot away. It wasn't just for the boy that John wanted her along in the morning, but for himself, too. But he wouldn't be pulled into another argument over Eddie Senior's surveillance. Reaching out, he grabbed her wrist, stroking the soft skin beneath his fingertips. She stilled. "The party ended so differently than how it began."

"Are you sorry that we had it?"

"I'm glad."

Their eyes moved to the papers she held. She waited, expectantly. The air swelled with anticipation.

"What are we doing, Sarah?"

As he moved forward, she swallowed and leaned back against his desk. He pressed against her, dipping his face into her hair. "You smell like strudel."

She laughed softly, yielding to his touch.

Taking the stack of newspapers from her hands, he set them down on the desk behind her, about to lift her into his arms. His journals caught his gaze.

He peered closer. "That's odd."

"What is?"

"My journal has reappeared. The one marked *Records*."

Blushing and twisting in obvious discomfort, Sarah opened her mouth to respond, then closed it again. When he frowned at her reaction, she dashed to leave. "I've got

to see to it that Polly and the other women are taking care
of the dishes.''

"The dishes can wait." He roared the words.

She raced away, but he caught her by the arm. Gripping
her firmly, shocked at himself that he could turn so
quickly to anger, he snapped her around to face him. ''It
was you. You took it.''

Her breathing came in shreds.

''Who the hell are you looking for, Sarah, and how did
you recognize that Angus McIver was carrying
Colt .35s?''

Sarah needed to escape. John's proximity, both physically and mentally—his wild but accurate guess that she'd
taken his journal—gripped her heart with looming dread.
Lord, he was an observant man. No wonder he was in the
force. Under any other circumstance she'd be extremely
proud of his skills, but not when he used them against
her.

Extricating herself from the long, tanned fingers dig-
ging into her muscled arm, she vowed she wouldn't let
him intimidate her. With determination in her stride, she
walked into the kitchen past the ladies scrubbing and
cleaning, then boldly left him gaping after her as she
stepped through the back door.

John followed her into the garden. Overhead, the moon
glimmered in the night sky like a big wax candle. The
sultry light draped itself across the raspberry bushes and
apple trees. Had John noticed the lovely fragrance in the
air, of ripe apples and sweet earth? Did he notice how
beautiful the evening was, or was he only interested in
pursuing his puzzle?

''I asked you a question.''

His breath rippled across the back of her neck. His civil

tone hammered through her chest. "You speak to me as if I'm a stranger." When he didn't deny it, the hollowness inside her multiplied. "You talk to me as if I'm a witness in the jailhouse and you're interrogating me."

"It's the way I speak, Sarah, and there's no difference between the way I talk to you and anyone else. I'm trying to be fair, which I do for everyone. If you're slighted, it's all in your imagination. And don't muddy the waters. I asked you a question."

She walked to the garden bench that they'd argued on earlier and ran her fingers along the smooth hard back. Where was the man who'd tenderly cared for a frightened boy only thirty minutes earlier? "You asked me two. Which do you want me to answer first?"

With a repressed moan, he placed a hand on his lean hip. His black leather vest parted, accentuating the silky white fabric of his shirt. She watched the moonlight dance across his golden skin, melting into the curves of his throat.

The wrinkle between his black brows deepened. "How did you come to recognize Angus McIver's guns to be Navy Colts?"

"My father carried similar guns while I was growing up."

"I thought you said he was a watchmaker."

"He was. He…he kept guns in the store to protect himself."

"Navy Colts?"

Among others. "Yes."

"Those are mighty fine guns for the average man."

"I guess my father wasn't average."

"And you knew the caliber of Angus's guns to be .35."

She nodded briskly then tried to step out of his glare. Reaching above her head, she snapped a large yellow apple from its branch, wrapping her fingers around the firm ball.

"Your father had .35 caliber guns, too, I suppose, and that's why you recognized them across the street."

"That's right."

"Aha. So you admit it was *across the street* at forty feet away. How could you see that distance?"

"You'd…you'd recognize them, too, wouldn't you?" He stumbled. "If I was looking closely, I would."

"So it's not entirely impossible."

"But I'm a policeman. That's my job."

"It was a lucky circumstance that I noticed them, I suppose. Guns have always attracted my attention." She'd been looking carefully at every gun she'd spotted in town, checking them for any distinction that might have been at Keenan's hand.

John scratched his stubbly jaw. "They've always attracted your attention," he repeated with disbelief. "Guns have."

She nodded and wiped the dust from the apple. Her mouth watered, ready to bite.

"What else attracts your attention?"

Where was this question headed? "The usual things… that attract a woman."

"Auction houses, ploughs and wagons?"

In panic, Sarah dropped the apple. How had he known she'd visited the auction house? The apple careened out of her hands. In a clumsy display of juggling, she twisted to catch it before it hit the ground, but missed. However, John also leaped for it, knocked his shoulder against hers, but caught the apple.

Straightening a foot in front of her flushed body, he held up the yellow fruit in triumph. "Did you think no one would tell me, Sarah?"

Flustered but unwilling to admit it, she reached to take it from his outstretched palm but he caught her wrist with his other hand and pulled her tight against him. Her breasts crushed against his leather vest. Penetrating her bodice fabric, cool leather slid against her nipples. The movement knocked the breath out of her. He wound an arm around her waist, making it impossible for her to run. Making it impossible for her to do anything but peer into his swirling dark eyes.

Controlling, twinkling, *arrogant* dark eyes. She longed to slap him. And kiss him.

Did he think he had caught her? She'd read in the newspaper that a plough was up for sale at the auction house. The ad had stated that a man named O'Neill was selling his farm equipment and moving to Vancouver. She'd gone, of course, to meet the Mr. O'Neill, and not to see the plough. When she'd gotten there, she took great care in pretending she was interested in many sale items, so as not to draw attention to herself. When she got to the plough, the ticket attached to it had been marked Tom O'Neill. Not her brother.

"Would you like a bite?" The apple reappeared in his left hand, although his right remained firmly ensconced in her back.

Her lashes flashed. "Of you or the apple?"

For a moment he said nothing. Then his head rolled back and the sound of deep laughter rumbled through the night air, pulsing through her skin. "You tempt me, Sarah. Is it because of your splendid body that I feel pounding beneath my own, or is it because of your energy?"

"Perhaps it's both."

"Maybe," he murmured, lowering his gaze to her throat. "Or—" he said, dipping his shoulders closer, his face so close she could feel the hair on her cheeks stir

"—is it because I've never met a woman like you before? Who are you? A sphinx or a criminal, or an innocent doe trapped in something she stumbled upon and can't escape? A woman who heats my blood with anger as much as passion."

She wiggled to get away but only managed to make him twist closer, so they were standing thigh against thigh. Lord help her for the images flying through her mind, of his bare skin pressed against hers. "You're being overly dramatic."

He laughed again. "Am I?"

When he bent his face closer, his lips a whisper away from hers, she gasped in submission. She melted back in her boots and closed her eyes, ready for the feel of his hot mouth as he took hers.

Instead she heard him bite into the apple. Her eyes flew open in utter humiliation.

Apparently he knew better than to laugh this time, but the upward curl of his full lips and the sparkle in his eyes told her how amusing he'd found her reaction.

She'd never yield to him again!

"Did you buy anything?" he asked after he swallowed.

She watched the mound of apple weave down his golden throat. She swallowed, angry at herself for noticing how masculine he was, how everything he did exuded power and poise.

"You went to the auction house yesterday, so I assume you went to buy something. What was it?"

"You know I wouldn't buy anything there without discussing it with you first. The items are large, and I have little money of my own."

"What caught your eye?"

"I—I saw a set of brooms for the kitchen I thought would look nice. And a poker set for the fireplace."

"Those are small items, Sarah. Most women would go directly to the mercantile to buy them. They probably wouldn't even think to look for them second-hand."

She gulped, floundering for a smart reply.

"The manager told me you were looking at his rack of guns."

Her feet pounded the earth. "Can I do nothing in this town without being spied upon?"

He moved in beat with her as she tried to step away. She heard the apple core hit the ground as he wove both his arms tighter around her back, pressing closer again. "No one is spying on you. These are my friends. They come to the fort on deliveries, they drop by the hospital with their ailments. They have a neighborly curiosity."

"Neighborly indeed."

His eyes searched hers, then lowered over her lips and chin. This time he swooped so quickly upon her throat she hadn't the time to anticipate it.

His lips pounded upon her skin, kissing and caressing and moaning in delight. He smelled of apples and leaves and trust and distrust.

She'd ached to be in his arms and now that she was, she trembled with agony. He made her body yearn for union; he made her wet with desire. Hope and longing burst from within her, from a place in her heart she'd tried to lock away. But she couldn't lock her heart away from John. She was too weak to fight him. When her arms came up around his shoulders, she dug her fingers into the back of his neck, playing softly with his hair.

"Sarah…" He responded with awakening lips ripping into her shoulders. She felt the heat of his mouth burning through the fabric. His chest tightened, his arms stirred against her spine and she knew he craved to be with her as much as she craved him. His mouth skimmed lower, and when she felt the moist heat suckling over one breast, she panted in surprise.

She would not yield to him.

She would not....

With a mighty heave, she clawed the back of his hair, the pressure breaking the hold his lips had over her skin. He surrendered and broke their clasp, choking for air, his broad chest lifting and subsiding with every breath. She fell back against a tree trunk, thankful to lean against something stronger than herself.

Now he knew how it felt to be taken to the edge and then refused.

They surveyed each other like dueling swordsmen.

He ran the back of his shaky hand over his mouth, as if they'd been in battle and she'd somehow cut him. "Who were you searching for in my registry?"

As if she'd ever say!

His body tensed and his voice reverberated with command. *"Who are you looking for?"*

She simply stared, unable to answer. She didn't want to fabricate a story, yet she couldn't trust him to be her brother's keeper.

"Then let *me* tell *you*."

Fearing what was coming next, she pushed off against the tree, ready to bolt for the house.

"You're looking for your cousin. The pickpocket you told me about."

Her muscles drained of blood. She turned around to face him. "What did you say?"

"It's been my experience that people come West for one of two reasons. Either they're trying to escape from something in their past, or they're looking for something. They might be looking for adventure, or a new life, or a person. Your cousin is the only family member that you've ever mentioned to me that you were close to. Is he still living in Halifax?''

''No,'' she breathed.

''Then where?''

''I'm…I'm not sure.''

''He's here, isn't he?''

Oh, God. Her skin turned to gooseflesh from the fear in her heart. John was so close in his guess.

''What's his name?'' he asked, wickedly calm. ''I'll help you find him.''

She stumbled, walking backward to the kitchen door for safety. He stiffened as he watched her leaving, colder than she'd ever witnessed him. ''You won't tell me his name, will you?'' His look was callous. ''Well, you don't have to because I know his surname is O'Neill.''

Her stomach quivered. ''How do you know?''

He scoffed. ''Because that's why you went dashing down to the O'Neill ranch the second day after we got married. That's what you're looking for in my registry. It somehow ties into the auction house, but what I can't figure out is how it all ties into guns. But give me another couple of days and I'll figure that out, too.''

Who would find him first?

''What's your cousin's Christian name, Sarah?''

''I can't tell you.''

''Why not?''

''I'm afraid of what you'll do to him.''

John winced. ''You won't tell me because he's still in trouble with the law, only this time deeper. Why didn't you tell me this before we were married? That's the real reason you came to Calgary, not to marry me.''

Is that what he thought? In the beginning, maybe yes, but not anymore…or was John right?

His look of despair and disgust made her wrench herself away from his harsh glare, but not before the damage of his next words echoed into her soul. *"How could you bring this into my house?"*

Chapter Fourteen

Sarah trembled with the knowledge that the race was on. She had to find Keenan before John did. She was hard-pressed to admit it, but shame was on her side—John's shame that he had a potential criminal in his family. His desire to keep the news to himself until he found that person gave her an edge she wasn't proud to have.

A cool September breeze ruffled her angora shawl as they sped by the mercantile's front glass window, she was seated beside John in the buggy. His long legs stretched beside her shorter ones. She watched the breeze blow gently across his hands, stirring the hairs at his wrists as he held the reins in capable fingers.

To observe the streets this quiet felt odd. At four-thirty in the morning, with the sun still hiding below the eastern horizon, Sarah strained her eyes to capture the details of buildings beyond their boxy shadows. The livery stables and auction house looked like one of the postcards David had shown her of the town, but with no people in it.

For the third and final morning, they were on their way to see Eddie Junior. Silently, Sarah laughed at her previous attempts of rising early to make coffee for John, for now it seemed he couldn't wait for their stilted meetings to end. As soon as they gave the young boy his treatments, John would take the buggy and be off for the day, while Eddie Senior walked Sarah home before his morning started in the livery stables.

And she...she would go back to the empty house, prepare for her morning at the jeweler's, then return midday to the same empty plate on the counter and solitary bread crumbs on the table.

During their morning walks, the elder Eddie had seemed as congenial as he had that first evening Sarah had met him, and she wondered what secrets he concealed about his gunshot wound.

John was ashamed of her. She saw the shame in his eyes when he asked her to pass the butter at the supper table, when he said hello to Eddie Senior and his wife while holding the door open for Sarah and pressing an arm to her shoulder in a false gesture of husbandly pride.

She struggled with the decision of whether to tell John everything about Keenan and take her chances. But what chance would that leave Keenan with? What right had she to find the brother who so obviously had said his good-byes to *her* twelve years ago?

She'd stayed put in the same residence for those twelve years, *easy to contact,* desperately searching the return address of all mail their household received, waiting for a telegram to call her to him, wondering if he was still alive and even if...he remembered his younger sister.

Maybe she'd never find Keenan. Lord, she never wanted to say it, but maybe Keenan hadn't made it this far west. If an accident had befallen him, why he might even be....

And yet, here was Keenan, an invisible ghost sitting as solidly between her and her husband as if Keenan were here in bone and blood.

Half of her craved to find her brother, the other half wanted to strangle him when or if she did. How could he just up and leave? How could he leave her behind to care for their folks alone? Especially to care for their ailing mother.

"What are you going to do today?"

John's voice startled her. She fidgeted with her shawl. "Nothing much. Work. Cook. The usual."

In the darkness, a sleek lock of hair fell forward across his temples. He needed a haircut. He hadn't had one in the weeks she'd known him. He probably hadn't had time for one. "I'm not interrogating you, Sarah. It was a simple question from husband to wife."

"Oh." She could no longer tell where the interrogations ended and the normal conversations began.

He was ashamed of her.

"They caught all the rabid dogs except one."

"Melodie told me."

The Mounties had put a curfew on the town. No children were allowed on the streets past six o'clock, until Dr. Calloway lifted the curfew. The last dog had to be found and all animals in the area cleared of potential risk. So far, they'd found no others afflicted. Logan, as the veterinarian, was seeing to that part of police duty. Everyone was encouraged to stay away from potential carriers—foxes, skunks, raccoons, coyotes and bats.

"John... I noticed...if you'd like a haircut anytime soon, I'm good with a pair of scissors. I used to cut my mother's hair, and sometimes my father's, depending on how the store was doing that month, if he could afford to go to the barber's."

"I'll keep that in mind," John said. "Here we are."

It seemed they had little to say after that. They arrived at the Dickson house, John gave the child his needle,

Sarah did her best to remain cheery around the child, then she and John went their separate ways.

Two weeks later, time had passed but nothing had changed. Much to her disappointment, John had come home one evening with his hair newly trimmed. It'd been cut by the fort cook, he'd said, who doubled as a barber when one was needed.

It seemed no one needed her for anything.

She considered giving up hope in her search for Keenan, as well. There was no hint that he'd ever lived in the area. She felt tired from searching, and the slightest criticism from John caused her nausea to return.

"Good morning, Sarah," said Mr. Ashford as she hung up her cloak in the storage room of the jeweler's the following day. "I've got a customer out here who's interested in getting his wife a gift. Would you help him? The mayor's dropping by this morning to pick up his broken locket and I haven't finished repairing it yet. Maybe you can show the customer one of your watches."

"Mine? But they're not ready."

"I saw the three you put together. They look good. The sooner you start selling them, the sooner you'll make a profit and the sooner I will." He added with a nod, "I imagine the doctor's mighty proud of you."

The truth was, she hadn't told John. Toying around with watch movements and gold cases and silver chains seemed so…miniscule in comparison to the scale of things that he accomplished.

Besides, they weren't speaking.

When she brushed by Clarissa, the young woman glanced up from wiping the counters. "I still think he was forced to marry you," Clarissa whispered in a grating tone as Sarah passed.

"Yes, Mr. Jones," Sarah said cheerfully to the cowboy

twenty minutes later as she bent over the glass counter. She forgot her own troubles while she concentrated on the sale. "This is the last one I have to show you."

"It's so shiny and thin." He poked a weathered finger at the glass, then stroked his broad mustache.

"That's the choice I made when I designed it. I wanted something slender that could fit into a woman's pocket, or be pinned against her blouse while she's cooking supper or shopping at the general store. It's not too heavy. See, it won't rip the fabric of her blouse."

"Specially designed, huh? Must be expensive."

Sarah brightened. "That's the beauty of it. It's the least expensive. The reason we can keep the price low is because I've made it from leftover pieces of other watches. You see, I took the movement from a Swiss watch and applied it to an English case, then had the tinsmith hammer a thin gold plate, which I cut into a ribbon for the broach pin."

"You think she'd appreciate it for a gift?"

"What's the occasion?"

"Over ten years of marriage with the likes of me."

Sarah laughed and nodded, and wondered if she and John would ever make it to ten years. Another wave of disappointment assailed her. "If I engrave it here with your wife's name, why, no one else would own anything like it."

"Engraved. I like that. I'll take it."

The thrill of her first sale bubbled through Sarah. After she engraved the *y* in Lily, she gave the cowboy a tiny cardboard box stuffed with cotton wadding and his wife's watch.

Smiling, he tipped his hat and made to walk away. The light shining through the barred glass windows glimmered over his holsters. When she glanced down at the guns strapped to his thighs, a shockwave rolled through her. She slipped out the front door and followed him. "Sir?"

Mr. Jones spun around in the bright sunshine slanting across the covered boardwalk. "Something wrong?"

"No, I—I couldn't help but notice those guns you're wearing. My father collected guns and I—I thought you wouldn't mind if I had a closer look. I enjoy fine craftsmanship. The checkering on the grip looks a bit unusual."

He narrowed his eyes. "My, you are a surprise, aren't you, darlin'?" Then he removed one gun and held it out.

Sarah hadn't seen gunsmithing done this well for over twelve years. A thin checkered pattern crisscrossed the stock. Not only meant as decoration, a good checking job would camouflage the wear where the hand met the wood for years to come and provided traction and a non-skid grip for sweaty hands. While running, a hunter needed all the traction he could get on his gun. She glanced up at Mr. Jones and wondered where he'd gotten them. Was he a hunter or a marksman?

The unusual diamond border was a pattern Keenan had often used, but what made it entirely unique was the spacing and the contours. Most amateurs spaced at sixteen lines per inch, but this one was checkered by a professional, at thirty. And no amateur would attempt to run the lines around the sharp curves to integrate the pattern on the two sides of the stock, like this one. There was a finely curled twist, almost invisible to the naked eye where each line met with the border, a twist that could only be made by a person who was using their left hand.

A left-handed gunsmith. The thrill of victory hit her square in the chest. *Keenan.*

More than two hours later, at the stroke of noon when her shift ended, Sarah bounced out of the jewelry store with her shawl slung over one shoulder, determined to find her brother. The astounding thought drew perspiration from her brow. She bumped into David on the boardwalk.

"David, don't bother me now."

He pushed back a handful of yellow hair and tickled Willie, who was resting on his skinny shoulder. "I've got a couple of questions left before I finish my article. I'll tag along quietly. You won't even notice I'm here."

"I don't know if you've looked in the mirror lately, but you've got a monkey on your back. How can I not notice you? Vamoose."

David laughed. "Why? Do you have a secret?"

"No." Sarah bit down on the inside of her cheek, trying to curb her annoyance. She kept walking toward home. Mr. Jones wouldn't tell her much about the guns. For some reason, he said he couldn't remember where he'd gotten them. Hah. That would be like a woman forgetting who gave her the rings she wore on her fingers. It would never happen. Why had he felt it necessary to hide his source? The only thing he did tell her was that he'd had the guns for two years.

Which meant Keenan had been in the area two years ago. Angus McIver's name had cropped up twice in the conversation, as had Slade Phillips's. Perhaps she'd begin her search by visiting those two ranches. She could visit on the pretext of saying thank-you to the wives for coming to her wedding party.

"There you are, Sarah." Melodie Sutcliffe waddled around the corner as Sarah turned down her street. "I've come to invite you for lunch."

Although always happy to see her one true friend, Sarah didn't need two people dragging her down at this precipitous time. She needed to find Keenan, alone.

"Great!" said David. "We can all have lunch together

because I have a few last questions for you both. For my article.''

Sarah groaned at the suggestion.

Melodie lowered her voice. ''It's just that, Sarah, honey, you and John have been avoiding my dinner invitations.''

Looking at Melodie standing there so serenely, nine months along in the family way, made another thought race through Sarah's mind, one she'd been avoiding for days. Sarah was late in her monthly time by a few weeks. Because she was often irregular, and motion sickness and its nausea were not uncommon for her, she wasn't sure whether it meant anything.

''I'm sorry,'' she said gently to her friend. ''John and I have both been busy…'' It was a weak attempt at an excuse, and Melodie's sharp gaze seemed to see right through it.

Sarah stepped forward and placed an arm around her friend's shoulders. ''I promise we'll get together soon. Thank you for the invitation. Now, if you'll both excuse me, I need—''

Melodie cried out. ''Ow!'' She turned pale and clutched her swollen belly.

Sarah leaped forward. ''What is it?''

''I think…'' Melodie groaned ''…it's the baby.''

John heard his name being called in a faint feminine voice. Propped on a stool, seated beside his patient in the hospital ward, John looked up from his suturing behind the curtain and heard someone burst through the doors.

''John!'' Sarah's voice echoed against the plank walls. ''They told me you were in here. Is it safe to come inside?''

Why was she here? Fear gripped his heart. He nodded

to the constable lying on the bed. "I'm in here. Is something wrong?"

Sarah slapped back the curtain. She apparently wasn't expecting John to be with a patient. When she glanced down at the three-inch bleeding hole in the constable's arm, and the tugging of the silk suture as John pierced the skin, she wobbled back.

"Sit down, Sarah. There's a stool behind you."

"I just—I'm sorry…" Heaving onto the stool, she bent her head between her knees, then took a deep breath in and out. Her navy skirt skimmed the floor and the cameo buttons at her collar pressed against her throat.

"Undo your collar, you'll breathe better." John was reminded of another time, eons ago it seemed, when he'd undone her corset for her so she could breathe. "Sorry, Todd," John said to his patient.

"It's all right. One of my sisters can't take the sight of blood, either."

John sped up his stitching. "What is it, Sarah? What's wrong?"

Undoing the buttons of her collar, she spoke with her head between her legs, her voice tumbling over the twelve-inch plank flooring. "It's Melodie. She's fine, but she's in labor."

"I see." John looked to Todd for a moment. Melodie had been progressing in her confinement with good health and vigor, each time John had checked her over the past three months. "Does Logan know?"

"I asked the corporal to find him. Logan is apparently in the stables."

"Has her water broke?"

"No."

It was Melodie's first child, and those labors always

progressed slowly; they likely had hours before she'd deliver.

"I know Dr. Waters isn't in any shape...isn't available," she corrected herself.

"Where is Melodie and who is she with?"

"I left her at her home with David and the monkey. Polly's over there, too."

John tied the final knot, snipped the thread with scissors, swabbed the entire thing with carbolic acid again, then looked for his gauze bandaging. "You're lucky the thief didn't have good aim," he told the constable—one of many he'd sutured in the last while. "If the knife had landed two inches over into your chest, it could have killed you."

John heard Sarah try to stifle a nauseous whimper. Due to her motion sickness, riding a horse wasn't a good idea for her, but he admired the fact that she had ridden here anyway to get him. She was strong-willed and valiant. No one could tell Sarah what she could and couldn't do. Including him.

Logan burst onto the ward. "How's Melodie?"

"She's fine, she just got started," Sarah said from between her legs.

Logan approached John, spotted Sarah and frowned. "What are you doing down there?"

She righted herself. The blood had pooled in her face and it threatened to burst from her glossy cheeks. Her bun had fallen out and her head of reddish-blond hair tangled around her cheekbones.

John was struck by how pretty she looked when she was caught in a vulnerable situation. Then the realization that he liked her tough and independent struck him.

As he bandaged Todd's arm, John wondered. How could he have it both ways? How could he demand she relent to him in his decision-making at home, but also want her to stand on her own two feet? The two ideals didn't go together. It troubled him that maybe he was being illogical and unfair in what he wanted from his wife.

No. He bristled. His experience as a doctor and a Mountie made him decisive and sure of himself, and there was nothing wrong with that. Besides, she still hadn't disclosed a word about her missing cousin, and John's disappointment in her grew with every passing day.

On the ride back into town, Logan rode Sarah's horse while John insisted she ride back with him in the buggy.

John flicked the reins as they drove beneath the fort's palisade gate. "Are you all right, Sarah?"

"I'll be fine."

"Still nauseated?"

She hesitated before answering. "A little."

"There's nothing much I can do for your motion sickness, other than make you a cup of chamomile tea when we get there."

She nodded, clenched the side rail, straightening the fabric of her skirt with her other hand.

Stealing a glimpse of her luscious outline beneath the soft cotton of her blouse, and the hint of her splendid legs beneath her skirts stretched before him, he realized he always wanted her at the most inopportune moments. He flicked the reins to go faster.

What could he do to bridge the troubled waterways between them? There had to be a way to mend their differences, to show her how much he *could* care for her, while still maintaining his confidentiality with his men.

Other Mounties had wives and families. How did they manage? But then, none of them had the distinction of being called Black-'n-White. Was he really that rigid?

When they arrived at the Sutcliffe home, Logan was

already there. He'd galloped ahead by twenty minutes and was at the back door to greet them. Melodie was resting in her bedroom, he told John.

Polly had left, but David met them with the monkey on his hip. "Can I stay and take notes?"

"Are you insane?" asked John. "Get out of here. And take that unhygienic ape with you."

"Hey. Willie's not unhygienic.... I guess photographs are out of the question."

The veterinarian held the door for David. *"Out."* As the photographer and his hairy assistant left, Logan scooped his tin cup from the pesky paws.

Entering the log kitchen, John spotted Melodie's sister, Francis, handling the boiling water on the cast-iron stove. She had her own toddler to attend to, who was clawing at her skirts and crying in desperate need of his afternoon nap.

John watched his wife take gentle control of the situation while he set down his medicine bag and quickly washed his hands at the counter. Sarah's paleness had left; color filled her soft cheeks again.

"Go put your child to bed, Francis," said Sarah. "I'll look after Melodie for a spell."

Frazzled by the child's wails, Francis patted her strewn black hair. "Would you? I'd be ever grateful. I'll be across the street at my home if you need me, but I'll be back as soon as his nap is over."

"Don't worry. I know where to find you. Take all the time you need."

Francis kissed Sarah on the cheek, took her child, peeked in on Melodie down the hallway to the right, then left.

Logan, in comparison, rattled around the kitchen, putting another log into the stove when he'd done so two minutes earlier. John nudged the younger man with a free foot. "How many foals do you figure you've delivered in your time?"

"Close to forty."

"Calves?"

"Twenty or more."

"Then what are you nervous about?"

Logan laughed. "I reckon because Melodie's my wife and I love her to pieces. You know the feeling." Logan peered from John to Sarah.

The two of them locked eyes and John felt the heat of failure and frustration rise up his neck. Stricken by an embarrassment John wished he could assuage, Sarah lowered her gaze to the cotton blankets she had pressed in her arms, then stepped into the hallway toward Melodie's room.

John followed. She was lying in bed, in the parlor that doubled as the bedroom, dressed in a starched white nightgown. Judging by the effort on her face, she battled a contraction.

"Hold on there, Melodie, don't push yet." With the ease and comfort of years of experience, John lifted the fresh sheets and checked her station. Surprisingly, her cervix was three-quarters dilated and had thinned nicely.

"You've been in labor a lot longer than an hour. When did it start?"

"I felt some tingles in the middle of the night, but I've felt them on and off for several weeks."

"You should have told me," said her husband. He sat on the other side of the bed, stroking his wife's long brown hair. John was touched by the ease between them. It only magnified the stiffness John and Sarah displayed.

The room was large and cheerful, with a fireplace along one wall, bookcases along the other and a huge desk in the center. Sarah sat down on the wide, beaten rocking chair beside Melodie and clasped her friend's hand. When the two of them began to whisper and smile, the men left quietly for the kitchen.

Ten minutes later, Logan's hands shook on his cup of coffee as he brought it to his lips.

"She'll be fine," John tried to reassure him. "Honest. She's healthy. I'm sure you've been checking your wife's condition for the last few months yourself, veterinarian or not."

Logan chuckled. The faint scars on his cheek, left over from his bullet wound, rippled. "She's got the best damn horse doctor in town."

"Now that's something to be proud of," John said, joining in the laughter. Gazing at his friend, John couldn't believe at one time he'd doubted Logan's abilities to be his makeshift assistant. Logan was youthful, energetic and took commands well. And his skills as a surgeon were growing.

Still, John wondered if the federal government would ever send him another medical officer.

When John went to check on his patient again, he overheard Sarah whispering as she placed a wet cloth over Melodie's sweaty brow. "You're going to pull through this just fine. You're the only friend I've got in this town and I'll do everything I can to help ease the pain."

For a moment John stumbled at being caught listening. Her only friend in town? *Wasn't he her friend?* He placed a cup of newly brewed chamomile tea beside Sarah's chair. The space at the bedside was cramped and they brushed legs, sending a tingle through his.

Wasn't he?

"What's this?" Sarah bent forward and inhaled the steam. Her waist twisted, drawing his attention to the swell of her breasts. When she opened her mouth to say thank you, she met with his intent gaze. He hesitated in confusion, swimming through a haze of emotions. For the first time he consciously realized how much he *liked* Sarah, as a woman and a person.

Yet she didn't seem to know it, and that struck him with a chord of utter discontent.

Melodie groaned in another contraction.

Forgetting all else, John placed his hand on her abdomen. The contracted muscles tightened beneath his palm. Her contractions were firm and regular and she surprised him by being ready to deliver.

"With the next contraction, Melodie, you can push."

Logan dashed to his wife in a momentary panic, making the other three laugh gently at his reaction.

"Calm down," Melodie said to her husband.

"I can't," he responded, nervous fingers winding across his stubbly jaw. "It's not as if you're a cow or a mare."

Melodie laughed. "What does that mean?"

And then another contraction hit. An hour later, with a lot of pushing and shouting, a healthy baby boy was born.

"Let me see," said the new mother, scrambling up on her knees to look at the baby that John held in his arms. The umbilical cord glistened in the towel. John rubbed the baby's tiny pink back with the towels nestled around him. Sarah came to hold the baby while he cut the cord, and they shared a smile of wonder.

When he looked up again, Logan was sliding to the floor.

"Logan?" Drenched in perspiration, Melodie craned her neck over the bed to see her fainting husband hit the rag rug. "Oh, dear."

Thankfully, Sarah took over Logan's care while John helped mother and babe.

An hour later, when the new family was settled together around the bedside and Logan's strength restored by a powerful cognac, John finally had the time to turn his attention to his wife. He hadn't realized it, but the room was hot and his shirt dampened with sweat. Sarah, her loose curly hair flowing over a curvy shoulder, was smiling at the cooing baby.

"Let's go for a walk," John said to her, clasping her warm fingers between his own and leading her gently out of the room.

Chapter Fifteen

Sarah felt John's exploring fingers winding between hers and pined for him to hold her. She squeezed tighter. He was so much taller than she, which always made her feel more feminine when she walked beside him. She wanted to respond deeper, to twirl around and to face him here in the sunset glow of the dusty street, but was afraid to open her heart. Every time she had in the past, they'd argued.

Listening to the crunch of her boots on pebble, when the silence ripened and her emotions swelled to the brink, she couldn't help herself. "Was there something on your mind, John? Where are we going?"

"To the train depot to see if my British journal has arrived. But that's just an excuse, really, to get you alone."

Emotions warred inside of her. The hope and promise of what he might want to talk about combined with the fear that he had something monumental to tell her—a separation perhaps?—added to the guilt that she was keeping Keenan to herself. But then, John *was* holding her hand and surely that had meaning.

They reached the boardwalk. John nodded to several

couples brushing past them, then dropped her hand in a self-conscious moment. It felt as if someone had severed them in two. As quickly as his embracing warmth had come, his shyness in public—like all men she'd ever met—quickly took root.

The thought that she may be carrying his child made her tremble. If he had no feeling for her, what then of the child?

John stopped, placed a hand on his back pocket and cleared his throat. While she waited with deepening breath, in the street above them, lamplight cascaded over the ample fabric of his expansive shoulders, over the suspenders cutting into the muscles of his midriff, over the tight, lean hips. "I don't think I've ever told you how helpful you've been to me in my practice."

Helpful. Grateful for an assistant, that's how he felt. She blushed, aware of the hot hand that came up to press against her spine as he led her around two customers exiting the mercantile. He'd been so passionate on their wedding eve, surely there was more to how he felt than gratitude.

"Melodie's been very good to me since I arrived," she babbled, increasing her pace and concentrating on her worn black boots. "I was thrilled to be of help to her this afternoon. Did you know that she and her sister insist on serving me lunch twice a week?"

His brows rose in surprise. "No, I didn't."

"Last week, they invited Superintendent Ridgeway's wife, Annabelle. My, she's a friendly lady. Then they gave me pointers on how to handle being married to a policeman."

The rugged muscles in his face piqued with interest. "Pointers? Like what?"

Sarah fingered the inside of her skirt's soft cotton

pocket, absently pulling at the corner threads. "They told me what they do to pass the time when their husbands get called away for lengthy duty, how they rotate spending the evenings at each other's homes. Also, how best to wash your uniforms, and how to address the commissioner when he comes to visit."

"You never shared this with me before."

"I wasn't sure you'd be interested."

He pondered that for a moment, running his hand through his slick dark hair. She noticed that the folds of his ear were lightly tanned and that his neck was taut with tension.

Was he upset about his work? "You said we're going to the train depot for a journal. You've been immersed in them for weeks. What are you looking for?"

With a gentle smile that erased his brooding tension, he studied her. "You're interested in medicine, aren't you?"

"I'm interested in the people you help more than the medicine itself. I—I can't say I'm very good at stomaching most of what I've seen you do."

"You were excellent with Melodie today. You kept a very calm head, despite your own nausea."

"So you noticed." He was a surgeon, after all. Had he also noticed…suspected that she was late in her monthly cycle?

No, how could he? They were practically strangers when it came to things like that, and she hadn't had a menstruation since they'd been married, six weeks ago.

"I notice *lots* of things about you," he whispered into her ear, sending a shudder through her body.

She sighed, afraid to continue in this vein of intimate discussion.

"For instance," he said, bringing a hand up behind her

neck, "I notice that when you rise with me in the morning, you brush your hair in that ridiculously tight bun, but if you rise on your own like you did today, you tend to wear it down."

When he wound his warm fingers beneath her mound of hair to tickle her neck, she felt every cell call to attention.

They descended the boardwalk stairs to cross the street for the train depot. The sun had set and the sky was that brilliant purple she adored, half twilight, half dusk. His hand shifted on her back, in parallel motion to her moving muscles.

He murmured, "It's down the way I like it. You've got gorgeous hair. Why don't you wear it for me like this more often?"

They stood in the street. Beneath her pounding heart, she barely noticed the team of oxen pulling a wagonload of logs, coming toward them.

"Out of my way!" shouted the driver.

John yanked her out of the path, pulling her roughly against him. To their left, a train rumbled past a crowded platform of waving people.

She gulped as John's voice grew raspy. "I also notice that when it's dark out and I look into your eyes, they're as shiny as mirrors. Especially when you're trying to hide something from me. Sometimes a person needs reassurance, Sarah."

John needed reassurance from *her?*

She had the feeling he was referring to many things in his life. "I've noticed some things about you, too," she offered, pulling away from his intensity and striding to the brown log walls of the stationhouse.

"Really?" He chased after her, around a fellow carrying two bursting suitcases strapped with rope, and another burdened with a bushel of corn. "What have you noticed?"

"You bounce when you walk," she said.

"That's not true."

"It is. When you're in high spirits, like you must be now, you bounce."

He laughed. Just then, two young women dressed in the latest fashions of silk bustles and feathered bonnets exiting the stationhouse, glanced at John's fine figure and whispered to each other. He had a captivating presence and Sarah couldn't blame any woman from being interested. When two passing gentlemen glanced at Sarah in the same interested fashion, John's eyebrows rose to tease her.

"And when you're angry with me," she hollered with her own mark of laughter, "you have a tendency to scratch your chin."

"What?"

"Sometimes when we wash the dishes together, you scratch your chin nonstop."

"I'll try not to do that any more."

"Promises, promises," she said in mock indignation. They entered the stationhouse. The back wall and its twelve-foot-wide doors gaped open, revealing a double set of tracks below. Dozens of travelers swarmed the wooden benches, the small café and the ticket booth. Some older men, unshaven and dressed in shoddy woolen suits, looked like vagabonds desperate for a good meal. They clashed against the opulence of first-class tourists traveling farther west to see the Rocky Mountains, their polished luggage neatly clasped at the sides of their accompanying servants.

Realizing she wasn't sure where they were headed, Sarah stopped to let John lead. To her amusement, he nearly toppled over her. "And what is that you carry around in your suit pocket?"

His polished veneer faded at her question but he didn't answer.

The heavy breeze of an incoming train roared past them. Her skirts ballooned around her legs. "The little ticket stub in your scarlet tunic," she called above the screeching wheels. "You know the one, it's wrinkled and faded, green with black writing. I've seen it often when I've brushed your suit. I always leave it in your inside pocket the way I find it, but I'm curious."

"Why it's…it's…"

Her loose hair whipped in the wind, masking her expression. Had she asked a delicate question? She hadn't been able to read the ticket stub because it was so faded, but she hadn't meant to snoop or pry.

Judging by his awkward shrug, John's discomfort multiplied. He indicated they join the queue to the ticket booth. "It's something that I… It's a good-luck token, of sorts."

A good-luck token carried by a man of John's caliber? A woman might carry something like it as a token of affection from a lover, or a fond remembrance of an outing. Was John remembering a woman from his past?

Sarah's heart squeezed with the possibility. Had he been in love before with someone else? How did Sarah compare?

The train screeched to a stop and Sarah didn't press him further. It was their turn at the ticket booth. Before John said a word to the stout, bearded man behind the cage, a pudgy hand appeared, holding a stack of three journals.

"Howdy, Doctor, here you are. Next."

John took the materials and they left for home.

Outside beneath the streetlamp, Sarah watched him skim the table of contents in the first journal. Sometimes, when he was immersed in his work like this, she found him irresistible. He worked hard on behalf of all his patients.

"Hmm. This one looks like it may be of use to me."

"Of use how?"

He gazed down at her face, only now seeming aware that he wasn't alone. "Sorry, I didn't mean to get lost in these. There's a blacksmith—a young family man with two children—who works for Angus McIver. He's got a strange neurological disorder that I can't pinpoint."

"Neurological?" She hadn't a clue when John spoke in long medical terms.

"A brain dysfunction."

"The poor man, that's awful."

"It's nothing contagious, I don't think, but the man's ability to walk and use his arms is sometimes compromised. He shakes, on and off, and I can't figure out why it comes and goes. I've seen the condition once before in a much older man, back in Toronto. No one knows what it is. Unfortunately, as a blacksmith, the man works with his hands."

"But you think you've found something?"

"Identifying the illness is half the battle. I'll have to tell him about this article that groups the neurological symptoms into an order I've never heard before."

"I hope it helps him."

"I'll tell him tomorrow, when I make my weekly call on Angus."

"Angus?"

"His gallbladder has been acting up for months. I try to check on him once a week."

A thought dawned on her of how she might tag along

so she could try to find some clues about the checkered gun she'd seen. "I've never been to the McIver ranch, and I was thinking since our wedding party, I'd like to call on the folks who attended to thank them personally for coming."

John closed his journals and peered at her. "Mr. and Mrs. McIver donated the steer we barbecued, and it would be expected that you call on them."

"Perhaps we could go together, when you make your medical call tomorrow."

"All right. I'll come home in the early afternoon to pick you up and we can go from there."

She responded with eagerness. "I could take your horse and ride to the fort, or walk to meet you at the fort, if it's more convenient for you."

"With your motion sickness the way it is, I'd rather pick you up."

She fidgeted with her fingers, knowing that the motion sickness might be something more this time. However, his concern was touching.

John grew thoughtful. "I've never told you this before, but it struck me when I saw you with Melodie earlier."

Anticipation whirled like a hummingbird inside her stomach. "What is it?"

"I like you, Sarah."

A knot of utter disappointment hit her throat and she stumbled. *Like?*

He stared at her as if expecting an acknowledgement of some sort. What could she say? She liked him back?

John liked her, but she was falling in love with him.

The realization hit her viscerally. And then came the drowning despair.

She would never—*never*—beg him for his affection.

"I suppose likability is an important aspect of marriage." How dismal she sounded. Listening to his heavy footsteps as they continued walking, she couldn't bear to glance up to gauge his reaction, nor allow him to see in her eyes what she'd just discovered herself.

She rattled on. "I think I'll wear my larger straw hat tomorrow when we go visiting. It shades better against the open sun."

There was a pause in his voice, as if he were disappointed, perhaps, that she'd changed the subject. "We've never talked about children."

Where was this leading? Sarah panicked. "Melodie and Logan seemed very happy to hold their little boy."

"We've never talked about children outright because I assumed you'd want…" He struggled to say what was troubling him. "But maybe I shouldn't assume things about you. Maybe that's where I've gone wrong. Do you think you'd like to, one day, have children?"

With him? The touching, gentle man he was at this moment? This was the vulnerable side of him he'd displayed before, not the gruff commander she'd fought with.

And to have a child she could smother with love with no restraint, who wouldn't question her motives and who would love her in return as nature had intended, made her voice catch. "Very much."

John nodded in simple pleasure.

Hope sprung from her bosom. They continued walking. "And would you like to have children?"

"One day, yes…" He grew still. "Not until we set things right between us. I supposed we should have discussed it on our wedding night, but thankfully it's not too late. We can't bring a child into the world unless we're committed to stay together."

She gulped at the pain that throbbed at his words. He obviously thought that since she hadn't confided any symptoms to him that their wedding night hadn't provided a baby.

"Are you ready to tell me about your cousin?" he asked.

His unexpected plea tugged at her heart. Everything in their marriage seemed to be in the balance of this question. "I'm afraid to."

He groaned aloud. "You ask me to treat you above my men, yet when I ask you to confide in me, you say you can't. Why not?"

Because I'm afraid you'll drive my brother away. Because family is the only thing I've ever really wanted in my life. Family is the very thing I want from you. "Because I'm not ready."

"If I've been rough with you, frightening you into thinking…I never meant to. I've tried to force it out of you, but now I'm asking nicely. Can't we settle this in a peaceful manner?" He tugged at his collar. "When you're ready, will you come to me?"

She swallowed. "…I'll try."

"Will you be ready soon?"

"I don't know."

His disappointment in her was palpable in the stilted air. But she was so close to discovering Keenan, she *felt* it.

After seeing the checkered gun earlier this morning, she realized her father had left her and Keenan each a working legacy. She could no more leave the jewelry business than Keenan could leave gunsmithing. No one checkered a gun like that out of necessity; quality workmanship arose from someone who loved doing it. As sure as the Rocky Mountains, Keenan was still involved with guns. And because the cowboy refused to say where he'd bought his, it meant he was hiding something. Perhaps illegal.

Sarah tried to lighten the conversation, but knew she and John had lost their intimate moment. She looped her arm through his as they walked. "What is Mrs. McIver's name, again? I'm afraid I lost track at the party with all the people I met. Please refresh my memory."

"Angus McIver is married to a wonderful woman named Sheila."

"Now I recall. They have no children, correct? Or was that Slade Phillips and his wife?"

"Slade Phillips has three children. The McIvers, unfortunately, even though they'd like to, have none. You'll also be meeting McIver's foreman and wife, Stuart and Martha Putnam, who came to our party. Then the blacksmith and his wife, Ken and Natasha Neal."

Sarah nearly tripped down the boardwalk steps. When she felt herself go ashen, she was grateful for the blessed cover of nightfall. Silently, she repeated the name she'd heard.

Ken Neal.

Keenan O'Neill.

It couldn't be…could it?

John steadied her with strong hands. "Are you all right?"

She nodded. Her eyes burned. She rubbed them with shaking fingers. After twelve long years, would she see her brother tomorrow?

She prayed it was him, lingering on the warm memories of Keenan helping her with her arithmetic and practicing for a spelling bee. Then, with a pang of sorrow, she prayed it wasn't him, for the Ken Neal, the blacksmith whom John spoke of, was in dire, questionable health. A family man with a wife and two children, a shaking palsy and a brain dysfunction.

Chapter Sixteen

"We've been robbed!" In pounding disbelief and outraged at the violation, John bounded out of his office two hours after they'd returned from the train depot.

Breathless, Sarah ran out of the kitchen to meet him in the hallway. With sleeves rolled up to her elbows, she held a thin screwdriver in one hand and the kitchen's temperamental clock in the other. "Are you sure?"

Choked with anger, John repeated his accusation. "Someone stole supplies from my office."

She tipped her nervous face toward him. Her wealth of hair toppled down her spine and glistened in the flickering light of the wall lantern. He didn't want to frighten her, but goddamn it he had to sort through this.

He touched her elbow lightly. "Have you noticed anything missing from your bedroom?"

"I'll go check."

She dashed up the stairs while he inspected the lower floor. Five minutes later, she returned, still flustered.

"Nothing's gone up there. The only thing I have of value are two vintage watches in my jewelry box. Plus my wedding band, but I'm wearing it."

John slammed the wall with an open palm, stalking

toward his office. ''There's nothing taken from the kitchen, either. The gold candelabra is still there, silverware still in the cabinet, the cash still in the cashbox behind it.''

By the blank expression on her delicate features, Sarah wasn't aware of his cashbox. She stepped inside his office. ''What's missing from here?''

He pointed to the row of glass cabinets. ''I had seven vials of rabies serum. Four I used on Eddie Junior, which should have left three. But there are only two left.''

''Maybe you miscounted.''

His jaw tightened. ''Not a chance.''

She looked to his faded leather medical bag. ''Maybe you left it in your bag.''

''It's not there. Someone had the gall to break into my house and steal—'' His words ran dry as a thought came to him. He raced out of the room to the back door.

''What is it, John?''

He played with the glass doorknob. It wasn't broken. When he raced to the front door, it was the same thing. The side light windows were intact, too.

''How did the bastard get in? Nothing looks tampered with.''

Sarah shifted behind him. When he turned around, she grasped her apron and looked at him apologetically.

Before she said a word, he blurted, ''You left the door unlocked.''

''I'm sorry. When Melodie went into labor pains, I brought her in here while David went to get Polly, but then Melodie insisted on going to her house to deliver. I must have left our house unlocked.''

He blinked. Then he told himself—*chastised himself*— that Sarah couldn't be a part of this. Not his wife. He refused to believe it. There was no logical reason why

Sarah would be involved in the disappearance of the serum.

"I'm confused," she said beneath his heated appraisal. "Someone broke in here and took only medical supplies. Why would someone bother to steal medicine? Why not come to you directly for treatment?"

"I suppose if they didn't have the money to pay...but any of the folks in town know I'd never withhold treatment for money. I'd treat them at my own cost. It doesn't make sense. Unless..."

Beneath the lit chandelier of the main hall, she fanned her fingers behind her then leaned against the stair stringers. "Unless what?"

He groped for the wall, needing to lean against something firm. "Unless they're hiding something. Unless they were in a place they shouldn't be when they got bitten, involved in a crime or something illegal that they don't want me to find out about."

"But couldn't they lie and tell you they got bitten during another time?"

"They could, unless it was too obvious to hide. Unless they were too scared to try and lie."

She rubbed her temple. "I haven't heard about anyone in town getting bitten recently."

Neither had he. "It had to have happened between now and twelve weeks ago. That's the incubation period, before obvious symptoms begin to appear. And once the gross symptoms appear, it's too late for treatment."

"How would the thief know what dosage and how to inject the needle?"

"First of all, we shouldn't assume there was only one thief. Secondly, they wouldn't necessarily know the correct dosage. They might guess."

"So if they underdose themselves, they might suffer from rabies anyway."

"It's possible. In which case, we only have to wait and see who in town develops symptoms. Then we'll find our culprit."

She shuddered. "That sounds gruesome."

"And dangerous to others if it gets that far." He stared at her again. "First Eddie Senior comes to me concealing a gunshot wound, then the fistfight between Angus and Slade—"

"What fistfight?"

"They've been enemies for years but they think no one else knows it." He paced down the hall into the kitchen, releasing some of his nervous energy. Sarah followed. "Then Eddie Junior gets bitten, and now the serum theft. Something doesn't add up, Sarah. It's a puzzle that fits together but I can't piece it. It's all related," he said adamantly, staring at her, judging her again as a stranger in his home and kicking himself for it. "All of it."

"How do you know? How can you be sure?"

"I *feel* it in my gut." He took two steps to the coatrack and donned his hat.

"Where are you going?"

"To the superintendent's house. I'm going to suggest we piece together every crime committed within the past twelve weeks to see what we come up with. Get your coat."

"How can I help you?"

"You can sit with Annabelle while I chat with the commander. I'm not leaving you behind when there was a robbery in here. I'll get a man to stand guard for a couple of days—"

"The theft seems almost harmless. I'll be fine, won't I? I'll lock the door."

"You never locked it earlier." The accusation rang out in the chilled night air and he couldn't snatch it back. He fought hard to dissuade himself from believing Sarah was in any way responsible. She couldn't have done it. *Wouldn't* have done it.

Her frosty glare shot an icicle up his spine. "Do you think I left the door unlocked to help the thief?"

He hesitated for half of a second. "No."

The pause must have been too much for her, for she cast her misty eyes toward the door and then back to him. "I'll be a moment in the bathing room, then I'll be right out. Just when I think things are getting better between us, you accuse me of something like this."

"You didn't do anything," he said. "I know—"

With the sound of the door slamming in his ears, he truly felt disgusted with himself.

How could John insinuate that Sarah had been involved in the theft of his own home? He'd denied it, but she could read the suspicion in his eyes.

Seated next to John in the jostling buggy the following afternoon as they rolled down the grooved road toward the McIver ranch, Sarah squinted against the unswerving line of the autumn horizon and tried not to let her humiliation overwhelm her. Golden wheat fields shimmered in the breeze as far as the eyes could see. Puffy white clouds ballooned overhead, moving with the gentle wind at their back, carrying the promising scent of a full rich harvest. Farmers had been blessed with a dry, hot fall. Sarah craned her neck to witness a team of horses pulling a wagon across the fields, surrounded by a dozen men cutting hay.

As the sun heated her hands pressing into her lap, it all sifted through Sarah's mind: her nervousness that she might soon see or catch wind of her brother, combined with her looming apprehensions about John.

How little John must think of her; how little he knew her.

What did she have to do to prove herself to her husband? A marriage might survive without love, but without a foundation of trust and mutual respect, theirs was doomed.

Would it matter to him if she told him she might be in the family way?

She patted her flat belly over her gingham country dress and wondered if there was a little baby inside. How much longer before she knew for sure? In a clinical examination, was there a way John could tell if a woman were pregnant, even though she might be only six weeks along? She'd missed her menstruation, her breasts were awfully tender and the nausea came and went.

She would love the child, no matter what. And despite the tendency for most folks to be shy about uttering their feelings, Sarah would declare her love openly.

At what point should she tell John? There didn't seem to be a point now since she wasn't sure, but in two weeks if her symptoms persisted, she would tell him. Despite their differences, she was adamant that as the father, John would have every right to know.

What hurt most was how much he trusted his fellow officers in striking contrast to her. John and his men worked together in life-and-death situations and she wouldn't want it any other way. But why did his instincts always look to her when there was a problem?

Would she always be a lesser partner in John's eyes?

Last night, John had come home more disgruntled than when he'd left, and she'd curled into her bed—*their bed*—alone and miserable, aching for a kind word.

This morning, she'd dropped by Melodie's to check on her and the baby. Thankfully, they were doing well. Francis was tending to them and, try as she might, Sarah wasn't able to suppress the feeling that she was unneeded there, too.

She hadn't asked John any more questions about the blacksmith or his family—she'd discover it on her own very shortly, without raising John's suspicions.

"Do you see the gate up ahead?" Breaking through their silence and the rhythmic clomp of the mare's hooves, John leaned in close to Sarah's shoulder and nodded toward the far right stretch of road. "That's the McIver ranch."

She saw the faint outline of whitewashed logs half a mile ahead. Peering to the tall outpost they were passing, she gazed at the crisscrossed rafters. "What's this?"

"It's a sentry post for Mounties. We've got four of them surrounding the town and for about a decade now we've used them to guard against invasion."

"From whom?"

"Originally, Indians and whiskey traders. Then rustlers. Currently, the Grayveson gang." Homesteaders were grateful to have the lookouts and John knew close police guard had been a big factor over the years in whether some settlers stayed or left the prairies altogether.

While the buggy lurched forward over a hardened rut, Sarah peered up at the empty platform mounted beneath the splintered log roof. "But there's no one inside."

John scowled. "At the moment, there's a shortage of men."

Sarah didn't reply. She'd heard John say that before in a tide of anger, and knew it was a sore spot. They'd been promised new recruits for over a month, but none had been dispatched yet from Ottawa or the closer town of Regina.

Ten more minutes got them closer to the gate. She dipped her body down between the leathered seat to pick up her straw hat. As she did, something whizzed by her ear.

John screamed, "Hit the floor!"

Frightened by the terror in his eyes, she stared in disbelief. Without warning, he shoved her down by the shoulders. "That was a goddamn bullet! It just ripped the back leather! Stay down till I tell you!"

When he unsnapped his shoulder holster to access his gun, Sarah closed her eyes in panic. Squished into a small lump at John's tall black leather boots, she trembled.

Her voice choked. "Who's shooting at us?"

"I don't know! Two riders from the back of McIver's ranch!"

Another shot rang out. This time she heard it. The mare spooked and the buggy tugged. The mare reared again then raced off like a bat from the dark side of the moon.

"Whoa! Whoa!" John tried tugging on the reins but the runaway horse wouldn't stop. "Whoa!"

Instead of slowing down, they sped up.

John cursed. "I think the riders are gone! Get up, Sarah, I need you before this whole cart tips over."

She jumped up to his side and he passed her the reins. She screamed above the wind. "What are you going to do?"

"We can't jump from here! I've got to stop the mare!"

With pounding heart and bile cutting her throat, Sarah tried to control the horse.

"Keep her steady! Don't fight her, I'll do the rest!"

When he jumped onto the sleek back of the chestnut

mare, Sarah let out a little scream. They would all be killed!

The wind snatched at John's hat and hurled it into the air. He didn't look back, but braced himself tighter and inched forward, reaching for the lines. Then John edged into a more relaxed fit astride the horse, patting the flanks. His lips moved in soothing sounds.

Slowly, their gallop slackened. The horse eased, with its muscles flexing and stretching beneath John's. Sarah fought for air as the rush of blood pumped in her ears.

"Slowly," John murmured to the horse. "Nice and slow. That's it."

When they finally came to a halt, her upper body heaved, drenched in perspiration. John looked back at her, slid off the horse, gave it another pat, then came to Sarah's side all the while scanning the prairie for intruders. "You can let go of the reins now, Sarah."

She stared ahead, frozen with the shock of what had just happened.

"You can let go now, sweetheart." He nudged her clenched hands and extricated the lines. "You did a good job."

Unable to move, she sat where she was.

"Come here." Gently he coaxed her off the seat, then lifted her to the ground. She slid against him and into the safety of his arms. "Are you all right?"

She nodded, still shaking, comforted by the strength of his touch, by his encompassing reach around her slim shoulders and the quiet calm he emulated.

John peered into the horizon from where they'd come, perspiration at his temples glistening against the billowing white clouds and intermittent blue sky. He withdrew his gun. "We better move. We don't know how many more there are. I've got a feeling there's trouble waiting for us at the McIver ranch.''

They walked alongside the horse. As they turned beneath the whitewashed gate with the initials A.M. burned into a wooden sign above it, two men on horseback galloped to greet them. John poised his gun, but quickly lowered it. He must have recognized the riders.

A cowboy, direly in need of a shave, asked, ''You all right, Doc?''

''Yeah.''

The other rider circled Sarah. ''And the missus?''

''She's shaken up but she'll be fine,'' John replied. ''Any men hurt on the ranch?''

''Two.''

John sighed. ''Who?''

''The blacksmith and his assistant. They were in the corral, shoeing horses when the riders appeared.''

''Oh, no,'' whispered Sarah, knowing the blacksmith might be Keenan. Her stance wavered but John reached out and steadied her.

''I've got my medicine bag. Take me to them. Take Sarah into the house.''

Sarah's back stiffened with renewed resolve. ''John, please, I'd like to help. You said yourself I'm a good assistant.''

''Yeah, but are you sure you're up to it?''

Her lips tightened. ''There are two men down and you'll need help.''

John spun around and surveyed the ranch. ''Yeah, I will.''

When they reached the stables, a dozen ranch hands were running in all directions.

''See if Angus is all right!'' one shouted. ''And find out where Mrs. McIver went!''

"I'll account for the steers!" called another.

"The horses in the stables are restless. Let them out for a run."

"Here they are," said a cowboy, leading John and Sarah to the two wounded men inside.

Seated in a mound of hay within a stall, the two moaned in pain. John and Sarah circled closer, facing the men's backs.

Both men looked to be around the same youthful age. One man was light-haired and heavily bearded, staring at his wounded foot. His boot and sock were removed and someone had brought a roll of bandages to his side. The other man, a blonde, had a chest wound. Leaning against the stall boards, his shirt had been opened to reveal a bloody matted chest. Sarah looked away for a moment to combat her nausea, then peered again at the wound. It didn't look so bad the second time. He was pressing a big ball of cloth against it, to stop the bleeding, while two others attended to him.

Were either of them Keenan?

Sarah peered closer. They both had the same light-colored hair he had.

"Sarah?" John knelt beside the man with the chest wound. He drew up a syringe of what looked to be morphine. "Can you hold back his shirt while I clean the wound?"

She dove to her knees on the straw. "Yes." It made sense to treat the man with the greater wound first. An injured foot could wait, but a chest wound might prove fatal.

"Pleased to meet you," she said to the man. "I'm Sarah."

He moaned and nodded. "I'm Davis."

He wasn't the blacksmith and he wasn't her brother.

Within three minutes John gave the morphine, assessed the wound as being a light graze, then cleansed it with solution. He left her holding a fresh gauze pad, applying pressure while he scooted to the other man.

Sarah strained across the ten-foot distance to look at the blacksmith, but his head was bent and his beard so thick she couldn't place him.

After giving the second man morphine, John returned to her side. "I'll take over here. Could you please soak Ken's foot with carbolic acid? Looks like he'll need a couple of stitches as well, but I've got to do these first."

Sarah nodded and did as her husband asked.

With the weight of twelve years of expectation bearing down upon her, she slid over to Ken's side.

"Howdy," she said, peering into the round, pale face.

When he looked up, his piercing blue gaze, so very familiar, nestled into hers. A lump the size of a rock formed in her throat.

He blinked at her. Then stared. He rubbed his eyes. His gaze raced from her, across the mound of straw to John's lowered back, then down her face and to her hands, which were moving over his wounded foot.

With labored breath, he slumped into the straw.

With a tremor, she dipped the brown bottle of carbolic acid against her clean cloth and whispered so no one else could hear. "Hello, Keenan."

Chapter Seventeen

John lost himself in his work, battling his hot temper at the vile men who'd shot at him and Sarah, and who'd done this to two innocent, hardworking men. Seconds after John got the chest wound bandaged, he ordered the others to carry Davis back to his bunkhouse bed, then sprang to Ken's side.

Crouching on his knees in the dank straw beside the bloody foot, John said to Sarah, "Lift the bandage and let me take it."

Beyond John's tight shoulder, he noticed Ken staring at Sarah. The morphine had taken effect, Ken's upper body beneath his loose overalls and short-sleeved shirt had relaxed, so John began stitching. "It's a small wound and fortunately you'll need only two or three sutures. Can't say I can save your boot, though." John glanced down at the hole blasted through the black snakeskin tip.

Ken attempted a chuckle.

"It'll affect your walking. Do you still have the cane you were using when you had that bout of palsy three months ago?"

Ken nodded, still gazing at Sarah.

Sarah coughed with discomfort. John wondered if she

were feeling ill again at the sight of blood. Still, she stuck to John's side like paste, and he couldn't deny how good that made him feel. "You've never been introduced to my wife, Ken. This is Sarah."

In a somber mood and somewhat distracted, Sarah nodded.

Ken didn't smile. His shaggy head of blond hair turned to the pretty woman. "Your *wife?*"

"Yeah," John said, knotting the final suture.

"I heard you got married, but I didn't know…how long ago was it?"

John clipped the threads. "Almost two months."

Sarah took the scissors from John before he had to ask. They worked smoothly together.

Ken asked her, "What made you marry a *policeman,* Mrs. Calloway?"

She didn't respond, but John heard the scissors clatter. She was nervous. It was a lot to ask, John thought, of a woman with no medical training to jump in whenever she was needed.

"She answered my advertisement," said John.

"A mail-order bride then?"

Sarah nodded.

"You've come all the way from Halifax?"

She nodded again.

John stared at the two. How had Keenan known that?

She must have mentioned it while John was attending to the other wounded man. In times of crisis, many injured folks just wanted to share a kind word or two with strangers. It always seemed to calm them, and it was a skill, John perceived, which Sarah had and he lacked.

Ken shifted his position, straightening his good leg closer to Sarah's gingham skirts. "Does a mail-order bride bring her family…her folks…with her when she travels?"

Sarah jerked away and fumbled with the cleansing solution. ''They've…they've passed away. Ma from consumption six months ago and…'' Her voice trailed off as she lowered her head over the injured foot.

Something in their voices made John peer up at them from wrapping gauze.

Ken's eyes glistened and his lips trembled. ''And Pa?''

''Eleven years earlier, struck dead by lightning.''

When Ken moaned, the doctor stopped. ''Am I pressing too hard?''

Ken gasped for air.

''You're in pain, I'm sorry. I'll give you another dose—''

''I'm fine,'' Ken insisted, but his hands shook. ''It'll pass.''

''Are you sure?''

The bearded man looked to Sarah who was openly sympathetic, then he nodded.

Sarah's teary eyes spilled over. She wiped her cheek.

''If this is too much for you, I can take it from here,'' John told her.

''No, I'd…I'd like to help.'' She remained where she was.

''What happened in the corral?'' John asked of Ken. ''How'd you get shot?''

Somewhat recovered from his bout of pain, Ken explained. ''Me and Davis were shoeing three new broncos. We were almost finished when up out of nowhere came the two riders.''

''How'd they get so far onto the ranch without being noticed?''

Before Ken could answer, John heard Angus's voice booming behind them. ''There you are. Hellfire, what happened?''

"I was just asking," said John, turning the foot slightly to assess Ken's remaining range of motion. With pain medication in him, his foot turned freely.

Angus gripped John by the shoulder and swung down to the straw, on their level. Several men circled behind them, talking to themselves. "I'm told Davis suffered a chest wound and you've…you've been shot in the foot." When the expletives rolled from Angus's lips, Sarah looked the other way.

John repeated his question to Ken. "How'd the riders get so far onto the ranch without being noticed?"

Ken seemed to lose his desire to talk. "I'm not sure." He looked to his boss, then cast his gaze downward, studying his bandaged foot.

"Well, what do the other ranch hands have to say?" asked John.

Angus removed his hat and slapped it on his hefty thigh. "I missed everything! I was visitin' the folks down the road, advisin' them on when best to take their steer to slaughter and goddammit, I wasn't here."

Ken didn't respond to his boss.

Angus continued. "I suppose with all the hired help on the ranches and farms for harvest, there's dozens more men comin' and goin' than usual. I'm not surprised they went unnoticed."

"Who do you think these men were?" John asked.

Ken shrugged.

"They were wearin' black bandanas around their throats, weren't they?" asked Angus. "That's what I was told. And when they came shootin', they lifted up their black bandanas to hide their faces. That's a mark of the Grayveson gang."

John believed the Grayvesons could be in the area. They'd been spotted two hundred miles to the south last week by an Indian scout, but it was confidential information whispered between the Mounties. No one else knew.

John packed up his supplies. "It seems strange that the Grayvesons would strike during the day, don't you think, Angus? The last time they hit your ranch, it was during the day, too. And this time, they never stole anything."

In a frenzy, Ken's gaze flew to Angus's. The injured man watched his boss answer very slowly.

"Who knows what they're up to. We gotta catch every last one of 'em, and I aim to put out a reward for anyone who knows anything about this."

A cold look passed between Ken and Angus, and John felt his gut quiver. Something deeper was going on between these two men. Ken might have thought he was masking the look of contempt for Angus in his eyes, but it hit John squarely in the stomach.

John had known Angus for nearly ten years, and he'd always trusted the rancher. Ken had been around for about two, traveling up from somewhere near the border, if John recalled correctly. What did their animosity mean?

"Where's your wife, Angus?" asked John.

"She's with her sister five miles away. The sister's kids have got a party of some kind goin' on."

"Birthday?" asked Sarah.

"I don't know. Might be a christenin'. No, no, she'd tell me about that. Somethin' to do with school, or one of their friends is movin' or somethin'…"

For a man who claimed he was deeply interested in children, Angus didn't pay them a lot of attention.

"Well, I should go see if she's returned. I better explain this to her because I don't want her to get worried by the fuss."

John stood up and offered a hand to help Ken to his feet.

Angus quickly followed suit to help the man rise, but Ken raised his hands in refusal. "I can do it," he said, barely controlling his disgust for Angus.

"I'm sure you can," said Angus, trying to laugh it off. "I'm sure you can." He turned to Sarah. "Well then, little lady, sorry to introduce you to the ranch this way, but when you're done here why don't you come up to the big house for a cup of coffee? If the missus isn't there, I'll get someone to ride over and get her."

"Thank you," said Sarah.

"I brought you the artichoke extract," John hollered to Angus's retreating back. "I'll see Ken to his quarters first, then we'll follow to the house."

Angus limped away, slightly doubled over to his right side, clutching at his belly.

John called, "You're not feeling well today?"

Angus choked out the words. "Let's just say I'm glad you brought the extract."

John watched the huge frail man shuffle away. Artichoke extract could do a lot to help the liver and to temper bile, but it could never get rid of gall stones. Angus needed surgery.

Ken stumbled to his feet, using the boards behind his back to steady himself. When he rose to his feet, almost at John's height, John stepped to his injured side and wrapped Ken's arm around his shoulders for support.

"Can you take his other side, Sarah? He can hop on his good foot, but just in case he wavers…"

Sarah tenderly took the burly arm and slid beneath it.

"Where are your quarters?" asked John.

Ken lifted his good foot and leaned into John as they slowly walked out of the stables into the bright sunshine.

Ken nodded in the direction of a group of weathered log buildings. "My wife and I got one of those. The single men stay in the bunkhouse, but those of us with wives and children are entitled to the...shacks." Looking to Sarah, Ken lowered his voice in shame.

John tried to think of something pleasant to cheer up his patient, but he realized he knew very little about Ken. They walked, shuffled and hopped toward the splintered log shacks.

"I've got good news about your condition," John said. "Good in that I've finally pinpointed what I think you have. And that's half the battle. Sarah and I discovered an article written in an old British medical journal. It's a study done by a British physician, a Dr. Charles Parkinson, in 1817 to be exact—"

"That sounds like seventy-year-old news. How can it be of help to me?"

"Another physician recently combined the research he's done with Dr. Parkinson's study. It sounds very similar to what you have. Tremors, rigid arms and legs, slowness when you walk, and difficulty maintaining balance."

"What does Dr. Parkinson say?"

"He died in 1824, but he left behind a sixty-six page paper, 'An Essay on the Shaking Palsy.' He grouped together the symptoms of shaking limbs. What you have has been labeled Parkinson's disease. No one knows what causes it, but most scientists believe the disease is due to some dysfunction of the brain."

"The brain?"

"It usually doesn't affect people until their sixties."

"Just my luck, then, isn't it?"

"There have been cases as early as twenty. The good thing is, yours seems to be mild. Let's hope it continues to come and go sporadically, as it does now." John stepped over a pebble in the grassy path. "Certain medications will help with the spasms. We can also treat the symptoms with arsenic, opium and other sedatives."

"That'll make me drowsy. I can't afford to sleep away my life."

"Have you noticed that if you go horseback riding, your symptoms ease?

"Yes," said Ken, "I have."

"Some doctors have discovered that relief comes during long train or carriage rides, so they've devised a trembling armchair."

"I got no time to sit in armchairs, either."

"I know. But maybe when your symptoms come, Natasha might join you on a horse ride or wagon ride. I'm sure your children would love to accompany you, as well, to help you with this."

Timidly, Ken glanced up at Sarah. Was he embarrassed to be discussing his illness in front of her? Maybe John should have been more discreet, more sensitive to Ken's pride.

"How many..." Sarah whispered, obviously touched by Ken's situation. "How many children do you have?"

"I got two. A boy and a girl," Ken said proudly. "The boy, Rusty, is eight, and the girl, Marianne, is two." His blond hair shifted around his shoulders as he turned to John. "Will this disease afflict my children, Doc?"

Sarah flinched. Her concern seemed to run deep.

"I'll tell it to you straight. I don't know. But I'm still looking. If the answer to that question is out there, I'll find it."

"At least you believe me. You believe that my symptoms are genuine."

John sputtered. "Why wouldn't I believe you?"

"Not everyone does."

"Who doesn't?"

Ken took a moment to answer. He seemed to weigh it in his mind before confiding. "Angus."

Thunderstruck that Angus could be so harsh, John halted beneath the oak tree shading the shack. Is that why Ken was fuming at his boss? Who wouldn't be?

The sound of hollering children interrupted their conversation.

Wheeling around, John watched the youngsters come dashing toward their father, arms outstretched, with Ken's fretting young wife at their side. With a smile at the welcoming sight, John glanced up at Sarah in time to see her face twisting with the strangest combination of regret and happiness he'd ever witnessed.

"Pa!" The young red-haired boy shouted as Sarah watched from beneath the fluttering oak leaves.

She felt like weeping, watching her nephew and niece race toward their father, two beautiful children she'd never met before, who didn't know a thing about her.

Keenan's slim wife, her long black hair tied loosely in a beavertail, hugged Keenan as he struggled to maintain his balance with bobbing children wrapped around his knees. The two-year-old girl, black-haired like her mother, couldn't speak much so couldn't know the severity of the situation. She tottered in her worn leather shoes, smiling and gurgling. "Papa," she said.

"What happened to you?" Rusty peered at the bandaged foot. "They told us you got shot."

"It was an accident at the corral. I'll be fine."

Rusty kicked at a mound of dirt with bare, blackened feet. Ripped overalls hung from his lithe body. "We were down at the creek pickin' berries when we heard the shots.

Then the ranch hands came runnin' after us to take cover."

Keenan's wife stared at him. "The Grayveson gang. *Again?*"

When Keenan nodded, Natasha came to his side and burst into sobs. There seemed to be deeper significance to her question, but Sarah couldn't fathom what it was.

John lowered his medical bag to the grassy slope. "The Mounties will do everything we can to catch them."

Only then did Natasha glance in their direction.

"This is Dr. Calloway," Keenan told her. "And his wife Sarah."

Keenan's short introduction multiplied Sarah's heartache. How could they resurrect all the precious time they'd lost as siblings? It was impossible.

But then…what had she expected? That Keenan would embrace her like a long-lost brother and joyously shout it to the world that they were related? She hoped her sacrifice in coming here to the prairies to find him wouldn't be utterly wasted.

Keenan looked old to her. It was the same dear brother she remembered, but he looked tired around the eyes, as if life had gotten to be too much for him.

Could she help ease Keenan's burden? She tried not to be selfish about his illness, tried to think of him and the difficulties he was going through rather than what his illness implied for her. But…what potential risks might her own children face? What about the child she might be carrying?

Trying to stifle her sense of loss—an ache for something buried in her past that perhaps should remain buried—Sarah nodded hello to Natasha, well aware *she* could be the one to speak up and identify herself, but she wasn't sure if it would create more problems for Keenan. Something was going on at this ranch, between Keenan and Angus and maybe even the Grayveson gang.

Guns were everywhere, revolvers strapped in holsters around the ranch hands, rifles displayed on racks in the stables, of every caliber and make. Smith and Wessons, Colts, handcrafted guns, she'd even spotted a brand-new British Lee-Metford Magazine Carbine slung in the boot of Angus's horse as they'd left the stables. Why so many guns?

Sarah glanced in John's direction. His muscled jaw flexed with sympathy, but his intense dark gaze darted past them across the compound of log buildings, assessing it from all angles. He felt the same tension in the air, Sarah was certain.

John patted the young boy on the shoulder. "Could you get your pa's cane for him? It would sure be a big help."

Rusty smiled and darted into the cabin.

"Can you show me where you were in the corral, Ken, when this happened? And show me the smithy where you work."

Keenan and Natasha exchanged a sharp, frightened glance.

When Rusty returned with the cane, Keenan asked them all to remain at the house while he showed Sarah and John his workplace.

There was nothing unusual in the corral, as far as Sarah could see. But John studied everything in detail, wanting to know the positioning of Keenan and his assistant when the riders galloped by, wanting to know which other men were working in the area, if Keenan had seen Angus that morning, even how far in advance they'd planned the shoeing and who exactly knew they were planning to work in the corral today right after lunch. Keenan shuffled in great discomfort with some of the questions.

Near the end, Sarah glanced up at the big board-and-batten house with the wrap-around porch, nestled among a line of pines and wondered if Angus and his wife sat inside. How odd, thought Sarah, that Angus wasn't joining the police officer investigating a crime on his property. Angus was a busy man, obviously, and attending to his wife to ensure she wasn't shaken up by the incident, but would he make an appearance before John left the ranch?

When Ken wobbled on his cane and led them into the blacksmith's forge, it took a moment for Sarah's eyes to adjust to the darkness. Along one wall, two small windows lit the dark space with tunnels of light.

The scent of burning peat met her nostrils, as well as the musky smell of grease and iron and mud. Sarah inhaled deeply. A wave of homesickness rolled through her.

The fire still roared from shoeing the horses earlier, the bellows and anvil awaiting Keenan's professional hand. Tools lined the walls, hammers, rasps, hand drills, crowbars. From the projects strewn about, Keenan's responsibilities lay in many directions: new forks for kitchen tables, fireplace trammels on which to hang pots and kettles, and wrought-iron work such as hinges, latches and nails. In passing, Sarah stroked the top of a wooden wagon wheel in which Keenan was setting new iron tires. It was an interesting feat in skill and precision, and one in frequent demand due to the bumpy country roads.

As John asked his questions and Keenan answered, Sarah walked around the anvil to a shelf tucked away in the corner. Lifting a blanket off the shelf for fear it was too close to the fire, Sarah halted in alarm at what lay beneath.

Well-oiled equipment, recently used. A metal saw file, slitting file, checkering file, squares, clamps, broken-screw extractors and taper-pin reamers.

Gunsmithing tools.

"Sarah!" Ken snapped. "Mrs. Calloway! Watch out for the fire!"

At Keenan's sharp voice, Sarah dropped the blanket and stumbled away from the heat.

When she looked up, Keenan's angry glare bore into hers. He wasn't concerned about her distance to the fire, he was upset she'd caught him red-handed. With a bevy of assailing emotions, Sarah's gaze swirled to John's. Had he seen the tools? Would he recognize them if he had?

Why was Keenan hiding them?

For one reason only. Because he had to.

There was nothing illegal about making guns. Folks had a right to protect themselves and their property. Unless…it all tied together to what Keenan was suppressing.

While John gazed at the tools on the walls, walking closer to the anvil and the blanket, Sarah waited, stricken with fear for Keenan, and guilt that she was hiding this much from her husband.

Keenan shook his head at her and swore softly beneath his breath. She noticed his arm begin to shake.

"Ken?" Two men popped through the wide-open doors. "Are the wagon wheels ready to go?"

John spun around to listen, and for the moment at least, his attention turned away from all else. Keenan breathed a sigh of relief. "They're right here. They just need attaching."

"We can get that for you."

The men strolled into the forge, heading for the wheels propped against the wall, when John stepped forward. "Mighty warm day out today."

They turned, one man short and plump, the other older, taller and thicker. The older man was sweating profusely, mopping his brow with a red-checkered hanky.

John stared at him, then glanced down to his long cotton sleeves. "Mighty hot for long sleeves, isn't it?"

Sarah stood perplexed, wondering what John was noticing. John had his long sleeves rolled up, most of the other workers did, too, but why mention it?

"Sir?"

"I can see the sweat pouring off your face. Why don't you roll up your sleeves?"

The man scoffed and reached for the wheel.

"You've got a fever. Undo your sleeves for me, please," John blurted.

"No. The hay's itchy on my arms."

"But you're not working with hay."

The man ignored him and rolled the wheel toward himself, stumbling a bit.

"You don't seem to be feeling well. I'd like to help you."

"No, thanks, I feel fine."

John cleared his throat and shuffled his booted feet in the dust, then slowly stepped out of their path. They walked by to the wagon propped outside, each anchoring a wheel to the back axis.

Unlatching his medicine bag, John handed Keenan a bottle of artichoke extract. "Could you please give this to Angus, and our apologies to his wife, but we can't make the visit today. This has taken up more of our time than I figured, and I'm needed back at the fort."

Keenan readily took the package, looking relieved that John and Sarah were leaving.

Sarah wondered when she'd see her brother again, how and where to approach him privately when they were both always surrounded by other people.

With a distant nod in her direction, Keenan walked

away, but not without some trouble balancing his cane and the bottle.

John tapped the younger man at the wagon. "Could you help Ken carry that bottle to the big house?"

When both men were twenty feet away, John grabbed his medical bag and walked around to the back of the wagon, where the sweating man was hammering on his wheel.

Sarah had the feeling John had planned it so he'd gotten rid of Keenan and the younger man.

"What's your name and position here?"

"Calvin Rutledge. I'm the stable foreman."

"Well, Calvin, I'd like you to pass the word around the ranch that all those rabid dogs we caught in town were destroyed except for one."

The man's hand slipped, he hit his finger with the hammer and swore at the same time that Sarah struggled for air. Now it made sense. John had wanted the man to roll up his sleeves because he thought the man was concealing a dog bite!

"The last dog is dead by now, for sure," John continued, calm and even. "They don't last long on their own when they're in his shape. But who knows what other animals he infected before his death. Best to be on your guard."

"I'll pass the word along."

"If any of you have recently been bitten, don't panic."

Calvin braced himself, then stood up to face John.

"I've got a rabies antidote right here in my bag," John said, inches from the sweaty brow. "There's a certain method to the dosages that needs to be observed."

"A certain method?"

"Yeah. It's *not* a one-time dosage. One dose won't cure you."

The man's eyes shot with panic. "How many doses does a man need?"

"You leave that up to me, I'm the doctor. All you have to do is say the word, and I'll treat you."

The man swallowed. "Yes, sir." He made to turn away. "I'll remember that, case any of us need it."

John's stance didn't slacken. "Calvin, I'd like you to accompany me and my wife back to town."

"I ain't goin'. I got work to do. But if you want the extra guard for protection, I'll send—"

"*No.* It's you I need."

John bent down to the ground at Sarah's feet, opening his medical bag and staring at a pair of handcuffs inside. For Sarah, the sight of handcuffs next to glass syringes was the startling epitome of everything John fought in himself and everything she struggled to understand about him: the harsh policeman versus the compassionate doctor. Which one was he? And how could he handle the struggle of trying to harmonize those qualities in himself?

He didn't pick up the cuffs, nor threaten to use them. He didn't need to. "You can come quietly, and no one needs to know, or I'll arrest you and take you back by force. It's your choice." Then John rose to his full six-foot-one-inch height and snarled like a dragon, breathing fire. "Have I made myself clear?"

Chapter Eighteen

Exasperated, John tried once more to ask Calvin. "Why don't you make something up if only to appease me?"

"Because it ain't a crime to get bitten by an animal!"

Standing in the fort's hospital ward beside the veterinarian, John clamped his hand around the syringe of rabies serum, threatening to shake the answers out of Calvin, the stubborn idiot. "For your own health, at least tell me *when* you got those three bites."

The lips thinned. "Two weeks ago."

"By a dog?"

"A fox."

"How many doses have you had already?"

"I don't know what you're talkin' about."

"Dammit, I'm trying to help you. Someone stole a vial from my home. So how many doses have you had?"

Calvin glared at the two Mounties at the foot of his bed. "One."

"Who stole it for you?"

"I ain't sayin'. They were tryin' to help me and all's they're gonna get is hell from you."

John muttered beneath his breath. He injected the serum in the man's abdomen then stepped away from the bed to consult with Logan. It was close to six o'clock and Sarah was waiting at the end of the ward, within earshot. All six beds were full and everyone glanced in John's direction.

Letting Calvin recover for a few moments, John then scooted to his side and clamped a handcuff around one wrist.

"Whaddya doin'?"

"We can't take the risk that you'll leave before your treatment's finished. Those are severe bites. It'll take a week of injections." Although John had only two vials left at home, the hospital ward was stocked with plenty more rabies serum.

"Let me go!" Calvin rattled the metal headboard.

"No," said the veterinarian, reinforcing John's decision.

John added, "If you leave and you get rabies, you'll put the whole town at risk and then...we might have to shoot you."

Calvin wailed at the surgeon. "But I thought you said we were gonna keep this quiet!"

"A change of plans," John responded. "I think we're going to spread the news instead. Since you won't talk about how or where this happened, let's see what your confinement drums up." John turned to Logan and said quietly, "Pay close attention to what Angus and Slade say about it."

"Goddamn Black-'n-White! What everyone says about ya is true! You got a lump of coal for a heart when it comes to police work!"

His blood bubbling with outrage, John spun around. "You're wrong. If I had a lump of coal, I'd tie you down *without treatment* until you told me everything!"

Angered that he'd lost his temper, especially at a patient, John spun around and marched out of the ward. He collected Sarah and they went home in the buggy, he silent and morose, she stealing glances in his direction whenever she mustered the courage.

When they reached the house, he waved to the constable on guard at the front door, then rolled into the back alley to approach the small barn. When he unhitched the horse, Sarah didn't immediately leave his side. She stood at the doorway, her shapely form silhouetted in dusk. "When we were at the ranch, what made you suspect Calvin had been bitten?"

"Low-grade fever is common during the incubation period of rabies. Plus the long sleeves. It was a hunch."

"You've got an instinct for trouble. You're so good at this, John."

He glanced up, somewhat cooler than he had been, realizing Sarah had done nothing to warrant his wrath. "Thanks for your help today at the ranch," he said in a tone colder than he'd intended. "With Davis and Ken."

His briskness chafed against her warm demeanor. She lingered at the door, watching him, looking like she wanted to say more.

"Something on your mind, Sarah?" He removed the mare's bridle and led it to the water trough, where it drank. With a dozen problems grating on his mind, he was weary and irritated. "Spit it out. I don't have time for any more games today."

Stung by his words, Sarah stiffened, then recoiled. He was instantly sorry for what he'd said, but like everything else going wrong this afternoon, she spun on her heel and left.

Another cold and lonely night alone, he thought with a snort. So what else was new?

Walking into the house from the back door, he eyed

the pesky monkey racing along the fence top. It was carrying something in its arms, which on closer inspection proved to be a folded newspaper.

When John slid inside the house, the monkey slid in, too.

''Come back here!'' John shouted down the kitchen, but the monkey kept going. For the moment, John let him be.

Unfolding the paper the monkey had dropped, John groaned when he read the headline; The Wild West Life Of A Mountie's Wife by David Fitzgibbon.

John had low expectations of David's journalist abilities. John hesitated to read it, but then supposed he should so he'd know what David had written about his wife.

Pouring himself a glass of water from the jug resting on the hutch, he heard Sarah's footsteps on the creaky planks above his head, then her soft voice as she cooed to the monkey.

She'd probably tell John that the monkey was more civil to her than he.

And maybe she'd be right.

John stared at the photograph on the front page accompanying the article. There was Sarah, in the midst of five other women, Melodie on one side of her, the superintendent's wife to the other, and two older women whose husbands were near retirement.

Expecting paragraphs of inaccuracies and shoddy writing, perhaps even comical to attract publicity, John began to read.

They come from every corner of the country. They travel in cramped trainloads, spend months in covered wagons, battle drought and locusts, yet it's near impossible to extract a complaint from any one of them. They are the Mounties' wives, and no man on earth could be more blessed with the grit and courage that each of these women display.

"What do you miss most about Halifax?" I ask Mrs. Sarah Calloway, the newest of the wives who's just set foot on prairie soil.

"The sound of the ocean at my door. Fresh seafood every day."

"What do you like most about Calgary, your new hometown?"

"That's simple. My husband," she responds with the integrity and unwavering resolve of a woman who's traveled nearly two thousand miles to respond to the mail-order ad of a man she's never met.

And yet no one here laughs at her unorthodox circumstance. Townsfolk pitch in to help celebrate their wedding, they provide work at the local watchmaker's so the young bride may occupy the hours she spends alone while her husband, the Mountie's Chief Surgeon Dr. John Calloway, spends every daylight hour at the fort.

"Why did you come?" I ask in honest confusion.

"Because I wanted a better life, to better myself. And because when I finally met my husband, he was more than I imagined."

More, indeed. The more you get to know this soft-spoken woman, the more you discover about her. For instance, when she's finished working at the jewelry shop, she tinkers with new watch designs in her home, and when her husband returns from the fort, she's often at his side late into the night tending to bullet wounds and rabies bites.

"I couldn't stomach it at first," she confides after much probing. "I was ill at the sight of blood for the first month.''

''Did your husband know?''

''It doesn't matter,'' she says, waving away the question. ''The only thing that matters is the patient.''

People, rest assured, we in the West are protected by the brawn and will of the North-West Mounted Police, and the sheer backbone strength of the women behind these men.

Another hardworking woman, Mrs. Melodie Sutcliffe…

The article continued about the other women, but John slumped back against his chair, shattered by the clarity of David's insight into Sarah.

Why hadn't John ever asked her these questions? Why had it taken a stranger to inquire about the most basic, personal issues at her heart?

Astonished at his undeniable clumsiness as a husband, John swelled with shame. He'd taken so much from Sarah, but had given so little in return.

Awakening from his haze, he jumped from his chair and bounded up the stairs. Clutching the newspaper, pounding on her bedroom door, he yelled, ''Sarah, let me in!''

''No! Go away!''

''You know me. I don't like getting no for an answer!''

''And you know me. I'll keep giving you one!''

He tried the knob but the door was locked. ''Let me in!''

''What for?''

''I…I want to talk to you.'' He pounded more until the entire house rattled.

The door swung open. ''For heaven's sake, what is it?''

He stared, openmouthed. Sarah clutched his quilt to her naked body, only managing to cover the essential parts. Her creamy shoulders glistened in the golden light of the wall lamp and that abundance of silky strawberry-blond hair rolled in waves around her cleavage.

"If you've got something to say, spit it out. I don't have any time for games." She mimicked his earlier words to her. "I've got water heating and I'm heading to the bath."

He gaped in enthrallment. It was the same quilt she'd clutched to her bosom weeks ago when David and Polly had walked in on them, the same quilt he used to wrap around his own nakedness on cold wintry nights when he'd had no woman to keep him warm.

"Ugh!" she muttered at his silence. She fumbled to wrap the quilt around her backside, but her arms didn't stretch that far and the quilt was slippery. "Oh, forget it," she said, walking in perfect dignity past him toward the stairs, as if nothing were amiss and she were fully clothed.

He watched in amazement and amusement as she walked by, totally covered up on her front side, but totally naked on her back. The muscled flesh of her white buttocks shifted seductively as she moved, and the dimples that ran up her curved spine beckoned for his hungry mouth.

He burned in need as he'd never burned for any other woman.

"Sarah!"

"Pardon me, sir, are you speaking to me?"

The chimp reached the handrail first and slid down. With a frown, John looked from the monkey to her. "Excuse me, miss, could you give me directions to the carnival? I have a feeling they're in town."

''Yes, it's straight out that front door. Please go take a hike.''

''But I think the entertainment's in here tonight.''

They reached the stairs and she stopped, indicating he should descend first.

But then he'd miss the beautiful view. ''After you, please, I insist,'' he said. ''Ladies first.''

''Thank you,'' she said with great ceremony, blushing at the way he gazed at her backside when she brushed by him. ''You are truly a gentleman. And they are hard to find in this house.''

''The pleasure is all mine.''

''I'm not sure you could afford the tickets this evening.'' She continued down the stairs, playing their charade. ''The entertainment can be awfully expensive.''

''I'll pay anything,'' he said with a sigh as they wound along the hallway to the bathing room.

''Don't sell your soul,'' she whispered, easing into the room and, with a quick snap, closing the door in his face.

Before he had time to yell, the lock clicked in his hands.

''That's not funny. Let me in,'' he commanded.

''Not by the hair of my chinny chin chin.''

''Then I'll huff and I'll puff...''

''You're out of luck, Mr. Wolf. My house is built of brick.''

''If I catch you, I *will* eat you.''

That silenced her for a moment.

He'd try another tactic. ''Have you seen the article in today's newspaper?''

''What article?''

''David's. The one he wrote about you.''

John had to wait only three seconds before the door

unlocked and she peered out. She squeezed an arm through the door, likely expecting him to pass the paper.

Instead, he tugged her arm then raised it to his lips and kissed her hand.

The door fell open, and her quilt with it.

God, she was heaven sent.

Her mouth opened in horror, she raced to grab the quilt, but he stepped on it first.

When she yanked on the fabric, her swaying breasts jiggled with her frantic movements. Giving up, she straightened, cocked a hand on each naked hip and glared at him. "What happened to the gentleman?"

"He ran away. You're left with the big bad wolf."

She spotted a blanket on the upholstered chair in the corner and snatched it around her shoulders.

Damn, she was too fast for him.

Twirling around, she pried the paper from his fingers. "Let's see the damage David has done. If he's said anything to embarrass us—" she said apologetically "—it wasn't because I didn't try my best. He…he had a way of getting into my hair and following at the most inopportune moment. And he didn't take notes very well," she blabbered. "He's probably mixed me up with the other women to boot…" Her voice trailed off as she read the article.

When she finished, she looked up slowly to meet his gaze.

"Why didn't you tell me how much you miss Halifax?"

She shrugged weakly.

"Of course you miss the ocean. I never thought about the difference in geography and what it must be like for you, surrounded by acres and acres of nothing but wheat."

"It's not so bad."

"Once in a while, at the end of August, we get train shipments of lobster from the east coast. Had I known, had I thought of it, I would have arranged to buy some."

Her eyes grew moist. "There's always next year."

"I suspected that you got ill at the sight of blood, but I didn't know for sure…"

"It's all right."

"What watch designs are you working on? If you'd…if you'd like to share them with me sometime, I'd like to see…"

She drew her blanket tighter and didn't reply. Maybe he'd pushed her once too often and she didn't feel like opening up to him again. Why should she? All he ever did was dampen her spirits when she sought his company.

John glanced past her shoulder to his uniform hanging off the rack in the corner. He strode into the room and removed a green ticket stub from the inside pocket.

"What is it?"

He pressed it into her hand. "It's the ticket from the fairgrounds my family played at before they all took ill. The last day we were together…as a happy family. It's a nice memory from my childhood."

"Um," she said softly. "Why didn't you get ill, John?"

"Just lucky, I guess. Or unlucky, as I thought for years when I was in my teens and wished I'd gone with them."

She grappled for words, and in the end, she said the kindest thing that could touch his heart. "I won't disappear on you like Beth and Hank and James. I'm not going anywhere…unless you want me to."

"I don't want you to." He was fully dressed and she was naked. As much as he yearned to stay and make love to her, to prove that he cared about her, he didn't want her to feel as if he were pouncing at the first opportunity. He didn't want her to mistake his emotions for simple lust.

Hell, he didn't want to mistake it himself.

Was he falling in love with her?

Lifting her warm, pliable hand into his larger one, he covered the ticket and clasped her fingers shut. For the first time in their marriage, he entrusted her with something very personal.

"I'm going for a walk to clear my head. Could you take this for me, for safekeeping? I'm not going to carry it around anymore."

"John," she murmured. "Thank you. Don't go, though. I—I've got something I'd like you to read. Wait right here."

She wrapped herself in the blanket and slid down the hall. He heard the ceiling above him creak with her footsteps, and when she came down, she held out a thin stack of envelopes. Her mail-order letters. "You can read them, if you like."

John found a quiet corner in his stable and while his mare chomped on oats, he read by the lantern's light, comforted by the soothing sounds around him.

If the tables had been turned and it was John who'd been fooled like Sarah, he'd burn the letters due to sheer embarrassment. Sarah's dignity had suffered in the prank, but she entrusted him to read what she'd written all those months ago.

The letters from John's men didn't interest him. He skimmed the phony words, incensed again with anger. Sarah's letters, however, kept him enthralled. She'd been open and warmhearted. He lifted her first one, printed on simple cotton rag paper with flowing blue ink.

March 30, 1889
Dear Dr. Calloway,
I'm writing in response to your ad of March 23 requesting a hardworking mail-order bride to join you in your home in Calgary. Normally, I wouldn't respond to such requests, but living on the wide prairie frontier and beginning a new life after the terrible loss of my parents appeals to me.

I'm not afraid of long hours of duty in the home, I have practical working skills of watchmaking, and like you, dream of someday having many children at my side.

It would be kind of you to respond to my enquiry, but should you choose another bride, best of luck and good wishes to you both.

Sincerely,
Miss Sarah O'Neill

John caressed the smooth paper. He'd once asked Logan why the men had chosen Sarah over the other fourteen applicants rumored to have responded to the ad. Logan had told him that Sarah had been the only respondent who'd wished John luck in his endeavors, even if he didn't choose her.

Her other letters went on to tell him more about her life in Halifax, living by the ocean's edge and her interest in collecting watches. She was thrilled that they shared a similar Irish heritage. By the time John reached her final letter, her tone had turned more personal. *She'd been tricked,* he wanted to scream. She'd been tricked, but in her letters, she'd remained steadfast and trusting.

July 14, 1889
My dearest John,
Thank you for your thoughtful letter. I'm so pleased you understood how difficult it was for me to confess

that you wouldn't be my first. If I could take that moment back, I would, but rest assured you will always be the only man I pledge my heart to.

My bags are nearly packed. Mother's few things have been shipped to the women's charity, and the creditors for the burial nearly paid. Thank you for the ten dollars you mailed in that regard.

I anxiously await to see the prairie wild rose as you described, and to touch your caring face.

Yours with great affection,

Sarah

Still thinking about the day's events, Sarah pulled one long leg out of the bath water. She grabbed a linen towel off the chair. When she heard a faint knocking at the front door, she glanced to the wall clock. Eight-fifteen. Who would be calling so close to bedtime? In order to get up at the light of dawn, most folks were preparing for sleep.

Unless it was an emergency for John. Wasn't he home yet from his walk? Her heart gathered speed as she prayed she wouldn't have to deal with any medical dilemmas alone.

Sliding into her red robe, Sarah headed to the front hall. When she opened the door, there stood Natasha in a black cloak, with her toddler and young boy at her side, shifting nervously as they all stared at Sarah.

Natasha held out a wicker basket with a blue cloth covering its lumpy contents. With trembling hands that belied her calm smile, she glanced to the watchful constable who was standing on guard, peering at the basket, then the women.

"I brought you fresh-baked scones from the bakery. You'll have to return the basket to them tomorrow, but I wanted to thank you for helping my husband today."

Sarah took it, gazing past her shoulder to the empty porch. "Why, thank you. Did you bring Keen—Ken with you?"

"No, he's recovering at home."

"Of course," said Sarah, brushing at her robe. "His foot is injured. What was I thinking? Come in, please."

She led the troop to the library, placing the basket on John's wide desk then lifting a corner of the blue cloth. "You didn't have to do this, but thank you very much."

When Sarah turned around, Rusty, in freshly pressed woolen trousers and spiffy leather shoes, peered closely at her face.

Sarah clutched at her robe's satin neckline, wishing she'd had time to make herself presentable, as they were all so finely dressed.

Rusty blurted, "Pa says you're our aunt."

Sarah felt herself flush down to her very bones. She wheeled around to look at Natasha, but met with a silent inquisitive gaze.

"You know?"

"Only Rusty and I know, and we've promised to keep it a secret for as long…as needed." At her feet, the toddler cried. Natasha pulled her up from the floor and into her arms. She kissed the girl's forehead. "You're tired, honey, it's past your bedtime. We'll be there soon."

"You don't look like my pa," said Rusty. "When I was small, he used to tell me you had short curly hair."

Keenan had spoken of her before this night? He'd told his family about her, after all. Tenderness welled up in Sarah's throat. She kneeled beside Rusty and stroked the fine worsted wool of his jacket sleeve. "I've let it grow long."

"Rusty," said his mother. "There's no time to discuss it or we'll be late." Her voice lowered to a hush. "We'll be late for our train."

"I don't wanna go."

"We're doing this for Pa."

Sensing danger, Sarah's stomach churned with fear. She stepped closer to Natasha. "Why have you come to me?"

"I told the constable at the door I wanted to thank the doctor for treating Ken's illness, but what I really need is to speak with you in private."

Sarah lifted the basket and led the group into the kitchen wishing to distract the children so she and Natasha could talk. She peered out the back door and whistled. When the monkey popped his head around the corner, she placed an onion in Rusty's hand, which led the monkey inside. To the children's delightful laughter, Willie entertained them while Sarah pulled Natasha aside.

Natasha poured out her problems. "Ken is in trouble. I thought maybe since you're his sister and you're married to the doctor, you might…" She played with the fingertips of her cloth gloves. "I'm on the verge of leaving him. I don't know who else to turn to."

"Leaving Keenan? Why?"

"Keenan you say?"

"That's what we used to call him when he was a boy. How long have you known him?"

"Nine years. We met when he was a drover, running cattle up from Texas. Angus McIver hired him."

"What trouble is Keenan in?"

Natasha buried her face into her gloves. "I've left our luggage hidden in your alleyway because I decided if I …if I spoke with you and you can't offer my family help,

I'm walking to the train depot with the children and leaving for the States.'' She glanced at the kitchen clock. ''In forty-five minutes.''

''Why?''

''For my children's safety, otherwise I'd never leave Ken's side. Ken knows I'm doing this. He agrees that Angus and his men are simply too big a group to fight any longer.''

''Angus? What has *he* done?''

Bitterness crept into Natasha's expression. ''He's behind it all.''

''Behind what? Keenan has told us that Angus doesn't believe in his palsy, but what I see is an ill, retiring rancher who has the continual misfortune to be a target of the Grayveson gang.''

Natasha's limbs grew shaky. She peered at Sarah as if weighing a decision. ''Angus was the one who ordered Ken shot today.''

Sarah whirled in confusion. The outrageous statement hammered against her brain.

''Angus wanted him shot in the foot, to save Ken's hands for gunmaking, and only enough injury for blackmail.''

''Oh, my God,'' said Sarah, finally understanding, finally recognizing the truth and what had been under her nose for weeks. ''Angus McIver *is* the Grayveson gang.''

Both women jumped at the sound of the front door creaking open, echoing down the front hall into the kitchen. The familiar thud of heavy boots met with the floor planks, getting louder as they headed toward the women.

John was home.

Feeling trapped in the middle of an impending storm,

Sarah rose on jittery limbs to face the doorway and prepared to greet her husband. What should she tell him?

"Hello, Dr. Calloway," said Natasha as he strode into the room.

Long-legged and bulky, he stopped in midstride. His suspenders pulled at broad shoulders. John rubbed his dark jaw. "Ken hasn't taken a turn for the worse, has he?"

"No, no, he's fine."

The monkey leaped from a chair and ran past John.

"Ma, can we go chase him?" asked Rusty.

Sarah answered for her. "Sure. Just be careful you don't hurt yourself on the stairway."

Natasha followed the children out of the room, weaving her slender frame behind her waddling little girl. "Make sure you don't break anything! There's a lot of fine things in this house!"

An opportunity opened for Sarah. Planting her warm hand on John's cool sleeve, Sarah pulled him aside.

He opened a cupboard door and slid her envelopes inside. "Thank you for sharing these with me, Sarah. I know it was difficult for you."

He was a complex man, and it wasn't easy to win his trust, but she felt closer to him. Now was not the time to discuss the letters, however.

"What is it?" he asked.

Beneath his steady scrutiny, she could barely think. "All these weeks, John," she said, fumbling for the right way to ease the news to her husband. "I wasn't looking for my cousin. I was looking for my brother."

Chapter Nineteen

John towered over Sarah, his brown eyes flickering with suspicion, making her feel as if her breath had been cut off. "Your brother is the pickpocket? The thief?"

Her face rose to meet his challenge. "He's no longer a pickpocket."

John rubbed his chin, the way he always did when he was angry with her. "Does this mean you've found him?"

With her stomach clenched tight, Sarah tried to steady her fears. *John would help them. He had to.*

"My brother is Ken Neal."

His jaw slackened. He stumbled away, groping for the chair back. Taking a second to decipher the news, he spun around to face Sarah. He impaled her with his raw gaze, and any closeness she'd felt after he'd read her letters seemed to vanish. "You knew we were going to visit your brother today and yet you said nothing to me? I just read your letters and thought you were the most honest—"

Her insides quivered. "I couldn't be sure it was him. But the name you gave me was so similar to his family name…Keenan O'Neill, I had to see for myself."

"Did he know it was you?" Then John laughed with

a shallow ring. "Of course he did, I saw that in his slippery eyes. Yet neither of you said a word to me."

"I didn't know what to say.... When we arrived, I was astounded that he'd been wounded."

"You played me for a fool."

"I didn't mean to."

"Did Ken—Keenan get a kick out of watching you dupe me?"

"That wasn't how it was intended."

"Needless to say, *it's how it played out.*"

She weakened beneath his accusation. "I wasn't sure if Keenan was still in trouble with the law, and you were so hard on me, so hard on everyone around you...can't you see why I kept it from you?"

"What trouble was your brother in that he had to escape Halifax?"

"Gunrunning."

"Was he caught?"

"Yes."

"Convicted?"

"No. I meant he was caught by my father, but not the authorities. They suspected him and came calling, but as far as I know, they never caught up to him, or charged him."

"But you put lives in danger, Sarah, did you think of that?"

"Whose life?"

"Your own! If the Grayveson gang was after Ken and his assistant—and I believe they were targeted on purpose, although I don't know why yet—then as Ken's sister you might have been next! Hell, you still might be!"

John was concerned about *her.* She tried to weigh the whole structure of events, trying to comprehend what he must be feeling.

"There are a thousand possibilities of danger when it comes to the Grayveson gang," he said harshly. "You know nothing of the horrors they've done to innocent people."

She backed away, clutching at the neckline of her robe, which was threatening to spill open. "We don't have a lot of time. There's something else you need to know."

"What?" He glanced down at the jumble of loose hair around her shoulders.

"Natasha's come to me—*to us*—for help. She says Angus McIver was behind Keenan's shooting today."

He was riveted by the accusation. She gave it time to filter in.

John crossed his arms and leaned against the counter. In a low voice devoid of warmth, he asked, "Why would Angus McIver have two of his own men shot?"

"Because," she said. "Angus McIver is the mastermind behind the Grayveson gang."

John flinched. By his rising stance and his calculating gaze, Sarah knew the truth had sunk in.

As Sarah spoke, Natasha had walked in, sobbing gently.

"How do you know this?" he asked Natasha.

"We don't know all the details. For two years Angus has been blackmailing Ken to supply guns for the gang."

"Blackmailing how?"

"Threatening to harm his family…to harm me."

John swore.

"When Ken developed the palsy, Angus was furious. He said Ken was making up the illness simply to get out of his gun-making duties." Natasha glanced at Sarah. "It's not true," she whispered.

"I know," said Sarah, weaving an arm around her sister-in-law.

"Ken has tried to deliver," said Natasha. "But the

number of guns keep multiplying and he can't keep up. He's got a dozen guns due in a week's time, but there's no way he can make them. Not only do his hands shake, but he can barely stand on his feet with just a cane supporting him. When he confronted Angus and told him he no longer wants to work for him, Angus threatened to have him shot. And his assistant.''

"Why is Angus doing this?" said John. "Why is he rustling cattle and horses and masking behind the Grayveson gang?"

Natasha unbuttoned her cloak, revealing a gray dress beneath. "In the beginning, the Grayveson brothers were acting on their own. About three years ago, Angus brokered a deal with them. He hired drifters and the gang to steal from him to make it appear as if…Slade Phillips might be behind it."

"Slade Phillips?" John called in disbelief.

Natasha held firm. "He's a wheat grower and wheat growers are getting the best of the grazing lands around Calgary."

"There's plenty of land to go around for everyone."

"Not according to Angus. Angus wants Slade to leave and to take all his grain-growing friends with him."

"Hell." John pinched two fingers in the air. "We're this close to arresting an innocent Slade Phillips. All paths lead to him."

"I don't know how, but Angus managed to head the gang within a very short period of time."

"Son of a bitch," said John. "Angus McIver is responsible for the death of Wesley Quinn."

The room went silent.

"Ken and I decided it was time for me to leave the country and to take our children to safety. I was headed to the train station to catch the nine o'clock out of here.

To leave Ken.'' Pleading to John, Natasha sobbed. ''Ken told me about his sister and the idea struck me to confide in her.''

Sarah floundered.

John walked to the pine table and slapped his palm against the battered wood. ''We need a person we can trust, not a Mountie who'd be visible, to deliver a message to Ken and to secretly pick up the guns he's working on. I'll get someone to finish the guns and deliver them to Angus as if Ken made them. This will save Ken from suspicion while the troops have time to build a case against Angus.''

''Thank you,'' cried Natasha.

John paced to the back door. ''Who can be our messenger?''

''Eddie Dickson,'' Natasha offered.

''The man who works in the livery stables?'' asked John. ''The man I bandaged? He's not to be trusted. Why, he lied about his sickle injury.''

''I know,'' murmured Natasha. ''He lied to protect Ken. Angus sells many of his horses to the livery stables. Eddie and Ken have worked together for two years. The night Eddie was injured in the livery stables, he was trying to knock sense into Ken to stand up to Angus. Eddie Junior was helping his father clean his guns and in the turmoil, the boy pulled a gun on Ken, thinking he was protecting his father. Eddie Senior tried to tell his boy that Ken was his friend and leaped for the gun, but got shot instead. Ken was sickened by it, and that's why he decided to finally stand up to Angus.''

''So Eddie Dickson is a good man,'' said John. ''How does Calvin Rutledge figure into this? He's still holed up at the fort, getting his rabies treatment. Is he a good man?''

"I'm not sure," said Natasha. "He doesn't confide in me or Ken."

"Then we can't trust him until we know for certain," declared John. "And who are we going to get to finish off the dozen guns?"

"I can do it," said Sarah.

"This is serious business. It's not clock design and it's not jewelry repair."

"You're forgetting my father was a clockmaker and a gunsmith. He taught Keenan and I *both* of these trades. I know how to make a gun."

"So does the blacksmith at the fort, but he's a trained policeman."

"But I know the intricacies of Keenan's designs, which the blacksmith can't know. Angus McIver won't be able to tell the difference in whether *I* fashioned his guns, or Keenan did."

John's gaze slid up and down Sarah, but he spoke to the other woman. "Natasha, you've got a train to catch."

"What?"

"You and your children are still leaving on the late train." He glanced at the kitchen clock. "You've got ten minutes to catch it."

"But I don't want to leave Ken now."

"I've got a plan and it involves you heading out." John glanced at the basket with the blue cloth lying on the table, as Natasha called for her children. His thick hair tapered neatly to his collar. "Sarah, very quietly, please go ask the constable at the front door to come in for scones and tea."

"I ain't takin' orders from a woman." The fort's blacksmith, Constable Longfellow, muttered his opinion as soon as John and Sarah set foot in the forge at eleven-ten the next morning.

"Yes you are," replied John as calmly as he could muster. He placed two heavy wooden crates on the working bench of the cool, dim interior. This morning, Eddie Dickson had secretly retrieved the batch of guns-in-the-making from Ken Neal on the guise of returning an ailing horse to the McIver ranch. "As your commanding officer, I'm telling you you're going to work with Sarah and do as she asks."

Sarah had the good sense to remain quiet. She found a crowbar and began to pry apart a crate. The hem of her dowdy dress swirled around her high-ankled boots, but the worn cloth clung to her upper body like kidskin gloves to familiar fingers. As concerned as John was that she was involved in this jeopardy, at least she'd be working within the safety of the fort, with dozens of policemen to protect her.

In a soiled leather apron, the blacksmith spun away to the anvil, cursing beneath his breath and hammering at a newly forged wrench. Although Longfellow was his actual name, because the blacksmith was barely five foot tall, he'd earned the nickname of Shorty. His greased hair clung in clumps behind his ears. Shorty was an excellent combination of blacksmith, chemist, metallurgist, welder, ballistics expert, plus he had an artist's eye for symmetry.

When John made no move to leave but began prying open another crate, helping Sarah unload the half-finished pieces—barrels and chambers and blocks of wood—Shorty peered up from his work. "Does Superintendent Ridgeway know about this?"

He was the only other person who did besides Logan and two others. John and Sarah had also decided to keep the news that Keenan was related to Sarah to themselves for now.

"Of course the superintendent knows. He'll be by later to see how you're making out. But this is a highly classified assignment and we can't trust anyone but you, Shorty. You can't tell anyone else what you're doing."

The blacksmith stepped to the firepit and worked the bellows. The fire roared. He inserted the wrench again to heat it before pounding it into shape on the anvil. He growled, "Don't worry, I ain't gonna tell anyone about workin' with a woman."

John looked to Sarah with relief. Shorty was in. When Sarah gave John a soft, knowing smile, a pulsing knot formed in his gut. She'd come to him, after all. He wasn't quite sure if he was livid that she'd kept Ken's identity hidden yesterday, or elated that she'd come to John as soon as Natasha had voiced a problem between Ken and Angus.

In the end, hadn't Sarah put her trust in her husband?

Or had she waited too long for it to be meaningful?

John fought with the conflict raging in his mind.

"I'll do the woodworking and stockmaking in the other room, Officer Longfellow." Sarah lifted the wood blocks and carried them past the firepit to the open doorway. "I know how wood chips and dust can make a mess of your metal-working machinery."

Shorty grumbled. "You know, miss, a gun is a lethal weapon. If poorly designed, it can kill from both ends."

"Yes, sir, my daddy used to say the same. If I find a gun in a dangerous condition that can't be corrected, I'll scrap it. But it appears that Ken has already worked many of the metal pieces. The chambers need to be assembled and balanced, and the barrels turned and polished. Then of course, all the grips need to be applied."

"Any steel parts need to be cut?"

"Looks like a few."

"How do you know so much about guns?"

"My father was a gunsmith. He used to say the main difficulty for the beginner was to properly visualize the steps in making a gun part. He taught me to look at the gun in one plane at a time. Slab off the surplus metal in that plane only, then turn the part at right angles and repeat the process in another plane. It isn't nearly as difficult as it seems if the work is broken up into simple steps."

"Not difficult, huh?" said Shorty. "We'll see. Did your father make a livin' at it?"

"I'm afraid not. There's not much money in it, if…you're an honest gunsmith. Sometimes it'd take my father three hours to fix a busted rifle to discover it was simply in need of a new ball bearing. Then he would only charge three cents. No one was willing to pay more."

John followed Sarah, walking by Shorty with another open crate. Shorty picked up a half-assembled gun. When Sarah returned from the side room, he asked her, "Why don't you show me what you can do by removing these two screws and polishin' the inside?"

Sarah frowned. "No, sir. I never remove any screws until I can figure a reason for doing so. I might release inside parts that are under spring tension. They might shift and lock the action and then maybe even *you* might not be able to get it apart without breaking something."

Good for her, thought John, biting back a grin.

Shorty didn't blink. "Well, you best get to work on those. Good thing they're new, you'll have no trouble assemblin' them."

Sarah laughed good-naturedly while she took out a ribbon and tied up her hair, preparing to work. "A new one takes longer to assemble than reassembling an old one."

"How could that be?" asked John.

"On an old gun, the parts have bright spots worn through where they've been rubbing against other parts, so the puzzle of assembly is easier to figure out."

Shorty muttered. "I guess I better go find me some tin plate for solderin' the metal."

Sarah looked at him and shook her head. "I think we'll have more need for zinc chloride, because it's the most common flux used for soldering iron and steel. But you already knew that, sir, and I hope I've passed your final test. If we wind up doing a lot of talking, we won't get much work done, will we?"

That silenced the blacksmith for good.

For a moment, John forgot about his personal problems with his wife and marveled at the change in her. That she could link guns and metal with such femininity and common sense made his legs weak. What a woman.

"I admit it's a problem, but let's try to come to an agreement that we'll all be happy about." Adjusting a trigger on a revolver the way Sarah had showed him, John squared off against Sarah and Shorty. After six days and nights working together, the two were driving John insane. John had spent most of his hours at the hospital, releasing Calvin Rutledge after clearing him of rabies, and attending to local townsfolk who kept dropping by for unexpected appointments, while Sarah spent eighteen hours a day working to save her brother. John had gone to see Mr. Ashford at the jeweler's to notify him that Sarah was needed at home for the next week or two, and Mr. Ashford had rearranged her hours without question.

A light breeze curled into the room, blowing in the cool morning air, nearly October, ruffling John's shirt. Sitting himself down, he groped for his shoulder holster in a routine gesture, then realized he wasn't wearing it. He never wore his guns inside the fort.

"Listen," said Shorty, propping his small boot onto the ledge of the workbench. "This woman is dang crazy. She's been workin' away at each gun as if it were a special oil paintin' for the judge's mansion. I'll be damned if I make these guns better than my own. It's a blasted gang we're buildin' them for. If I had my way, I'd make them all misfire."

The morning light caught Sarah's cheek, accentuating the dark circles beneath her eyes. "But there are good men behind these guns, too." With her hair tangled in knots and greasy from three days of practically living in the forge, she ran a grimy hand along her cheek, smearing it with oil. "What if...what if someone who's trying to help us gets his hands on one of these guns and it misfires, killing him or one of the Mounties?"

John knew she was thinking about her brother. He sympathized, but he also agreed with Shorty.

Sarah held a finished revolver in her palm. Her fingernails, once buffed and polished, were outlined with black dirt. "Ken Neal isn't well enough to finish these on his own, and if we do anything phony, the Grayveson gang might catch on."

"Maybe it's better to sacrifice one man than dozens of police."

Sarah nearly gagged. She turned blindly to John, but he tried to remain on an even keel.

"We're not sacrificing anyone, Shorty," said John.

Shorty had been told about Ken Neal but was still unaware of his relationship with Sarah. The superintendent had told the blacksmith about the Grayveson gang, and half a dozen more Mounties had been briefed. From here to Fort Edmonton and down to the U.S. border, the

Mountie patrol bustled with the new information and the gathering of evidence. Nothing was conclusive yet.

With a cry of frustration, Sarah wiped her hand on her soiled skirts. "Let's put our differences aside for a moment and get to the stockmaking of the two rifles."

"That's another thing," Shorty complained. "Have you heard what your wife wants to do with the rifles?"

Sarah rolled her eyes. "It's what Ken would do!"

"How do you know?" hollered Shorty.

"I've...I've seen his work."

John stepped to the table that Shorty indicated. John's muscles strained with exhaustion and lack of sleep. After today, he hoped like hell that the three of them could catch up on their rest. Being tired and weary grated on everyone's nerves. "What does Sarah want to do?"

"She wants to fit the rifle butt to the size of the customer."

"How do you know who the customer is?" John asked.

Sarah tucked the finished revolver into the crate of straw. The revolvers were packed and ready to be delivered this morning, with only the rifles remaining. "Eddie Dickson dropped by yesterday and said the two rifles were intended for Angus McIver and Lincoln Grayveson."

"You're makin' a big deal over nothin'!" Shorty repeated.

"Ken Neal would fit the rifle to the man. If we do otherwise, it'll raise suspicions."

"See what I mean?" hollered Shorty.

"How do you propose to fit the rifle?" asked John, scouting for the crate lid and hammer and nails.

Sarah walked to the worktable and began to sketch on paper what looked to be a template for the rifle stock. "I can guess by their shirt size."

Shorty walked away. "For cripe's sake."

"No, listen to me," she urged. "I guess that Angus wears about a size seventeen shirt collar, and I hear that Lincoln Grayveson is a much smaller man, perhaps a size fourteen or fifteen."

"Go on," said John, perplexed but wondering where she was headed.

"A rifle stock for the bigger man would measure, say thirteen and a half inches from the center of the trigger to the center of the butt plate. The comb would be slightly thinner than normal to compensate for Angus's full face. We'd accommodate a drop at the comb, a drop at the heel, and adjust the cast-off. The smaller man's would be suited accordingly."

John stared at her.

"Ken would do it," she said firmly, bringing out a steel ruler to measure her sketch. "To do work beneath his capabilities would bring him to the devil's door."

"She's right." John signaled. He placed the lid over the crate and hammered. "Do as she says."

Shorty trudged to the stack of brushes and cans. "Why don't I start the final coat of oil finish? I've got linseed—"

"No!" said Sarah, looking up from her work. "Ken would never do a London oil finish. On this open-pored walnut, the linseed oil wouldn't be much good. It gets soaked up and penetrates clear through so it doesn't offer much protection against moisture."

Shorty shouted, "Then what do you suggest, Your Highness?"

"Equal parts of white shellac and *boiled* linseed oil."

Shorty dragged his heels to the cauldron and poured in a tin of oil. "You're makin' this more complicated than it needs to be. I think these guns are overdone, and once the Grayveson gang gets their paws on them, they'll smell somethin' in the air and your Ken Neal will have hell to pay.''

Sarah jarred from the rebuke. She didn't move, then stumbled onto a bench. With her weary head propped between her soiled hands, she moaned to John. ''Are we doing the right thing? Are we helping Keenan or making things worse?''

''We're doing the right thing,'' John whispered, sagging onto the bench beside her, wishing he felt more confident. The planks beneath his seat buckled with his movement. Because his time was spent mainly in the hospital, his clothes weren't nearly as soiled as hers. ''When you get caught up with your sleep, you'll see it clear again. Are we almost done?''

''About six hours for the rifles, then drying time.''

''I'll send the revolvers now then, with Eddie Dickson, and leave the rifles for tomorrow.'' Six more hours of torture, then he'd be able to close his heavy lids.

A sound at the door startled them. John rose to meet the corporal who entered. ''What is it?''

The young corporal squinted in the dim light, adjusting his gaze from the brightness outside. John, however, could see that the man's face was ashen. ''It's Constable Pawson, Sir.''

Sarah jumped to John's side and listened.

John bristled to alert. Constable Pawson whose leg he'd saved, who'd fought gangrene and had won the battle? Had the man's leg worsened? ''Yes, what is it?''

''Sir…'' the corporal's voice cracked ''…he's been knifed.''

John turned blindly, grasping for footing. Sarah leaned into him. ''How bad?'' he asked.

''His throat's been slit.''

Sarah cried out in anguish as John trembled with fear. "Murdered?"

"Yes, Sir."

"Who's responsible?" John asked in horror, certain he already knew the answer.

"We think the Grayveson gang."

John flew into action. He hurled out the door. "Stay with my wife," he shouted to the corporal.

"Where are you going?" Sarah screamed.

"To get my guns!"

Chapter Twenty

Sarah had never seen so many men hushed with reverence.

Clouds of dust rose behind the herd of magnificent horses carrying forty-two policemen out of the fort gates as they surrounded the prairie town, desperately searching and guarding against the gang who'd killed one of their own. As the afternoon ended, punctuated by an apricot sunset filtering through the hues of the Rocky Mountains, bank tellers left their posts, barbershop chairs emptied, saloons thinned and everyone whispered and waited for what might come.

Crossing the cracked dirt path of the fort's square, Sarah sympathized with the young family Constable Pawson had left behind. She prayed no more men would die, but refused to even consider that John might be one of the next.

Not when she thought…when she was certain she was now carrying his child. She arose with morning nausea, despite an appetite that rivaled any Mountie's. Thankfully, the nausea left by breakfast, so she was able to conceal it from John till now.

She spotted him in a circle of men standing by the

jailhouse, discussing what had happened earlier that morning. She'd never forget his effort in helping Keenan.

As she approached to let John know she was finished with the rifles, one of the men was saying, "Maybe Pawson had information on someone. Where would he get that information?"

"He spent a lot of time convalescing in the fort hospital," said John. "He never mentioned anything to me."

"Who was there with him?"

"Folks come and go with their ailments. I've been treating everything from broken limbs to burned arms to gonorrhea to…rabies. Do you think there could be a connection between Pawson and Calvin Rutledge?" asked John. "They both spent time in the ward together."

The men pondered it, some with eyes glazed in concentration, others shrugging.

John turned to two men. "Find Rutledge and bring him here." When he looked past their shoulders, he spotted Sarah. "Excuse me," he said, weaving past his men.

"We're finished with the rifles," Sarah whispered to her husband, still wary to keep her business to herself. Whatever John had chosen to disclose or not disclose to his men would be his choice; she wouldn't tamper with it. "The shellac is drying, but there's nothing more for me to do."

He glanced at her soiled clothing. "Go home, then. Clean up and try to concentrate on something else. I'll make sure you're escorted and that a man stays with you at all times."

She squinted against the fading sun. She wanted time alone with him, to tell him that they were about to bring a child into the world, despite the horror of the current situation, to tell him how she felt and how much she loved him. "I can't leave you."

He lifted her hand, smiled at the dirt beneath her nails, then kissed it lightly. "I appreciate that, but this could go on for days. Maybe weeks. We've all got to go about our business. We'll get the slimy vultures who did this."

"Will you be home this evening to join me?"

Wear registered in the lines of his face. "If I'm not needed for any emergencies, there's nothing I'd like more."

She'd tell him tonight, then. She'd soak in a tub and do her nails and brush her hair till it shone like a mirror. She'd offer to rub his back and to make him dinner, and then she'd spill her heart and hope that he would return some of what she felt for him. They had a lot to talk about, since discovering Keenan's identity and the present chaos of the fort.

John looked up to study the streaking beauty of the evening sky. "Under any other circumstance, I'd consider this a breathtaking night."

She nodded softly, knowing exactly how he felt. It was a bittersweet moment, trapped together in the swirling confusion, feeling John's pain at the death of one of his friends, aching to tell him the joy of what the future might hold.

Two riders on horseback distracted them. The men rode in through the gates and captured all attention. In the fading light, Sarah didn't recognize them.

However, she noticed recognition dawn in John's eyes. He stepped in front of Sarah, almost protectively. Unease settled on her shoulders.

"There you are, Doc. We'd like you to follow us back to the ranch."

"Does Angus need something?"

Sarah felt the heat of fear. Angus McIver's ranch?

When the revolvers had been delivered this morning, had Ken been discovered?

"Why?" asked John.

"Angus is in an awful lot of pain. Bring your instruments. He might need surgery."

No! When Sarah gasped, the riders tilted their silhouetted forms in Sarah's direction. Darkness shielded the strangers' faces, but she felt the drill of their violent stares. She shifted with discomfort at how filthy she must look. Her breathing grew unsteady.

"Your wife's lookin' like she's been workin' hard, Doc. What have you been gettin' her to do?"

"She's been helping the cook," John said smoothly. "He's got a garden and she's been uprooting potatoes. How long has Angus been in severe pain?"

"About an hour."

"Anything different than the usual?"

"It don't seem so, other than more pain, like he says."

"Is he taking the laudanum I left?"

"Yup."

"Good. We've got a bit of time to get to him then."

They nodded then turned their attention back to John. "Any word on who killed Pawson?"

John's jaw throbbed. He clenched his fists at his sides and Sarah saw the rage threatening to burst. She stepped beside him and wove her arm into his, hoping to shield his fury.

"Not yet," John drawled.

One of the riders tipped the brim of his hat. "What a shame."

John's arm stiffened, about to lunge, but Sarah gently held him back. "I'll help you get your instruments ready, John."

When they raced into his office, several men followed.

"John, you can't go," Sarah pleaded. "McIver might not be sick. You might be playing into their hands. The revolvers have arrived. Maybe they mean to harm you." She looked to the three other Mounties standing there, hoping one of them would help convince her husband to stay, but they only helped him with his gear, one lifting John's medicine bag to the table, the other stuffing bandages and scissors as John directed. Panic assailed her.

"I'll bring other men with me for protection," John replied.

"They may get to you anyway."

"We don't have any hard evidence against McIver. He may be innocent, despite…despite what Ken Neal says."

Sarah winced.

"On second thought, I think McIver is guilty as hell. Maybe I can trick him into confessing," John continued. "To give me any scrap we can use against him. If he *is* ill, the morphine I'll give him does strange things to people. Sometimes it makes them speak the truth."

When Logan strode into the room, John kept packing. "How's the wife and baby?"

"Both fine. Listen to me, John." Logan strode to the glass cabinet and removed a bottle of chloroform. "I just heard. I'm coming with you to assist, but I have to say…one slip of your hand on McIver's artery and he could be gone forever. No one would have to suffer at his hands anymore."

John gave him an incredulous glare. "What the hell are you suggesting I do?"

Logan backed away, placing the bottle inside one of the traveling leather pouches. "Nothing. I'm just pointing out how convenient it could be."

Sarah understood Logan's hatred. Of all the men here, Logan had been captured and chained up for six months

by the Grayveson gang, half his face had been blown off
by them when he'd escaped.

John's muscles twitched. "I heal people. I'm a doctor,
not a hired gun."

"You also seek justice," said Logan. "You're a man
of the law."

Sarah's mind spun with the reality of the difficulties
John faced. No wonder he was the man he was. Although
she found him overbearing at times, she now understood
why he had those qualities, and how they must have
helped him over the years in his police work. Praise the
heavens he was this strong.

They could work out their marriage difficulties…
Please, she silently begged. *Please don't take my husband
away from me.*

"As much as I believe McIver is guilty and as much
as you do, too," John said to Logan, "it's for a jury and
judge to decide his fate."

"Don't go," Sarah begged. "Don't put yourself in the
position where you have to choose."

"I've got to go. There's no one else who can do this."

Even in her state of alarm, she knew deep down in her
heart that there was nothing she could say to keep this
man from helping another person in need, or from flying
straight into the face of danger to expose a criminal.

"You can't come with me, Logan," said John.

"Why the hell not?"

"That'd put the only two medical officers we have into
jeopardy. If this turns bloody, who'll patch up our team?"

Logan's eyes glistened with compassion. "But a cho-
lecystectomy is major surgery. You'll be hours on your
feet. Who's going to administer the anesthesia? You can't
do it all yourself, it'd be barbaric."

John nodded to the man holding his medical bag. "I'll take Sergeant O'Malley and show him what to do."

"Hell, John," said the sergeant, squealing in disgust. "I can't watch you slice open someone's guts. Pardon my language, ma'am. And I'm afraid *my* hand *would* slip. I'd like nothin' better than to see Angus McIver dead."

John sighed. "Then I'll insist we bring McIver here to the hospital. I'll stress the importance of hygiene and the surgical assistance I'll need."

"Yes," said Sarah, bounding with hope. "Bring him back here where you'll be surrounded by armed police."

"It's a good idea," Logan agreed.

Battling a heavy cloud of despair that she might never see her husband again, Sarah followed him outside into the brisk night air to his horse. Gooseflesh rose on her arms. She needed a coat. But as cold as she was, she was more torn by whether or not she should tell him about the baby. To give him the dignity of knowing about his child before he left for battle.

Standing beside the massive horses, Sarah felt dwarfed. "Don't take any risks."

John glanced at her turbulent face, then cast his eyes downward over her greasy clothes. "I won't. Let the men take you home. Logan, make sure she's under constant supervision."

Five other Mounties rose to their saddles beside John. It was all the men they could spare, she'd heard them whisper, but she was happy nonetheless to see the numbers accompanying John.

McIver's ranch hands frowned. "You don't need to bring your friends."

"They're for my protection," John said bluntly. "You never know who's lurking in the woods, ready to ambush. Draw your weapons," he ordered his men.

Out came the Enfield revolvers, the police-issue Navy Colts, the Winchester rifles.

McIver's riders, nothing more than black shapes atop their horses, shifted in their saddles looking at each other, but they didn't argue.

John turned to his wife. "You could use a good soak in a hot bath. Wait for me at home. I'll return as soon as I'm finished." With a kiss on her mouth that left her breathless, John mounted his bay stallion.

Churning with indecision and frightened beyond her wits, Sarah tugged at his sleeve. Perhaps if she gave him reason to return, he'd be extra cautious.

He dipped down over the horse so that his ear pressed close to Sarah's mouth and she could whisper to him. "Please get through this alive. You've got to come home to me, John. I think…I think I'm carrying our child—"

"Let's go!" McIver's men called, moving forward.

Then her beloved John was swallowed by darkness.

An hour later as John entered the McIver home, walking behind one of the riders who'd brought him and two Mounties, Sarah's words still burned in John's head. *Pregnant with his child.*

Marriage to Sarah had thus far brought him many unexpected turns—the lovemaking, the desire to see her at the end of every working day, the painful arguments, the heated debates over the shabby way he'd treated her in comparison to his men, and now the blissful longing for a tender baby.

He was getting soft. How else could he explain the throbbing of his heart and the quickening of his pulse when he thought of his wife, his Sarah, bringing another life into the world? Their baby, conceived during a tide of passion that had been so stormy, yet, full of serene promise for the future.

How pigheaded he'd been, not to be able to see past his own needs.

He'd had her drilling guns and polishing weapons when she should have had her feet propped up on pillows, eating vegetables and fruits. The urge to see her again, to drive away her nightmares and to apologize for all the wrongs he'd done to her, controlled him.

"Right in here," a man indicated to John. "Your man can stay out here."

Alone, except for McIver's man, John stepped into Angus's den, in which he'd stood dozens of times before, drinking toasts to Angus's beef fortunes and examining the hefty man when his condition had flared.

Now, Angus McIver sat in a leather wing-backed chair dotted with shiny studs, cowering beneath a blanket.

He'd lost weight in the two weeks since John had last seen him. Excess skin sagged around his eyes and his yellow pallor looked frightening.

"Thanks for comin'." McIver lifted his head slowly as John knelt to examine him.

"Where's Sheila today?" asked John, forcing a smile.

McIver grumbled. "At her sister's." Something about the way he said it brought an eerie feeling to the room.

John examined McIver, confirming symptoms of abdominal pain, vomiting, heartburn and backache. It hadn't been a ruse to get John here. McIver was gravely ill, but John wondered how much good surgery would do.

"Help me," said McIver.

"That's why I'm here."

"You've always been a good man. You do what's right and you help people get better."

John tried to stomach the flattery, wondering if it came

from a man who'd ordered Pawson killed, and Wesley, and who knew how many innocent others who'd gotten in the path of the rustlers.

"How long have I known you?" McIver clenched his teeth in another wave of agony.

"Ten years."

"Ten years is a long time to cultivate a friendship, don't you think?"

"It can be."

"I'm not ready to die. I got a lot of livin' in me yet."

Had Wesley been ready to die? Had any of the others? "Did you know one of our men was killed this morning?"

McIver's yellow eyes narrowed. "So I heard."

"Do you know anything about it?"

"What would I know?"

"People say it was the Grayveson gang."

"Are those—" McIver grimaced and doubled over "—bastards back in town?"

John blinked. "Did they ever leave?"

McIver flinched. "I heard they did."

"Who'd you hear it from?"

The older man withdrew his arm from John's support. John placed his stethoscope over the frail heart. "You're having a gallstone attack."

"Why does it feel worse than the other times?"

"You've let the gallstones linger for too long. Your fever worries me."

"Why?"

"It's an indication of infection. The gallstones are likely blocking the ducts, causing a backup of bile, which is causing your pain and nausea. And they've been left to fester like this for weeks."

"But you can fix me up, right?"

"I'll try. You definitely need surgery to remove the stones and the gallbladder sac."

McIver nodded quickly in agreement.

"Have you ever met Lincoln Grayveson?"

"You don't pull your punches, do you, sonny? No."

"I heard you were together at the auction house two years back."

"What the hell is this?" McIver snapped between his groans. "An investigation or an examination? Maybe I met him once, how am I suppose to remember?"

"What about his brothers Sid or Zane? Ever met them?"

"No. Sid's in jail, isn't he?"

"Yeah. He got twenty-five years for attempted murder of a police officer when he blasted Logan's face."

Finished with his exam, John returned his thermometer and stethoscope to his bag. He turned to the ranch hand. "Help me get Angus up and into a buggy. Logan's waiting at the hospital to assist."

"I ain't goin' nowhere," McIver called. "You can do it here."

John tensed. "It's more sanitary there. Plus I'll have an assistant and ready supplies."

"I thought my men told you to bring your supplies." The withered old man looked past John to the floor where his three bags lay. "Looks like you brought everything you need."

The door opened and two more hands stepped into the room, with guns drawn.

John swore. When four of the five Mounties accompanying John walked in with their hands above their heads followed by more of McIver's men, John wobbled in his boots. "What's this?"

"What's it look like?" McIver strained to talk.

''Why'd you have to bring your men? It could'a been nice and quiet, a doctor visiting a patient. Now you force me to…''

John couldn't believe his men had been caught. Why and how had almost all of them relinquished their guns? And then he saw the reason.

Calvin Rutledge came around the corner and pushed Sarah to the floor. She fell in a heap at their feet. She looked up in horror. John leaped to help her.

One of McIver's men stopped him with a gun. ''Not so fast.''

John's heart pounded against his ribs. ''You son of a bitch, McIver.'' He whirled around, tempted to spit in McIver's face, then spun back to Sarah. His gaze shot to her belly. It was slightly rounded, no more than normal. She wasn't showing yet. Tenderness pulled at his throat. The sight of Sarah rising to her feet, in her red robe and half-soaped hair tangled in knots around her, sickened him.

He quickly pieced it together. They'd captured her in the bath, and it was because of *him*. He'd suggested it to her in front of McIver's men as they'd left the fort. The bathing room was one of the only places she would demand privacy from Mountie supervision, and the room had an exterior door that Rutledge had probably used for her capture.

McIver coughed and looked to his men. ''Where's the other Mountie?''

''He took off on foot. He's hidin' on the ranch but we got our men lookin' for him.''

McIver swore. ''Well, at least you got her. Now I know I'll be safe in the surgeon's capable hands.''

''Let her go,'' John pleaded. ''I'll do my best to help you.''

"You'll do even better with her here."

"Doc," said Sergeant O'Malley, his hands clasped behind his head, motioning to the man with the pointed revolver. "Have you met these men before?"

What was the sergeant getting at? "No," said John, barely able to look past Sarah's frightened gray eyes.

The sergeant explained. "The man behind me is Lincoln Grayveson and the one beside him is his brother Zane."

Dressed in dirty western gear, the men shed their hats, revealing two heads of greasy blond hair. "At your service."

McIver moaned in pain, but nudged John in a chilling display of power. "You'll do the surgery here."

Short and wiry, Lincoln Grayveson pointed his barrels at Sarah's head. "And just so ya know, Doc…if Angus dies on the table, so does she."

Chapter Twenty-One

"Hold out your hands." Motioning to the men in the room, Angus struggled to rise from his chair. The air sparked with heat and energy. Sarah slid her fingers around her robe's neckline, separating the sticky cloth from her clammy skin.

What sort of request was Angus making? Was the man going insane from his illness? Taking a shaky breath to still her thrumming heart, outwardly she remained quiet, scanning the room for escape possibilities. Other than the guns held by Angus's men, there were no other weapons visible.

Except...in a display case twenty feet away behind a window of glass, she spotted a rifle. It looked ancient, a cavalry rifle, but shiny and well taken care of. She wondered if it was loaded and the glass doors locked. She motioned to John, and he slowly turned in the same direction. With an urgent frown, he indicated that she should remain still, out of danger.

Her eyes stung with tears. Mentally she applauded the honorable qualities of her husband and the deep commitment she saw mirrored in his gaze. To come this far and to think she might lose John...lose their baby...

Angus shrieked again. "Hold out your hands! All the men!"

The four Mounties lowered their arms to midair. Angus shuffled along, passing by some hands, stopping to stare at others. When he was finished, he examined the hands of his three men—Calvin Rutledge and the two Grayveson brothers.

Finally, Angus pointed to Sergeant O'Malley. "After the surgeon, you've got the cleanest fingers and the steadiest grip. You're gonna be the one to assist him. But if anything happens to me, you're dead, too."

Sarah shuddered.

John lowered his tanned hands and Sarah longed for the protectiveness of his embrace. "We better get started, before your fever gets too high."

"All right." Angus turned to Lincoln Grayveson, the younger brother with the handlebar mustache. "Take the doctor to the kitchen—no, make that the dining room, the table's bigger—and send the rest of them, including his wife, to the barn cellar."

"No," said John. "I'm not doing this unless they're at my side where I can see them."

"Not a chance. Take them away."

"Then at least my wife, or I won't help you."

The strength of John's honor wrapped around her, giving her the stamina to hold her head high.

Angus groaned in pain. "You're a stubborn son of a bitch, John. Okay, the wife stays, along with O'Malley. Take the rest out."

It took them twenty minutes to set up in the dining room, to boil water for sterilization of John's instruments, to wipe down the glossy oak table and to get Angus up on it. Despite John's solemn expression, she sensed his fury at being held at gunpoint.

"For hygienic reasons," John told his patient, "you need to remove your clothes."

"I'm not doing this naked. I'll lower my belt, it's good enough. And I want a pillow."

"A pillow's no good," said John. "Your airway is easier to keep open if your head is flat on the table. I'll put a thin blanket beneath your head to soften the surface."

"The table's cold and hard. I want a pillow."

"Fine. Get the bastard a pillow."

"Is this your best bedside manner?"

"It's the best I can do under these circumstances. When did you get so damn greedy, Angus?"

Angus actually laughed. Then he pulled his gun from his holster and with a frightening expression, pointed it straight between John's eyes. "Do a good job, you hear me?"

John's expression was a mixture of torment and grief. When he glanced at Sarah, she suddenly realized John was uncertain about Angus. Was he uncertain that surgery could save him?

If Angus died, they were doomed. If he lived, they might be doomed anyway.

O'Malley stuffed the soaked cloth over Angus's mouth and Angus went to sleep. Contrary to Angus's demands, John immediately cut open the trousers and had the sergeant remove the pillow.

"What are you doin'?" McIver's men cocked their guns.

"He can't breathe properly with this lumpy thing. Look, I'll roll a towel under his neck. He's comfortable and breathing steady."

They relented, and John began to cut. Sarah couldn't watch. She looked away, but the sound of snip snip snip and an occasional slurp of fluid seemed to amplify tenfold.

Would John deliberately nick an artery as his men had

suggested? Would the sergeant "accidentally" press too hard with the cloth over Angus's mouth?

May God forgive her, but she struggled with her belief that it would be for the best. How could John take it, trying to save the life of the man he hated?

Perspiring profusely, Sarah felt the sweat dribble beneath her arms. She tried to think of other things. Where was the fifth Mountie?

And how was Keenan? Natasha and the children had left him that night by train and he must be tortured over the loss.

Glancing up at one of the Grayveson brothers, Sarah recognized one of the revolvers. So her gun delivery had been made. And just as Shorty had predicted, the guns were being used against the wrong people.

What had Sarah been thinking, convincing John and the others that the guns needed to be constructed and delivered to protect her brother? What had made her think they could compete and outwit these opponents?

Three grueling hours later, well past midnight when she could barely sit on the chair any longer from the ache in her backside, when the Grayveson brothers had rotated keeping their drawn guns on John and the sergeant for a hundred times, when John had remained steady on his feet with barely a spoken word, she heard his voice.

"It's nearly done. This is the final layer of suturing." John coughed loudly. "I'd love a glass of water."

"Shut up and finish your job."

Ten minutes later when Sarah glanced up, she caught a blur of blood and sheets and a pale man lying on the table. The lamp beside them was nearly drained of oil. John's back was completely drenched in perspiration. It followed his spine from his broad shoulders down to his lean hips. When she glanced to the splattered carpet, a shiny object caught the light.

A small knife!

When John had coughed, he must have thrown a surgical knife in her direction.

Sarah rose to her feet.

"What are you doin'?" asked Lincoln.

"I've got to stretch my legs." She rubbed her neck, slowly stretching and gingerly stepping onto the knife. She shielded it with her boot.

"Sit down!"

"All right, all right." She slid the knife over to her chair, sat down and kept her foot on the knife, waiting for the next distraction when she could pick it up.

"There, you see, Angus survived." John indicated the men should look at their boss. "Now you can let us go."

Lincoln grinned. "Not so fast. He'll need your help through the night."

John went to the counter and washed his hands in the awaiting basin. The distraction allowed Sarah to pick up the knife and slide it into her robe pocket. Her only hope was to somehow get the knife either to John or to the sergeant.

Just when her faith was rising, the fifth Mountie, caught and trapped, burst through the dining room door with his arms in the air in a gesture of surrender.

Sarah moaned in despair. Shielded by the Mountie, one of Angus's men followed behind, obviously jabbing the gun repeatedly, judging by the stilted way the Mountie moved. "You'll never guess what I found outside, boys."

It was Keenan's voice and he was the one holding the gun on the Mountie!

John's head snapped up from the wound he was bandaging as quickly as if he'd fallen through the trap doors of a gallows.

His gaze skewered that of the constable's being pushed through the door in front of Ken Neal. It took seconds for it to sink into John's brain. Did the constable know that Ken was on *their* side?

He *was,* wasn't he?

John had immediately thought so, but gazing at Ken's battered expression had John imagining the worst.

"Well, well, well," said Lincoln, running a hand over his damp face and ogling their latest catch. "Good work, Neal."

"I found him sniffing around out back." Ken limped into the circle of dim lighting. He used no cane. By his half-grown beard, he hadn't shaved for a week. "Took me a while to catch him. I had to knock him around the head a few times before he told me what was goin' on in here."

The captured Mountie swore and Lincoln laughed.

Ken glanced to his sister. John saw her eyes flicker. Then McIver moaned on the table. For a split second, while all eyes riveted on the heavy-set man coming out of his anesthesia, Ken grabbed the opportunity.

Ken threw a gun to Sergeant O'Malley, shot Lincoln Grayveson, ducked while the newly captured Mountie rolled to the floor and withdrew the gun hidden in the back of *his* waistline, allowing John to lunge on top of Sarah, knocking her to the floor.

A blast of gunfire roared in John's ears. Sarah shook beneath him as he agonized over whether she'd been hurt.

With superhuman strength, John threw her beneath the table, rolling with her to stay out of the line of fire. He didn't stop until they'd reached the corner, shielded behind a sideboard.

"Sarah, where's the knife?"

She looked down at her bloody leg.

"Oh, no," he whispered. "You're wounded."

"No, my leg scraped against the knife." She withdrew the blade from her pocket, indicating she was fine.

The gunfire stopped.

John swallowed hard. Bracing himself and the knife firmly between his fingers, he stepped out, ready to fight.

The smell of gunpowder singed his nostrils. Ken and the sergeant were standing above the fallen men. All three of the ranch hands were down on the floor, twisted and still. Angus groaned from the table.

"It's all right, Sarah," said John, lifting her to her feet. "They won't hurt us anymore."

With a quick look at Sarah's thigh and comforted that the cuts were superficial, John placed a clean gauze strip over her leg. "Keep pressing."

While Ken comforted his sister, John searched the fallen men for signs of life. He nearly slipped in the spilled blood on the floor. All three men were dead. Lincoln Grayveson, his brother Zane, and Calvin Rutledge.

Angus rolled his head from side to side.

The bastard deserved to suffer, but John hadn't the heart to allow any human being to come out of major surgery without the benefit of pain medicine.

Sifting quickly through his medical bags, John drew up a syringe, rolled up McIver's sleeve then injected.

The rumbling sound of quaking earth startled everyone. The sergeant flew to the darkened window. "Sweet Jesus."

"What is it?"

"It's a huge silhouette coming up the laneway and two acres across. A herd of horses and Mounties so numerous

I can't count 'em all. Must be close to sixty. I'll go direct them to the cellar.''

John picked up a gun so that he and Ken were both armed. John, Sarah and Ken drew closer to the table.

McIver's eyes fluttered open. For a moment his eyes didn't appear to focus. Then slowly he turned his head to the floor and his fallen men.

In a bizarre twist he reached for his guns, but of course he had no holsters. When his weak gaze focused on Ken, he looked stunned. ''Neal…take out your guns…shoot someone.''

Ken stepped closer and slowly trained his gun on Angus.

''Don't shoot him,'' John urged, watching Ken struggle with self-restraint. ''It's all over. We've got him and we'll make sure he stands trial.''

Ken lowered his barrels and Sarah wove her arm beneath her brother's.

''John,'' Angus whispered softly. ''John, you're going to help me, aren't you?''

''I'd like you to meet my brother-in-law.'' John patted Ken on the shoulders.

''Brother-in-law?'' Angus closed his eyes.

John leaned in close to the old man's face to make sure Angus understood. ''I've got one question for you. Keep in mind the judge will treat you a whole lot better if you tell me the truth. What did you do with your wife? Where's Sheila?''

Angus whispered something inaudible. John pressed closer to listen. He heard the man answer then choke for air.

Despite everything John tried to do to save him, Angus McIver died five hours later in a cold house surrounded by early morning fog.

Chapter Twenty-Two

"You're going to wear a hole plum through my windowpane if you keep staring through it like that."

Sarah laughed gently at Melodie's comment as she let the kitchen curtain fall back into place. It was getting dark, but there was still no sign of John or Logan. They'd been at the fort all day, tending to the three officers who'd been injured in the shoot-out.

A fire sputtered in the woodstove, warming the evening air and gently brewing tea as Melodie breastfed her baby in her big, lazy rocking chair.

Sarah went to the stove and poured two teacups, straining the leaves in the small sieve, then adding honey and one touch of milk for her friend.

Two officers stood outside as a precaution, although in Sarah's heart, she no longer felt in danger.

They'd discovered Sheila McIver at her sister's ranch, beaten and bruised by her late husband, but stoic in taking the news of Angus's death. It seemed Sheila had wanted to leave Angus permanently, for whatever reasons she had, and had confronted him last night. Their argument and his beating of her had caused his gallbladder attack, and he'd gone into spasm just as she'd left for her sister's.

Angus hadn't left behind any children, but at least Sheila would inherit the ranch once the court proceedings were finished and his estate settled.

Sarah took the baby from Melodie's grasp and switched chairs with the young mother, smiling and sighing into the gurgling face.

"Are you sure you're all right?" Melodie sipped her tea.

"Better than I've ever felt." After Sarah had cleaned up at home and changed from her robe into a pleated blouse and skirt, she'd come here so that she and Melodie could wait for their men together.

Comforted by the weight of the infant in her arms, knowing she'd soon have one of her own, Sarah held a moving finger above the baby and tried to get him to follow the movement, but his glistening blue eyes simply stared at her. She laughed and kissed the softest cheek she'd ever felt.

Sarah hadn't told anyone else the news of her pregnancy because she wanted to discuss it privately with John first. She felt like a schoolgirl waiting for her first beau to arrive.

"They'll be home soon enough," said Melodie across the kitchen table as she measured two cups of flour, standing by her bread pan about to bake a loaf.

"Do you remember the last time we waited for our husbands together?" asked Sarah.

"As I recall, it was your wedding night and we were waiting for the groom to show his face." Melodie smiled at her dearest friend. "Was it worth the wait, Sarah?"

Sarah's eyes watered and a lump arose in her throat. "More than I ever imagined."

"You've found a brother, now, too."

Sarah nodded tenderly, having told her friend the entire story in the last few hours.

While Sarah had stood by listening at the ranch, John had told Keenan what he'd discovered about Parkinson's illness. Even though it wasn't a perfect guarantee, the odds were high in Keenan's favor that his children would *not* get the illness.

When Sarah had breathed a sigh of relief, John had tenderly hugged his own pregnant wife at the news and then informed Keenan that his family was waiting for him ninety miles east of town at the first train stop. Two officers were guarding them, and Keenan could retrieve them as soon as he was capable. He'd claimed he was capable immediately and left on the first train out.

The kitchen door latch clicked and both women jumped with apprehension as Logan, then John, entered the house. Seeing John's exhausted but smiling face sent waves of excitement through Sarah. She drank in the comfort of his safety and his nearness as he bent down and brushed his lips across her cheek. His dark hair glistened in the lamplight. Being two days awake with no sleep, he'd grown dark bristles on his jawline, but he'd never looked more striking.

When he looked down at the baby in her arms, John tipped his finger beneath Sarah's chin and forced her to look into his penetrating brown eyes. *A baby. Their baby.*

"Let me see how this feels," John said, sliding the youngster into the wide crux of his embrace.

The parents looked on proudly. "Looks good in your arms," cooed Melodie, obviously hinting at the future.

Sarah felt herself blush. Then her stomach tingled with the prospect that she and John would soon be alone to say what they so desperately needed to say.

The veterinarian stepped beside John and scooped up

his son. Sarah watched the two proud men, awed by the splendor of a father's love.

Melodie kissed her baby while her husband held him. "Did you discover what happened to Constable Pawson?"

John pulled up a chair beside his wife in the rocker, stretching his legs so that one of his boots pressed hers. "It's sad. Sarah's brother had overheard at the ranch that the day Calvin Rutledge had been released from the hospital ward for his rabies treatment, Pawson had come in for a checkup to his injured leg. When Rutledge and the man who'd come to get him made an off-hand comment about Rutledge being bitten by the rabid fox in the vicinity of a ranch that the rustlers had attacked earlier, they suspected Pawson had overheard. So they'd dragged him from the hospital ward into the woods, never giving him an opportunity to relay the information before they'd killed him."

Sarah shuddered.

"The good news is, we've got twelve more men in custody, and in McIver's safe we found several stacks of stocks and bonds in U.S. accounts. No wonder we hadn't been able to trace anything to Angus McIver. He'd kept his money in a Montana bank, and Lincoln Grayveson had been the one who'd run the money to and from the bank when needed. That's why the brothers were both in town yesterday. It was a huge payday. With the help of the U.S. authorities, we've got enough evidence now to piece it together."

As the women filtered the information, the only sound in the room was the creaking of the wooden rocking chair. "What happened to Slade Phillips?" asked Sarah.

"He's innocent and just as shocked as the rest of us at Angus's true identity. It's over," said John, placing a hand over Sarah's. His hand felt wonderfully warm and reassuring.

Logan tried to lift their spirits. He nudged John. "I don't think the nickname Black-'n-White suits you anymore. From what I heard, you were building guns for the enemy and putting your faith in previous gunrunners like Ken Neal. And the John Calloway I once knew might have been harsher to Angus McIver during surgery *and* while the man was coming out of it."

John grinned and tried to shrug off the comments.

But Sarah understood what Logan was referring to. She'd witnessed the tenderness John had displayed to the man he'd despised. The kindhearted doctor had won out over the unrelenting policeman.

"Let's see, what name would be good…" Logan continued. "How about Big Heart?"

"Don't you start," John threatened. He tugged Sarah to her feet and wrapped an arm around her. "The name John will do fine. Let's go home, wife."

Sarah giggled, warmed by his enthusiasm.

"How's your leg?"

She ran a hand over her skirt, feeling the pad of bandages. "A little sore, but it's only a small scrape."

"Can you walk?"

She laughed. "It's just a scrape."

"Your husband's worried about you, honey," said Melodie. "It would do them good to worry about *us* for a change. Oh, my aching back," she added to her husband. "I sure could use a massage and rub-down."

"Well," said John, taking the cue. "We'll leave you two alone then."

As John and Sarah stumbled out the back door, still laughing, he draped Sarah's coat around her shoulders then put on his duster.

She rested her head on his chest, loving the feel of his moving muscles beneath her ear.

"Are you tired?" she asked him.

"Tired for some things, wide-awake for others."

"My goodness, Doctor, I think I know what you mean."

"John! Sarah!" someone called in the dusky distance.

John groaned and pulled her tighter. "What is it, David?"

"May I take your photo?" he called over the fence.

"Now's not a good time."

"Perhaps tomorrow?"

"I've got forty-eight hours' leave as ordered by the commander, starting now, and I don't want you knocking on my door for any of those hours. You hear me?"

Two days of uninterrupted time with her husband? Could life really be this good?

"Yes, Sir. Perhaps the day after?"

"David?" said John.

David hesitated. "Yeah?"

"You're a good journalist."

"Thank you, Sir!"

"I've been waitin' for you two to return all day," said David, coming into the light of their porch. "I wanted to give you this." He held out a leather bound book.

"What is it?" asked Sarah, taking it.

"A wedding album. Remember those pictures I promised you from the wedding party?"

"How lovely. Thank you very much."

David disappeared and John unlocked the door. When Sarah moved to step inside, he whisked her up into his arms and carried her over the threshold. "I never did this the first time around."

Sarah kissed his neck in response.

When they entered the quiet house and they were finally, peacefully alone, Sarah whispered in the darkness. "John, thank you for trusting my brother."

"If he was your brother, I figured he couldn't be all bad."

"Will there be any charges laid against him?"

"No, he was blackmailed."

"And how about his previous problems in Halifax?"

"The one thing I like about your brother is that when I asked him about his previous life, he told me everything, every detail I wanted to know. His crimes were petty, no one was injured and it happened twelve years ago, so no charges are pending. He told me he fled Halifax when he was being chased by the law in order to protect you."

"Yes, he told me today that's why he never wrote to us."

"Do you know who else dropped by the fort today?"

"Who?"

"Dr. Waters. He felt awful about the raid and came by to offer his services. Even though he walked straight and acted sober, I could smell the liquor on his breath. But for the first time since I've known him, I asked him *why* he drank."

"What did he say?"

"At first, he bawled like a baby. I should have asked him a long time ago, like you once told me, but I was too pigheaded. He told me his drinking started the day after he'd lost his second patient in surgery. The first died post surgery when the patient had an artery obstruction. The second died on the table with too much blood loss due to a mauled leg. Dr. Waters blamed himself, but I think there was nothing he could have done. And I told him so."

"Did you accept his help today?"

"Not in surgery, but he was a help in bandaging and

tending to the bodies. There are some things he's good at. We came to an agreement that if he cuts back on the liquor, he could help out in the hospital under my supervision. Maybe he'll get back on his feet.''

She was breathless with happiness for John. ''That would be wonderful. You need so much more help than you have.''

He lit the wall lamp, then the portable lantern. Golden light ricocheted off the walls and tumbled with their shadows. ''Sarah, I'm sorry that it took me all these weeks to come to my senses and realize that you're my first priority.'' He placed his limber hand on her flat tummy. ''And our family.''

''I'm sorry, too, for not coming to you straight from the beginning about Keenan—''

''How could you have? I would have thrown him in jail. And if I could do it all again with you, I'd write my own mail-order ad.''

She laughed. ''What would it say?''

''One hell of a strong woman needed. One who can stand by my side without complaint, but one with the determination to find her own path and to strike meaning into her own life. An equal partner in every way.''

They kissed. He *did* understand her.

''And…'' he added with a devilish glint, ''one with beautiful breasts.''

''I don't think you can write that.''

''Sarah?''

''Mmm?''

''I love you.''

She sighed softly. No one had ever said those words to her. She hadn't needed to prompt him, or to say it first, or to *ask* him how he felt. He offered it willingly, and it poured into her soul. ''I love you, too.''

This is what she'd always dreamed of, being held in John's arms while he whispered endearments into her ear, making her heart beat stronger. With those three words, she felt as if he were promising her the world.

He dipped his head and nuzzled hers, rocking her and waiting for the rest of what she struggled to say.

"I was wrong in thinking that you weren't behind me. Why, you were behind me all along, silently supporting and hoping that I'd turn to you instead of going my solitary way. Creating a family isn't a one-step process as I first thought when I answered that ad. It takes time to develop bonds. Family involves more heartache and difficulty than I ever imagined. But I cherish belonging to a family, and being your wife."

He pressed his caressing lips to hers and she was lifted onto a cloud. "I can't wait for the birth of our child."

She looked up into his gentle face, overjoyed that she would bear his children. "I can't wait to run you a bath."

John laughed as Sarah tugged his free arm, leading him down the hallway and into the back room. Savoring every moment, together they lit the fire, lit the candles, drew the water and hung the cauldrons.

"A little more to your left." Sarah coaxed John thirty minutes later, after they'd filled the tub and the windows were steamed from heat.

"There?"

"Six inches to the right."

"How about there?"

"Six inches back."

"Now?"

"Perfect." Sitting in the upholstered chair, Sarah tilted the full-length mirror and nodded to John that he'd finally found the perfect place to stand on the Turkish carpet in front of the blazing fire. Now she could watch him slide off his shirt while fully enjoying the view from all angles.

Oh, she would enjoy this.

The damp fabric of her blouse clung to her chest as she watched him slide off his white shirt. She recalled the first day she'd met him, waiting for him in his bedroom at the fort as he'd entered like this, shirtless and muscular and glistening with sweat, beckoning for her touch.

Her breath came warm and fast.

He unbuttoned his pants. "Come here and jump in the tub with me."

"I can't. My bandages would get wet."

"Then at least take off that proper Victorian blouse."

"Why, don't you like it?"

"I love it. Take it off."

"Seems to me, you love a lot of things this evening."

He growled and lunged at her and she dashed out of his reach. When he caught her, he pressed her up against the door with her arms above her head, holding them down with one hand while using his other to trail soft circles along her waistline.

Her body rippled in response. Struggling to no avail, she sucked in her breath as he yanked her blouse out of her skirt. "Miss, you're under arrest," he said playfully.

"Dear heavens, Officer, what have I done?"

"Resisted my advances."

"What's the punishment for this crime?"

While she wriggled between him and the door, he nibbled on her neck, the heat from their bodies fusing them together. "Removal of your clothing." He unbuttoned her blouse, beginning with the bottom one. With agonizing slowness, he worked his way upward, stopping when he came to the top of her corset. He dipped his finger into her cleavage, teasing her until she felt like exploding.

The muscles of his thighs were hard against her legs. When he kissed along her ear, he shifted his position and she felt his arousal. "But, Officer, you're still wearing your gun."

His kiss broke as he laughed into her throat. The bristles of his unshaven jaw scratched along her cheek and she startled.

"Sorry," he said. "I need to shave."

"You better take your bath first, or this won't get you anywhere."

With a long sigh of pleasure, he tugged her blouse down over one shoulder, then the other. When he kissed the swell of her upper arm, tingles rolled along her flesh.

Then in a flash before she knew what he was doing, he slid her corset down three inches so the white lacy fabric slipped off her breasts, but the whalebone strips held firm around her stomach, uplifting her naked bosom.

Her mouth fell open in shocked amusement.

"That's nice. Keep it like that while I bathe."

"I thought you didn't like corsets."

"I didn't say I didn't like them. I said you can't breathe in them. But I think I've found a solution for you."

They stared into each other's eyes, his dark and intense, hers warm and loving. He turned around, slid off his trousers, then dipped his muscular legs into the steaming water. Sarah marveled at the beauty of his body, the way his muscles moved together and every sinew and nerve seemed to work in combination.

"Hmm, feels so good."

She strode to the counter behind him.

"Where are you going? Come back here where I can see you and enjoy you."

While he washed his hair, she returned with a bowl of lather and a straight razor. When she knelt on the plush carpet before him, he swallowed hard. "You're going to give me a topless shave? If I've died and gone to heaven, please don't wake me."

She understood what was happening to him, for the same pleasures were quaking through her body. She dipped a washcloth into the warm water, then patted his cheeks. When she began to shave him, she felt her breasts sway with every movement, every twirl of her wrist. The exhilaration of the steamy air on her cool skin and the thought of being naked with her lover made her senses soar.

With a groan and a twinkling in his eyes, he reached out and grabbed one breast, softly, gently, pulling at the nipple.

"You're hired to do that every night," she whispered, teasing him into a smile.

He grew hushed while she finished the shave. Then with feverish determination, he slid out of the water, draped a towel around himself, threw it off when he was dry, then picked her up and carried her up the stairs.

She'd managed to lift the portable lantern and the light rocked in her hands.

When he brought her to his bedroom, she fell back onto the feather cover as he lowered his naked body along her length. "I've been wanting to make love to you in this bed from the moment I carried you to it that first night when you fell asleep at my table."

His eyes were filled with love as she stroked his belly. The muscles beneath her fingers tightened and she felt him shudder, delighted at the thought that she could affect him this much.

They took their time. He cupped her breast, kissing and suckling, making those small delicious circles that drove her to succumb. He unbuttoned her skirt and wove his fingers beneath her bloomers, tugging them past her feet, then doing the same with her skirt and petticoats. "Tell me that you love me."

Off came her corset. She lay naked on top of him, hearts beating, he caressing her bandaged leg, she guiding him into her body, rocking with his rhythm. "John...I love you...want you...need you in my life...."

They rolled silently together. He grasped her hips and pulled her closer, tighter, more urgently. Her lips fell open, she gasped with that incredible thrill of ecstasy, and he followed shortly after.

The room grew still as the warm light fizzed and cascaded across their golden skin. This time, during their lovemaking, she felt utterly, completely fulfilled. Gone was the loneliness she'd felt on her wedding night. She tried to preserve this moment in her memory, to hold it in her heart forever for she knew there would never be another man for her except Dr. John Calloway.

He reached up with a stroking hand and brushed her mass of tangled hair from her dampened brow. "I love you, mail-order Sarah."

Epilogue

One year later

"Look straight at the birdie!"

Standing in the Calloway home surrounded by a circle of watching friends, David Fitzgibbon clicked his portable camera at Sarah, John and their son. The magnesium flashlamp flared in a gust of smoke and ash, and the baby in her arms wailed in discontent. Sarah smiled at his timing.

John leaned over her shoulder and cooed as she cradled the warm, bundled infant. The tiny limbs felt so good, so secure in her arms.

Beyond David's shoulder, a fire roared in the dining room as Melodie and Natasha placed the champagne bottles on the table beside the bowl of colorful, dried gourds. Their children were playing outdoors as the adults inside prepared for the evening's celebration of the permanent arrival of twelve new police recruits in Calgary.

None were medical officers, but John still held the hope that one or two would arrive within the year.

Sarah kissed her son's cheek. "Are you hungry, my little tiger?"

Colton Calloway wailed in his charming way. Big mouth, lots of lungs and a cry that'd pierce a rhino's ear.

"What's all the wailing?" asked John, pressing close enough so she could breathe his wonderful scent. No matter how many times she'd seen her husband in full scarlet uniform and dark tight breeches, she'd never grow accustomed to the breathtaking sight.

"It's your son, he's hungry."

John filled the room with grace and laughter. "Well, unfortunately, I can't help him there. That's something only his mother can supply."

The warmth and promise of a wonderful evening together with friends filled her heart. There were also a few officers present she didn't know except by name—Inspector Zack Bullock, a youthful, commanding man who stood alone sipping his drink. Then talking in the corner were Travis Reid and his brother, Mitchell, both dark and striking Mounties. There was a definite lack of women in the West, but she was fortunate that she and John had found each other.

When John took the baby from her arms and held him in the air, Colton squawked some more. "Are you keeping your ma busy?" Then with a swoop and holler, John smothered his son with kisses. "Sure would like to give you a little sister." He turned to Sarah's laughing face. "Come with me, both of you," said John, taking Sarah's hand and leading the way upstairs to the nursery. "I'll help you get set up with the feeding."

"I'll finish with the rest down here," hollered Melodie. "You go ahead!"

Sarah smiled at the friendly faces, taking special care to make the new wives welcome. Three women had arrived today on the train with their recruited husbands, sitting stiffly in their chairs now, glancing awkwardly about the room.

It had come full circle for Sarah. Even though she'd only lived here for a year, she was now one of the more senior wives, helping the newest arrivals to find their footing on the harsh frontier.

David sat beside one of the quieter women and as Sarah passed, she heard him ask, "What brings you here all the way from England?"

He was still at it. His articles on the Mounties's wives had multiplied across the country, popular from one coast to the other, and it hadn't taken much for the townsfolk to convince David to settle permanently in Calgary.

Sarah was touched that John would rather spend his time—these precious thirty minutes—with her and the baby than to have an ale with his waiting friends. After the first two struggling months of their marriage, John unequivocally let her know that she was his partner, his priority.

When they were finished, in their tiny world of three, John took the baby and led his family outside. David had just finished taking indoor photos of the entire group.

Keenan's children—Rusty and Marianne, who could now speak—clamored around the baby. John crouched low around the outdoor fire to let them touch their cousin, advising the children on the best way to hold Colton. In the firelight, a delicate necklace and locket, which Sarah had designed for her niece, flickered around the young girl's neck. Over the past year, other folks in town had requested Sarah's designs.

While she looked on in blissful pleasure, adding her own words of advice and hugging the little girl, Keenan came up and threw an arm around Sarah. His hand was shaking lightly from the palsy, but his hug felt good.

"Ever since I've had children of my own, I've missed my own sister the most," said Keenan. "I'm sorry we never got a chance to know each other as we grew into adults."

"We know each other now." Sarah said a silent prayer, offering her gratitude that Keenan's condition hadn't worsened.

Keenan nodded, and when Melodie called out that dinner was served, he led them back into the house.

"Did everybody remember to bring what I asked?" Sarah said after the baked cinnamon apples were devoured.

"Yup, I've got ours," said Natasha.

"Me, too," said Melodie, with her toddler at her side.

The men groaned in unison. "Do we have to do this?"

"It'll be a lot of fun," the women insisted.

"Let's pour some drinks first." John poured as the women pulled out their family photographs. Sarah had ensured that the newer wives received the message to bring any photos they might have to the party, too.

An hour later, amid much laughter, pointing at their solemn faces in the stark photos and how old they seemed to look, John stared at the lovely woman at his side.

"Do you remember that evening on the garden bench?" he whispered into her ear, staring at the photograph David had taken on the night of their wedding party.

"I'll never forget your reaction when I pinched you."

She smiled and John was caught by such a moment of nostalgia, for her arrival that first day in the barracks, and for the friends he'd lost in the raids over the past two years, that he couldn't speak.

"We're indebted to a lot of people tonight," he said in a rough voice. "Especially to one man, to what he was trying to tell me before he passed away, and to how he brought us together by placing a simple ad."

She nodded, the splendor of her fine cheeks and unwavering gray eyes holding his gaze.

"I'd like to propose a toast," John said to his circle of friends. They lifted their crystal flutes, all filled with champagne except for Sarah's, which was filled with warm milk.

"To Wesley Quinn," said John with unbridled emotion.

Of those who knew Wesley or knew *about* him, the women swallowed tightly, trying to rein in their sentiments, while the men blinked in solemn respect.

Twenty crystal glasses clinked together. "To Wesley Quinn."

* * * * *

Be sure to watch for more romances from Kate Bridges featuring the Mounties, coming only to Harlequin Historicals in 2004.

Author Note

The characters and events of this novel are fictional. However, the idea was inspired by a real-life incident. As a prank in the late 1800s, a group of North-West Mounties placed an ad in an Eastern newspaper and ordered a mail-order bride for their commander.

When the bride arrived, clutching a piece of paper in her fingers with the commander's name on it, he was shocked by what his men had done. Sympathetic to the woman, he apologized, explained that it was a hoax, then quickly paid for her return train ticket and sent her home.

This novel explores what might have happened—in a fictional situation—if the mail-order bride had refused to go home.

PICK UP THESE HARLEQUIN HISTORICALS AND IMMERSE YOURSELF IN THRILLING AND EMOTIONAL LOVE STORIES SET IN THE AMERICAN FRONTIER

On sale January 2004

CHEYENNE WIFE by Judith Stacy
(Colorado, 1844)

Will opposites attract when a handsome
half-Cheyenne horse trader comes to the rescue
of a proper young lady from back east?

WHIRLWIND BRIDE by Debra Cowan
(Texas, 1883)

A widowed rancher unexpectedly falls in love with
a beautiful and pregnant young woman.

On sale February 2004

COLORADO COURTSHIP by Carolyn Davidson
(Colorado, 1862)

A young widow finds a father for her unborn child—
and a man for her heart—in a loving wagon train scout.

THE LIGHTKEEPER'S WOMAN by Mary Burton
(North Carolina, 1879)

When an heiress reunites with her former fiancée,
will they rekindle their romance or say goodbye
once and for all?

Visit us at www.eHarlequin.com

HARLEQUIN HISTORICALS®

HHWEST29

eHARLEQUIN.com

Looking for today's most popular
books at great prices?
At www.eHarlequin.com, we offer:

- An **extensive selection** of romance
  books by top authors!

- **New** releases, Themed Collections
  and hard-to-find **backlist.**

- A sneak peek at Upcoming books.

- Enticing book **excerpts** and **back
  cover copy!**

- Read recommendations from other
  readers (and post your own)!

- Find out what everybody's reading
  in **Bestsellers.**

- **Save BIG** with everyday discounts
  and exclusive online offers!

- Easy, convenient **24-hour shopping.**

- Our **Romance Legend** will help select
  reading that's *exactly* right for you!

**Your purchases are 100%
guaranteed—so shop online
at www.eHarlequin.com today!**

INTBB1

From Regency romps
to mesmerizing Medievals,
savor these stirring tales from
Harlequin Historicals®

On sale January 2004

THE KNAVE AND THE MAIDEN by Blythe Gifford

A cynical knight's life is forever changed when he falls
in love with a naive young woman while journeying
to a holy shrine.

MARRYING THE MAJOR by Joanna Maitland

Can a war hero wounded in body and spirit find
happiness with his childhood sweetheart, now that she
has become the toast of London society?

On sale February 2004

THE CHAPERON BRIDE by Nicola Cornick

When England's most notorious rake is attracted to
a proper ladies' chaperon, could it be true love?

THE WEDDING KNIGHT by Joanne Rock

A dashing knight abducts a young woman to marry his
brother, but soon falls in love with her instead!

Visit us at www.eHarlequin.com

HARLEQUIN HISTORICALS®

HHMED34

HEAD FOR THE ROCKIES WITH

Harlequin Historicals®
Historical Romantic Adventure!

AND SEE HOW IT ALL BEGAN!

COLORADO
CONFIDENTIAL

**Check out these three historicals
connected to the bestselling Intrigue series**

CHEYENNE WIFE
by Judith Stacy
January 2004

COLORADO COURTSHIP
by Carolyn Davidson
February 2004

ROCKY MOUNTAIN MARRIAGE
by Debra Lee Brown
March 2004

Available at your favorite retail outlet.

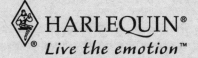

HARLEQUIN®
Live the emotion™

Visit us at www.eHarlequin.com

HHCC

COMING NEXT MONTH FROM

HARLEQUIN HISTORICALS®

- **CHEYENNE WIFE**
  by **Judith Stacy,** the first of three historicals in the *Colorado Confidential* series
  Alone and broke after her father died on a wagon train out west, Lily St. Claire knew her future was bleak. Until North Walker, a half-Cheyenne horse trader, arrived with a bargain for Lily: if she would tutor his sister, North would escort her back to Virginia… unless she lost her heart to him first!
  HH #687 ISBN# 29287-2 $5.25 U.S./$6.25 CAN.

- **THE KNAVE AND THE MAIDEN**
  by **Blythe Gifford,** Harlequin Historical debut
  Sir Garren was a mercenary knight with faith in nothing. Dominica was a would-be nun with nothing but her faith. Though two people could never be more different, as Garren and Dominica traveled across England on a pilgrimage, would they discover that love is the greatest miracle of all?
  HH #688 ISBN# 29288-0 $5.25 U.S./$6.25 CAN.

- **MARRYING THE MAJOR**
  by **Joanna Maitland,** Mills & Boon reprint
  Back from the Peninsular War, Major Hugo Stratton was scarred and embittered, much altered from the young man Emma Fitzwilliam had fantasized about over the years. Now the toast of London society, Emma inflamed Hugo's blood like no other woman. But could this beautiful woman see beyond his scars to the man hidden beneath?
  HH #689 ISBN# 29289-9 $5.25 U.S./$6.25 CAN.

- **WHIRLWIND BRIDE**
  by **Debra Cowan,** Harlequin Historical debut
  Pregnant and abandoned, Susannah Phelps arrived on Riley Holt's doorstep under the assumption that the widowed rancher planned to marry her and make her child legitimate. Problem was, Riley knew nothing of the plan and had no intention of marrying again— especially not a pampered beauty like Susannah!
  HH #690 ISBN# 29290-2 $5.25 U.S./$6.25 CAN.

KEEP AN EYE OUT FOR ALL FOUR OF THESE TERRIFIC NEW TITLES

HHCNM1203